PENGUIN BOOKS

Last Christmas at Ballyclare

Emily Bell is an *Irish Times* bestselling author who grew up in Dublin and moved to London after university. She has had various jobs including tour guide, bookseller and pub singer, and now writes full time. She lives in north London with her husband and daughter. She is the author of *Baby It's Cold Outside* and *This Year's for Me and You*, winner of the RNA Christmas/Festive Holiday Romantic Novel Award.

Last Christmas at Ballyclare

EMILY BELL

PENGUIN BOOKS

PENGUIN BOOKS

UK | USA | Canada | Ireland | Australia
India | New Zealand | South Africa

Penguin Books is part of the Penguin Random House group of companies
whose addresses can be found at global.penguinrandomhouse.com

First published 2023
001

Copyright © Emily Bell, 2023

The moral right of the author has been asserted

Set in 12.5/14.75pt Garamond MT Std
Typeset by Jouve (UK), Milton Keynes
Printed and bound in Great Britain by Clays Ltd, Elcograf S.p.A.

The authorized representative in the EEA is Penguin Random House Ireland,
Morrison Chambers, 32 Nassau Street, Dublin D02 YH68

A CIP catalogue record for this book is available from the British Library

ISBN: 978-1-405-95267-5

www.greenpenguin.co.uk

In memory of my parents,
who loved the Wicklow Mountains

The heart that has truly loved never forgets.

Thomas Moore

I

There was something very romantic about an airport at Christmas, Natasha decided. It wasn't just the commercial trappings, lovely though they were – the softly playing Christmas music and the perfume counters with their scenes of couples under a tree, laughing over a ribbon-wrapped box. It was the fact that everyone was there to be with the ones they loved – either travelling with them or to them. No wonder airports featured in so many romantic comedies. She felt as if she was in a romcom herself, one about two friends heading off on a trip that was going to show one of them – at least – his true feelings.

'That's fourteen pounds twenty, please,' said the cashier.

Natasha paid for her extra-large Toblerone, her traditional homecoming present to her mother and sister, and made her way back to Ben, who was browsing the bestseller section. He was standing in the posture that was so familiar to her: dark head on one side, hands in pockets. Her heart seized and squeezed with painful feelings of love for him. How many bookshops had she been to with him? Dozens – from the one in a converted train station near her flat in Isleworth to the

Waterstones in Notting Hill, near the independent cinema where they both worked. That was how they had become friends, over a year ago, when he saw her battered copy of *Love in a Cold Climate* and asked if it was any good. She'd thought he would consider it too girly, but he read it and over coffees said he found it funny.

Shared coffees and lunch breaks had turned into evening drinks and walks, as they bonded over books and more: both feeling like outsiders in London, both drifting in their careers and late twenties, and both recovering from heartbreaks. Natasha was getting over her confusing romance with Stewey, a former flatmate, and Ben had broken up with a fellow New Zealander called Lucy. They both worked at the cinema, manning the box office and concession stand, but Ben had ambitions to be a screenwriter while Natasha had studied acting and had occasional bit parts in fringe theatre. Now they were in the WHSmith in Heathrow, Terminal 5. They were both flying back to Ireland, where she had invited Ben to spend Christmas with her family.

The plan had taken shape back in early August, when Ben had first mentioned that he would be staying in London over Christmas. 'Are you kidding?' he had said, laughing, when she asked why he wasn't flying back to Auckland. 'It's, like, a thousand pounds.'

'But won't your flatmates all be going home?' Natasha had asked; she knew they all lived more locally, having spent so many evenings there hanging out with them and Ben.

'Yeah, but it's fine. I'll just watch movies and read. It'll be good to have me time.'

Natasha was horrified at the idea of him spending Christmas by himself, and then overjoyed, because this was the perfect excuse to invite him home to Ballyclare. After checking with Aileen, she had suggested it to Ben on their very next shift together.

'Won't your mum mind, having a stranger for Christmas?' Ben had asked, as he refilled the popcorn machine.

'Oh, God, no,' Natasha had said truthfully. 'The more the merrier. She's always inviting people. Otherwise it's just me and my sister Doon. And my mum will love you,' she added, which was completely true. Nobody could fail to love Ben. He was sensitive, soulful, sweet – an all-round nice guy. She could picture him sitting at the long pine kitchen table, chatting with them late into the night. He would love seeing the countryside and learning all the local history, of which there was plenty. Ballyclare was over two hundred years old, after all.

'Is it, like, a stately home?' Ben asked, sounding awestruck. He loved castles, ruins and everything to do with history. He was more likely to spend his free evenings doing walking tours of London than going clubbing – another reason Natasha loved him.

'Oh, no – sorry,' Natasha said. 'We don't really have those in Ireland. It's just an old house – Georgian.' She thought how inadequate the words were. How could she describe Ballyclare, which was to her the best house in the world?' 'It's very rural, up a winding lane in the middle of the woods. You can't see any other buildings from the windows, just the Wicklow Mountains, and from my room you can see the sea. And when the snow comes, it hits Ballyclare first. We might get a white Christmas.'

Ben looked charmed. 'It sounds awesome. Count me in,' he said.

'Brilliant,' Natasha breathed. She could see him falling for the old house, for the garden and the monkey puzzle tree outside, and then ... maybe ... for her? Not that Natasha would have voiced such a hope out loud, even to herself. But she couldn't help but wonder. He had told her, more than once, that nobody else 'got him' in the same way that she did. That she was the only person he could stay up all night talking to. He had even said that she was the inspiration for the main character in his latest script. Of course he was hurting over Lucy and understandably unwilling to jump into anything else too soon. But since making the plan back in August, they had grown closer and closer, and Natasha had grown more and more hopeful that there was more between them than just friendship.

'Hey,' Ben said now, turning from the bookshelf. 'I was going to buy something to read, but there's nothing good ... it's all this modern stuff.' Ben had a policy of only reading books published before 1992, which Natasha realized could seem a little pretentious, but which she found endearing.

4

'Um . . . yeah. This is supposed to be good, though –
for something different?' She pointed to *Book Lovers* by
Emily Henry, hoping it might help plant a subliminal
message in Ben's mind.

Ben laughed and Natasha did the same, pretending
she had been joking. 'Ah,' he said, picking another one
up. *Zen and the Art of Motorcycle Maintenance.*

'That's meant to be good!' she said.

'Actually, it's crazy to spend money on new books,
isn't it? I'll get it second-hand somewhere.' He put the
book back. He was extremely careful with money, a
trait that Natasha didn't share but admired. She was
rubbish with money, and also time-keeping; she had
once actually missed a flight while sitting at the departure gate, as her sister Doon never tired of reminding
her. But that had only happened because she was so
tired from getting up early for the flight. It wouldn't
happen today.

'I'm just going to check if our gate is up yet,' she
said, and nipped outside the bookshop to check the
departures board. There it was. Flight EI106 to Dublin,
Gate 402. It was a real luxury to be flying Aer Lingus
and she congratulated herself for booking the flights
so far ahead and getting such a good deal. *See, Doon, I
can be canny*, she said to her sister, who lived in her head.

She made her way back to Ben, who was transfixed
by his phone.

'Hey! Our gate is listed – so we can go there now if
you want. No rush,' she added quickly.

Ben looked up, his face suffused by an unfamiliar expression; he looked almost scared but happy too – in fact, Natasha thought, he looked *radiant*.

'Actually,' he said, 'you won't believe this, but . . .'

'Yes?' Natasha prompted, when he stopped short.

Ben's face changed into a kind of guilty grimace. 'I think I'm going to – go.'

'Go where?' said Natasha. 'To the loo? Or Pret? That's fine, I'll wait for you.'

'No.' He shook his head and said, 'To Lucy. To be with Lucy.'

Natasha swallowed. The air around her seemed to swim and she put out a hand on the bookshelf to steady herself, as she tried to rearrange his words into something that made sense. Maybe Lucy was in the airport and he wanted to go and say hello? Or it was another Lucy? He couldn't mean Lucy, his ex, who he'd sworn he never wanted to see again. 'Do you mean – Lucy Lucy? Your ex?' she asked, and as he nodded she felt herself grow light-headed again. This couldn't be happening.

'But, Ben – we're getting a flight.' Her mind tried to grapple with the practicalities; surely he wouldn't just leave the airport? If she could only get him on the plane, all this would blow over. 'Can't you go and see her after we get back?'

'I could, but – she's on her own for Christmas. She says she wants to see me. And I know it's short notice, and I'm really sorry about letting you all down, but . . .

6

if I leave *now*, if I make her a priority, I can show her how serious I am. A grand gesture, I suppose.'

'Like in *Love, Actually*,' Natasha said, feeling as if she'd been stabbed in the heart. With his curly dark hair and earnest blue eyes, Ben did look a bit like the guy who turned up on Keira Knightley's doorstep with his handmade sign.

'I haven't seen that,' Ben said.

Natasha found this hard to believe but now wasn't the time to berate him for his spotty knowledge of romcoms. 'But can't it wait till after Christmas?'

'No. If I leave it too late . . . the moment will be gone. I don't want her to change her mind. Please tell your mum I am really sorry, though. I hope you're not upset?'

'No!' she lied. 'I'm not. But, Ben . . .' She had run out of words. How could he do this? His bedroom had been made ready – the blue room at the front of the house, with the small iron bed, one flight down from hers. Aileen would have put some flowers in a vase, set a fire. It was all going to be so perfect; how could he give it up for that horrible Lucy? How could he even trust her after what happened between them last time? But she couldn't say that, so she said, 'But what about your bag?'

'I didn't check one in,' he said. 'Hand luggage only!'

'Oh.' She hadn't actually realized that as Ben had been running late and they had checked in separately. Perhaps she should have taken that as a sign that he wasn't fully on board with this trip in the same way she was.

'But your ticket! You won't get a refund, you know.' Surely thrifty Ben, who would only drink in the cheapest pubs and shopped from the 'reduced' aisle, wouldn't throw away the price of a ticket? But it seemed he would, for Lucy.

'I'm really sorry, Tasha,' said Ben. 'I know that your mum will be expecting me . . . but . . . you understand, don't you? When it's someone you care about this much . . .'

'Of course not. I mean, of course I do,' she said. She swallowed, wondering if she could tell him the truth now: that she didn't want him to go, that *she* cared – much more than Lucy ever could. But the words stuck in her throat.

'Is she even expecting you, Ben?' she asked. 'What if – I mean . . .' She imagined Lucy shrugging her shoulders and turning away from his handwritten sign, which almost made her feel more devastated for him than she was for herself.

'Not exactly,' he says. 'But we've been messaging. And she just sent me this – look.'

He held up his phone and showed her. She could only bring herself to skim the chain of messages, but she saw the words 'try again', 'be together' and 'want that too'. Words that she knew would be branded into her memory forever, like scenes from a horror film. She blinked back the threatening tears.

'Well!' she said, trying to gather the shreds of her dignity around her. 'If you're sure that's what you want to do.'

'Yeah, I am.' Ben looked guilty. 'I am really sorry, though . . . You're sure you don't mind?'

'Oh no. Of course not. Absolutely not.' Lies upon lies, but who cared? She just wanted this to be over now so that she could cry in peace.

'So . . . how do you think I get out of here?' he said, looking left and right.

And then, without understanding how, she was helping him with his mission; walking with him to find him a security guard, who called someone else, who called someone else who said he was going to have to leave through a special exit.

'I'm really sorry,' he kept saying to Natasha. 'Oh, crap. I never paid for this.'

He was looking at the book in his hand – *Zen and the Art of Motorcycle Maintenance*.

'It's OK, I've got it,' she said, reaching out her hand.

'Really? Thanks so much, Tasha.' He smiled gratefully and put it in his coat pocket.

'What?' she said, before realizing he had mistaken her offer to put the book back for a far more generous offer to pay for the thing. She felt too miserable to even try to set him straight, let alone grab the stupid book to have it scanned. She would just have to sort it out somehow.

'You're a star,' said Ben, looking at her with affection.

'Safe travels. Please give my best to your mum. And your sister. Tell them I'm really, really sorry – again.'

'Absolutely,' she said. 'No problem!' Congratulating herself on her composure, she gave him a quick hug and told him, with a voice that wobbled only slightly, 'Happy Christmas. I'll see you soon.'

Then she turned and started walking back to the bookshop, where she had to try to explain to a very confused cashier what had happened.

'He's left,' she explained.

'His flight left?'

There was no point in getting into it, and at least she didn't have to tell this person the full story. 'Yes. His flight left.'

With that out of the way, and her card £7.99 lighter, she made her way to the gate, feeling so keenly humiliated she could hardly lift her head. What an absolute idiot she was. She and Ben had been in a real-life Christmas romcom, but she was not the love interest. She was the romantic obstacle, the Miss Wrong.

She sat down at the departure gate and looked out of the window at the aeroplanes and tarmac under the grey winter sky. She tried not to imagine the magical scene that would be taking place soon in Lucy's flat. The ring on the buzzer; Lucy trudging down the steps expecting yet another Amazon package for her flatmate but seeing Ben. Her shock turning to joy; their kiss. Meanwhile, on the other side of the Irish Sea, Natasha arriving alone to be met by her sister at Dublin airport; the confusion, the questions, the amused sympathy. Not that she could admit to Doon that she had harboured romantic hopes for Ben. Doon was the worst possible person to admit a failure to. She would try to be sympathetic for two minutes, and then she would tap her fingers, with their giant engagement ring, and get judgemental, and she would be right. Here was Natasha, twenty-eight, still in her crappy job, no sign of a career, a house of her own or a relationship. She should have known that Ben didn't feel the same. She had packed so many hopes into her suitcase; he had been hand luggage only from the start.

Stop. She would replace these images with another. One that had always helped her in the past. She thought of Ballyclare. The approach up the driveway under the bare winter trees, tyres crunching on the gravel. The square white house, half coated in Virginia creeper, the porch with its red door adorned with a Christmas wreath. Mum waiting for her in the kitchen at the back of the house, where the fire would be lit and a space cleared for the Christmas tree that they would all buy together. She could almost hear the crackling logs burning in the fireplace, feel the heat from the range, and smell that particular mix of smoke and polish and baking that was just home. Being there would make everything better; it always had. As the call sounded for passengers to Dublin, she felt herself channelling Scarlett O'Hara and thinking, *I'll go home, to Tara.* Or rather to Ballyclare, her Tara. Where things would somehow be all right.

2

Doon sat in the arrivals lounge, clenched with anxiety. She was parked illegally in the set-down zone, which was a risk she would never take normally, but she had been running late; Natasha's flight was supposed to have landed half an hour ago and she had hoped she might have emerged by now. But she should have known better, because this was Natasha. No better woman for taking the scenic route. While other passengers were getting their bags, she would be deep in chat with some security guard or gazing out of the window at some particularly Instagrammable clouds. Doon existed in a constant state of tension while travelling, wary of taking the wrong exit or losing her ticket, but not Natasha. She breezed through life, missing trains and planes and yet somehow always arriving more or less where she had planned, mostly thanks to other people's efforts.

Doon sighed and tried to bring her thoughts back to her breath, as her yoga teacher was always telling her to. This Christmas would be different. She would not get irritated by her sweet little sister. She would accept her exactly as she was, along with her random friend or boyfriend or whatever he was. And she would count her own blessings. Her job – a dream one, senior data analyst for a multinational organization. Tick! Her home, a cottage in Ringsend – affordable and close to the GAA sports club where she trained with her running group every Wednesday. Tick, tick! Her friends. And, of course, Ciarán, her fiancé, a wonderful guy. And their wedding! That was the biggest blessing of all; it was also her biggest worry, but that was normal.

She drummed her fingers, noticing that the diamonds on her engagement ring were looking cloudy again. That was one thing she hadn't realized about diamonds: how soon the sparkle faded and how often they needed cleaning. Ciarán had even bought her a little machine that was meant to clean them with sonic waves; but somehow she could never see the difference afterwards. She thanked him profusely anyway, because it was so typically thoughtful of him. No detail was too small to escape his attention, either in their relationship or in the Irish-language school where he was deputy head. And he was very understanding, even when Doon had told him she wanted to spend Christmas at home with her own family this year, rather than with him at his parents' place as they had initially planned. He told her that this was actually in keeping with tradition; apparently you were meant to spend the Christmas before getting married with your own family. She loved that Ciarán knew these old traditions. Even more importantly she loved that he understood that family was paramount. He would make a brilliant father when the time was right.

In fact, Ciarán was so good that he didn't even mind when she had explained that she would be going to her mother's a few days early. She had planned to spend that weekend hanging out with him in Dublin, and then head down to Ballyclare on the Sunday, which was Christmas Eve. But at the beginning of December, Aileen had asked her if she would pick Natasha up from her London flight on the Friday and drive down with her that evening, so they could all have dinner together. And Doon, dutiful as always, had said yes.

It was pretty inconvenient to drive from work in rush-hour traffic all the way to Dublin airport and then back down to Wicklow. But Doon thought her mother must have some good reason for asking. Aileen would normally have preferred to have her youngest daughter all to herself for their first evening together again, even if she did have some guy in tow. Their relationship was like a long-distance romance, all anguished partings and much-anticipated reunions. Whereas with Aileen and Doon, it was more mundane: ups and downs, routine and compromise. Aileen could see Doon any time she wanted, so why did she want her there for Tasha's first night home? It had been a mystery, until Doon had gone Christmas shopping in Dublin with her mother on 8 December. They had tea afterwards in Bewley's, an annual tradition. Aileen had seemed so preoccupied that Doon had become paranoid that she was ill. Doon was always worrying about her mother – that she would twist an ankle during one of her solitary walks, or get burgled and attacked – but now she was imagining much worse: doctors, scans, diagnoses.

'No, no. It's nothing like that . . . I wanted to tell you and Tashie at the same time,' said Aileen, looking stressed.

'You're scaring me now, Mum,' Doon said, and her mother had finally confided in her.

A few months before, Aileen said, she had been alarmed to see some cracks in the drawing-room walls. She had finally decided to get in a structural engineer to take a look, and spoke to a friend at Wicklow Council who recommended someone. He had come out that week, and it had taken him ten minutes to identify subsidence.

'How much to fix it?'

Aileen put down her mince pie and dabbed her lips. 'Two hundred thousand, he says.'

Doon felt sick. The Christmas carols warbling in the background suddenly sounded distorted and harsh.

'What about the house insurance?' she asked.

Aileen covered her eyes with her hands. When she lifted her face a minute later she said, 'That's the thing. It lapsed a year ago. They sent me some paperwork but I must have overlooked it. I'm really sorry, Doon.'

They looked at each other as the enormity of it sank in – a white envelope, which looked like nothing but would have made all the difference.

'Don't say that. It's not your fault, Mum,' said Doon. And she meant it. She felt more inclined to blame herself. Aileen was practical-minded; she'd had to be, as a single parent all these years. But she also had a blind spot when it came to paperwork, letting it pile up in a letter rack beside the telephone on the hall table. Doon remembered seeing the pile one day and making a mental note to offer to go through it with her. But she hadn't wanted to offend her mother either, and she was busy herself, so she had forgotten all about it – and now it was too late.

Over tea that day they faced the facts. Aileen had a good job, teaching art in the local secondary school; she would draw a good pension if she retired at sixty in three years' time. But she only had four or five thousand in savings. That wasn't terrible, but it was certainly not enough for such extensive repairs. Doon, conscience-stricken, remembered the three thousand euros that her mother had given her towards the costs of her wedding.

'Mum, I can't believe that was such a big chunk of your nest egg. Let me give you that back at least.'

'No, no, no.' Aileen patted her hand. 'I wouldn't hear of it, chick. That's yours.'

Doon argued the point but to no avail. It wasn't as if the sum itself would make much difference in any case. Suddenly she found herself thinking of her grand-mother, their father's mother, who had died the previous June. She had been a wealthy woman, but Doon hadn't thought about the possibility of a legacy until now.

'What about Granny McDonnell's will? Anything there?' she asked.

'Oh, no, chick. That woman, her cousin, told me it was all going to charity.'

'Are you serious?' Doon shook her head. Aileen was the sole relic of this woman's son; she and Natasha were her only grandchildren. Their grandparents' house in Waterloo Road had been sold for 2.2 million a few years before; Doon had seen it written up in the *Irish Times*. It seemed extreme to give all of that to the Missions or whatever, if that was the case, but you didn't speak ill of the dead. Doon knew Aileen wouldn't want her money anyway.

'Do you really think you can raise that much money, Mum?' Doon asked. 'Wouldn't it be wiser to sell?'

'I don't know. I go back and forth,' Aileen said helplessly. 'I need to talk to the bank about a loan. I haven't had the heart to do it yet. I want to get all my ducks in a row – then do it in the New Year.'

'I see,' said Doon, not sure what ducks Aileen could mean, but understanding her not wanting to face it yet. 'I'm really sorry, Mum. I'm glad you told me.'

'I wanted to tell you both together, like I said,' said Aileen. 'But I'm actually glad now that you know. You can help me break it to Tashie.'

'Sure,' said Doon, her heart sinking.

'Thank you, love,' her mum had said. 'You're so practical. But you know how she feels these things.'

Doon said nothing but she was a little hurt at her

18

mum's assumption that she didn't feel things too. To Natasha, Ballyclare was heaven on earth; Doon's memories of it were a little more complex. But it was her childhood home too, and she felt sad at the idea of losing it after so many years. Not that it was their ancestral home or anything; they weren't old money but suburban blow-ins. The family had moved there when Doon was nearly four. There were photos of her and their father Dan standing proudly outside the house, then a wreck with roof tiles missing and at least one broken window. And one of Aileen up on a small stepladder painting a wall with the newborn Natasha in a sling. Doon could remember that day, and her anxiety lest Aileen and the baby topple down to the ground together; she had wanted to stop her but she knew she was too small and powerless. And she felt the relief that engulfed her when her dad had appeared to hold the ladder steady. That was one of her earliest and best memories of him. After he left, or more accurately went missing, there was nobody to catch Aileen when she fell – or any of them.

Doon gave herself a shake. That was ancient history and there was no point in brooding over it. She was about to duck back out and move her car, when she saw Tasha finally coming out of arrivals. Doon's irritation faded at the sight of her sister's heart-shaped face, a prettier version of Doon's own, her thick light brown curls pulled back in a velvet scrunchie. Her denim jacket looked hopelessly impractical for a Christmas visit, but that was fine. There were enough old clothes at Bally-clare to kit out an army, provided said army was willing to go to battle in Aileen's 1990s knit dresses. But where was this guy she was bringing?

'Tashie,' Doon said, giving her a hug and breathing in the cocktail of duty-free perfume; she must have tried a dozen. 'How are you? Where's your friend?'

Natasha's face fell. 'Long story,' she said. 'I'll tell you in the car.'

Doon nodded and they made their way towards the car park through the festive crowds. There was nowhere like Dublin airport at Christmas. The home-made signs, the tearful faces, the wordless hugs. Doon wasn't often overcome by emotion but it always got her. Her little sister was home and Christmas had begun. She was almost glad that this guy hadn't shown up; she would be able to catch up with Natasha in peace, before they got home and the bad news had to be broken.

Soon they were on the road and heading towards the M50, Sunshine 106 playing '2,000 Miles' by The Pretenders – a melancholy song that seemed to match Natasha's mood.

'So what happened with your friend?' Doon asked. 'Was he sick or something?'

Natasha let out a sigh. 'He . . . realized that he wanted to be with someone. His ex. He had this sudden lightning-bolt moment. And he left the airport to go and, I suppose, declare himself.'

'Gosh,' said Doon, thinking that this guy sounded as

impulsive as Natasha herself. 'That's . . .' She was about to say flaky, but realized Natasha might be insulted. 'That's romantic, I suppose,' she said instead, feeling pleased that she'd been diplomatic.

The silence from Natasha told her that this was, in fact, the wrong thing to say after all.

'What's wrong?' she asked, but she could guess, even before Natasha started to explain in a choked-up voice. 'Oh, Tasha. Were you – did you like him? I thought he was just a friend.'

'He was. I mean, we were friends, but I thought it could be more . . .'

Oh, Natasha, thought Doon. She was sorry for her sister, but also, sadly, not at all surprised. All her affairs of the heart seemed to come with an inbuilt self-destruct button.

'I'm sorry, Tash,' Doon said. 'But I think you're better off. Honestly, he sounds like a flake. Why couldn't he just wait till he got home before going to see her?'

'He was being romantic. Like you said,' said Natasha.

Doon could hear the gritted teeth and knew she should drop it, but she wanted to explain herself. Aiming for a gentler tone, she said, 'But that's not real romance. Real romance is . . .' Doon paused, trying to think of a good definition. 'Planning. Being thoughtful.'

'OK, thanks, Doon. I don't need a lecture on romance from you.'

Now Doon was insulted. 'What's that supposed to mean?' Did she mean that Ciarán wasn't romantic? Or was she blaming Doon for not being wedding mad?

The wedding had been a slightly sore point from the start, with Natasha getting upset over not being told early enough. She had intended to text her sister after calling Aileen with her news, but she had been distracted by a work email, and then Ciarán had inadvertently spilled the beans by tagging Doon the next day with a Facebook announcement. Doon had later heard, from Aileen, that her sister was upset at not being told by her first. Doon apologized, but she simply couldn't understand the big deal. What did it matter who told who when?

Natasha made no reply, so she continued, 'I'm just saying he's not worth it. And at least now you won't be getting your hopes up. Imagine if you'd spent all Christmas with him, and then –'

'Please, can we just drop it?' Natasha reached for the radio, which was now playing 'Last Christmas' and switched it off.

Doon sighed, and they drove on in silence. Poor Natasha. If she was in such a state about some guy, how was she going to take the news that her beloved house might have to be sold?

'Anyway,' Natasha said, obviously wanting to make peace, 'what's new with you? Are you going back up to Dublin tomorrow, or is this you for Christmas?'

'This is me for Christmas,' said Doon, wondering

how it was that Natasha didn't realize how inconvenient it would be for her to drive all the way back up to Dublin tomorrow just for one night. But it wasn't worth mentioning.

'Cool. And what else . . . ? Any ideas yet about bridesmaids' dresses?'

Doon swallowed. This was just one of the many wedding problems she didn't know how to solve: choosing a dress to suit both her curvy sister and her tall, athletic best friend. The hen do at least was planned; it would be a night out in Dublin in May, organized by Amy. The dress was the part Doon was happiest about; it was a white slip dress from Calvin Klein that Aileen had found in the Brown Thomas sale. But wedding planning was like a hydra; no sooner had you planned one thing than three others popped up, like the question of bridesmaids' dresses.

'I'm not sure . . . I'm just thinking I might just ask you both to choose something for yourselves. That would work, wouldn't it?'

'Well, sure. If you really don't mind. Hey, don't feel like you're being a bridezilla,' Natasha added, seeming to recover her good mood somewhat. 'You're allowed to get excited and take up people's time. You could even go mad and set up a WhatsApp group. Nobody would judge.'

'Thanks,' said Doon absently. She was thinking about a school friend's wedding she had heard about recently: six people in a registry office, then lunch at the

Shelbourne. She had nearly died of envy. But even Ciarán, who was so understanding, couldn't see why she wanted such an unconventional affair. When she had suggested that they keep the guest list to thirty people or so, he had looked bemused.

'But your extended family! You must have more people?' he had asked.

Doon had to explain that, no, it really was just her sister and mother, and an aunt and unknown cousins in Canada. Her grandmother on her dad's side, her last remaining grandparent, had died the previous summer. They hadn't been close; Natasha hadn't even come over from London to attend the funeral, which Ciarán thought, again, was strange beyond belief. He was from a massive Mayo clan with both parents, three grandparents, three siblings, fourteen uncles and aunts, and uncountable cousins and second cousins, all of whom expected an invitation, along with his entire GAA team and teaching colleagues. He had suggested a castle outside Dublin with capacity for two hundred guests. Two hundred! Doon felt sick. But she could understand that Ciarán's family set-up was different; he genuinely couldn't get away with a small do as too many relatives would be offended. So they had compromised on a chain hotel and one hundred and fifty guests, most of them from his side. It was still far too many. But it was too late now; that was the compromise, and the deposits had been paid. It would all be fine.

Now they were in Wicklow proper, and she felt

reassured by the familiar landmarks: the Silver Tassie with its Christmas lights; the signs for Powerscourt and Enniskerry lit up in the darkness. Not long now until she could get Natasha inside the house and break the news to her. At least it would distract them all from the absence of this guy – and from the wedding.

As they rounded a bend, a business card fell off the dashboard and Natasha leaned forward to scoop it up. '*Charles Cuffe, Property Developer*,' she read out. 'No way! That is hilarious.'

'Why so?' asked Doon, her heart beating wildly.

'Oh, you know Charlie. He was always the class joker; it's funny to see him all business now. But you know what his family's like . . .'

Natasha stopped short, remembering that of course Doon knew, because Charlie's older brother David had shattered Doon's heart irrevocably when she was sixteen.

'Sorry. Um, but why've you got Charlie's card?' Natasha asked.

'Oh . . .' Here was one of Doon's weaknesses; she was a truly terrible liar. Racking her brains, she said, 'I met him in the Spar and he gave it to me . . . He said . . . he said he would like to catch up with you?'

'Charlie did? That's nice.' Natasha seemed to perk up a little, and Doon felt guilty about the lie, while also relieved that Natasha wasn't suspicious as to why Doon had the card of a property developer. Doon had been given his card by her friend Amy, who lived in the village. It was a sign of how serious the situation was with the house that Doon was prepared to do business with one of the Cuffes, when she would have preferred never to deal with any of the family ever again.

'Ah, look. Looking good, Rathowen.'

They were driving through the village now, the narrow main street with its colourful shopfronts all lit up for Christmas. It was regularly voted the prettiest village in Wicklow, and for the season Rathowen had gone all out. Tinsel twined around every window; fairy lights were festooned over each colourful window display. In O'Connell's pharmacy the traditional Victorian street scene was out: a model of the main street in miniature complete with tiny fur-clad shoppers under wrought-iron lamp posts.

'You weren't here for the switching on of the Christmas lights, were you?' said Natasha, craning her neck around. 'They got that DJ to do it this year; he's hardly local. Enniskerry, I think he lives in.'

'How do you *know* all this?' Doon asked, not even bothering to ask Natasha why she thought she might have driven all the way from Dublin to witness the switching on of the lights.

'I don't know. It was on my Rathowen chat maybe . . . Oh, and I follow the Rathowen Tidy Towns Association online. They're hilarious, very pass-agg,' Natasha said. 'Oh, look, there's a new beautician! Ladybirds must be raging. Unless it's the same gang.'

Doon could see her devouring every detail with avid,

almost hungry eyes, Ben momentarily forgotten. She pondered the irony, that Natasha, who had ended up moving to London, was so much more plugged into the community here than she was. While Doon had always felt their status as blow-ins, and, especially after they lost their father, as not quite normal.

Why didn't Natasha just move back? Doon wondered. There wasn't much work locally, of course, but she could surely get some kind of local job or work remotely. Or maybe it was one of those long-distance loves that worked better with a sea between them. And, in any case, after this Christmas there might be no 'home' to move back to. Doon was dreading telling her, but it had to be done. Only another few miles and it would finally be out in the open; then Doon could stop agonizing about how to break it to her little sister, and focus on what to do next.

3

Pulling her ancient fake fur coat round her, Aileen stepped outside to gather some parsley. The parsley was looking a bit sad and withered at this stage in the winter, but weren't they all? It was still alive at least, which she decided to take as a reassuring sign. As was the presence of Orion, swinging his form over the fir plantation to the east, as he did every winter. Aileen looked up, trying to find a similar comforting parable here. She tried to tell herself: no matter what happens, whether I lose the house or manage to save it somehow, Orion will still watch over the winter nights at Bally-clare. It sounded good, but it wasn't any real consolation. So she gave up on Orion and threw some crumbs to the tame robin, Bobbin, who had adopted her and the house earlier that winter.

Back indoors, she chopped the parsley with quick efficient movements and then put it in a little ceramic dish ready to sprinkle over the fish pie later, now bubbling and hot in its Corning Ware container. She reflected that for all her failings and regrets, at least this was something she had taught her girls: proper knife skills and that a sprinkle of herbs improved any dish. Or maybe not. Maybe they would just shove ready meals into microwaves and use the blender to chop an onion, as she had observed Doon doing on one of her recent visits to her place in Dublin. Maybe if asked in later years what their mother had taught them, they would come up with a blank except for the one life lesson she would soon be teaching them through her failure: don't end up homeless, having let your house insurance lapse out of pure stupidity.

Of course there was no guarantee that the insurance would have paid out anyway. And maybe it was for the best. She was no idiot; she understood that she wasn't getting any younger and it made no sense for her to occupy a six-bedroom house on her own, with fuel prices going through the roof. She was fifty-seven now, which seemed like some kind of clerical error, because she still felt thirty-five, but there you were. And there was a chronic shortage of housing up and down the country. So her head told her to sell – if she even could sell, of course, given that the house was falling down.

But, oh, her heart. Her heart was so sad at the idea. The sadness struck her every day when she thought how this could be their last Christmas here. And when she thought of how she had brought the house back to life all those years ago, when she had taken the wreck that it was and made it into a home.

It had been Dan who had spotted it, returning from a drive to Blessington one Easter Sunday. He had seen the for-sale sign, and had driven up the driveway, more weeds than gravel, and they lifted Doon over a low stone wall to approach the place itself: a square white Georgian house, now sadly faded and neglected. They had peered into one broken window and seen a dusty room with bare floorboards, high ceilings and dusty plasterwork.

'What do you think? A lick of paint and it could be a beauty,' he said.

'You can't be serious,' she had said, laughing.

'Look at that,' he had said, pointing to Doon, who was climbing a low-branched monkey puzzle tree nearby – the kind that had obviously been planted by some well-travelled Victorian former owner with a waxed moustache and Malacca cane. 'This is what she needs. She can run free here; there's a stream at the bottom of the garden – she can be barefoot all summer.'

'That's true,' said Aileen, the dangers of the stream not yet crossing her mind. She was thinking of their terraced cottage in a west Dublin suburb, where she had recently twigged that the local lads hanging around the street corners on a Friday afternoon were selling drugs rather than swapping marbles as she had quaintly believed. She put a hand on her midriff, thinking of the new baby growing in it. 'Let's see how much they're asking for it.'

'No – let's tell them how much we're prepared to offer,' Dan said, his tone making him sound for a minute exactly like what he was: the son of a wealthy family, a Dubliner like Aileen but from a different social stratosphere. That very afternoon, he phoned up the estate agent who said that they were asking 95,000 euros – a bargain indeed, owing to its state of disrepair. Dan had inherited a lump sum on his twenty-first nine years ago and had invested it. With that as a deposit, and his salary as a solicitor – they could swing it. Sure, the trip to the office in Ballsbridge would be a pain, but that was what the car was for. The motorbike would be sold; he would drive instead and use the tape deck to learn Greek during his commute.

Aileen smiled, swept up in his enthusiasm and vision. She was used to his high optimistic moods, even though they were sometimes followed by down periods; she had accepted them as part of his personality. She hadn't realized, because his illness was still latent, that these highs and lows would become increasingly pronounced, with catastrophic effect, in the years to come. But that was a way away still. They would have five happy years at the house, or mostly happy ones. Until the day in August 1997 when Dan left, and never came home.

In the early years after they lost Dan, her greatest fear was that his illness would have been passed on to one of the girls. She watched with huge relief as Doon grew up serious and practical, sitting at the kitchen table doing her homework as calmly and competently as she now did her mysterious work in IT. Nothing ruffled Doon. But Natasha was a different story; the mildest peril in a story or cartoon sent her running to Aileen's lap or kept her awake with nightmares. Aileen was deeply relieved when things seemed to settle and her childhood terrors gave way to the usual teenage dramas about friends and boys. Aileen just wished that she could find her feet somehow, either in work or in a relationship, rather than drifting from one job and flat-share to the next.

Aileen sighed. You were only as happy as your least happy child, of course, but she would probably always worry about Natasha. And now she had to break it to her about the house. She had been worried about doing it with a stranger there, but perhaps Ben, the friend, would give her some moral support. Perhaps he would even prove to be a romantic prospect. She would try not to get her hopes up.

She took a last look around the house, which she had spent all week getting ready. The fir garlands and red ribbons were wreathing their way down the banister; ivy and mistletoe hung on each picture frame. The drawing room had a crackling wood fire in the grate, and its mantelpiece was also wreathed in holly and ivy, studded with a dozen red candles. The only thing missing was the Christmas tree, which they would all buy together tomorrow, as tradition demanded.

Her ruminations were interrupted by the welcome sound of car wheels crunching on the gravel. With a cry of pleasure, she took off her apron and ran to the hall, ready to open up the front door.

There she was. Looking just the same as ever; her hair a bit longer, maybe her figure a bit fuller, but her little girl nonetheless. She ran forward and gave her a huge hug, beaming over her shoulder at Doon, who

33

didn't smile back; she was opening up the boot with a look of grim concentration. She hadn't told her already, had she? But no, clearly not or Natasha wouldn't look so happy.

'Wait,' Aileen said, remembering. 'Where's your friend?'

'Oh,' Natasha said, deflating. 'I need a glass of wine before I can tell you that one.'

'Well, come on in and let's all have one. Are you all right with that bag, Doonie? Good woman. Come in, girls.' Aileen led them inside, feeling thrilled to have them both here.

They went into the kitchen together, Natasha seeming to perk up a little as she entered her favourite room.

Aileen looked around, seeing it through her daughter's eyes. Whitewashed walls with exposed stone, red earthenware floor tiles and a white Belfast sink nestled under a small dormer window, framed by red-and-white gingham curtains and looking out over the mountains. The furniture had been the same since the girls were tiny. The long scarred pine table sat eight mismatched chairs comfortably and twelve at a pinch. The wooden dresser held old Belleek and willow-pattern china mingled with the everyday stuff from Dunnes. At the other end was the living area, beside the wood burner, whose flames flickered over a rocking chair and an ancient red-velvet couch, shredded by the claws of long-gone cats. Aileen had considered replacing them when Pangur, the last one, died, but she relished the freedom of not having to look after anyone but herself. Tonight, though, it was a pleasure to feed her daughters.

They all sat down at the table in their usual places. Aileen poured wine for herself and Natasha and sparkling water for Doon, who didn't drink, and they started eating. She watched with pleasure as Natasha demolished two platefuls of fish pie and praised the ice cream churned with chunks of brown bread, which, she said, you could never get in London.

'So what happened, Tashie?' Aileen asked. 'With Ben?' She thought he must have had some terrible news or family illness to cancel his Christmas trip, which would explain Natasha's sad face.

'He just . . . had a change of heart.'

'Oh! Last night?' asked Aileen.

'No. At the airport.'

It took a few more repetitions before Aileen could literally comprehend what Natasha was saying: that this boy had actually got as far as the airport – been checked in for the flight! – before deciding to leave, to stay in London and see his ex-girlfriend. It was like something out of a film.

'Well, maybe he'll come another time?' she offered, wondering why Natasha looked so upset.

'I doubt it,' said Natasha, looking depressed.

Aileen suddenly realized how dense she had been. Of course. This boy wasn't just a friend to Natasha. She had feelings for him. Unrequited feelings obviously.

'I'm sorry, my pet, that's disappointing.' She wondered whether to say anything more explicit, but she didn't want to encourage Natasha to feel more upset about it than she already did. 'You never know what's a good thing,' she said instead.

'I suppose,' said Natasha.

Aileen silently cursed this unknown Ben for messing her around. She was hearing more and more stories like this from the younger women she taught with; all her boys were great, but when they reached their twenties they seemed to become flakiness personified. Maybe this was just what men were like now? Or – a worse thought – was this the inevitable legacy of what happened with Dan, of the hole that was left in her daughters' lives? She sometimes wondered if Natasha's chequered love life had something to do with her losing her father in such traumatic circumstances when she was only five. Doon, who was eight going on nine when it happened, didn't seem to have had the same issue, but Doon was sturdier perhaps.

'Maybe you're right, Mum,' Natasha said. She sat up a bit and seemed to be trying to talk herself into a better mood. 'Anyway . . . maybe it's nice that it will be just the three of us. I can't remember the last time we did that. Last year? Oh, no, we had that German teacher from your school. How is school, Mum?'

'It's grand, thanks, love,' said Aileen, distracted. 'We have a TikTok now. I'm learning to make videos for it. It's quite fun actually.'

Catching Doon's eye, Aileen could tell she was waiting to break the news about the house. For the first time she noticed how tired Doon looked – for all the world as if she, not Natasha, had just got off a flight.

'Tashie,' she said, when they had finished the last morsel, 'there's something we need to tell you. That I need to tell you, I mean. It's about the house.' She took a deep breath.

'What about the house?' Natasha said, glancing around at the kitchen.

'Well, you see these cracks on the wall? They've appeared here, and in the drawing room, in the last couple of months,' Aileen said. 'And I decided to get in a structural engineer, to take a look. So he came out – this is just a few weeks ago – and he took a look, and apparently there's subsidence. Do you know what that means?'

'Of course,' Natasha said. 'It's when the foundations are sinking into the ground.'

'Well, yes,' said Aileen, surprised and then rolling her eyes at herself; look at her treating Natasha as if she was a child, when she was closer to thirty than twenty. 'So it's going to need major repairs.'

'Oh no,' said Natasha. 'That's a pain, Mum. So you'll have to move out for the duration of the works? I'll ask around. I'm sure somebody has a room going, or you'd probably want your own place, would you? Let me think.'

Doon shot Aileen a look or rather a glare, and she could almost hear her: *Tell her now, Mum.*

Aileen sat up straighter, refusing to be intimidated by her older daughter. She would do it her own way.

'I'm afraid it's more serious than that, pet. The repairs are going to cost big. Around two hundred thousand euros, he said. And I don't have that sadly. I'm planning to go and see the bank in the New Year about a loan,' she added. 'But it's not guaranteed that they'll lend me the money. And if they don't, then I might have to sell.' It was a case of will, not might, but she wanted to soft-pedal it a bit, for Natasha.

Natasha made no sound at all but she looked ashen. *It could be worse*, Aileen told herself. *It could be a lump in my breast, not a crack in the ceiling. It's just a house. It's bricks and mortar. I have a lot more than most people.*

But Natasha's next words took her by surprise.

'Did you get a second opinion?'

Doon and Aileen looked at each other, startled; both that Natasha had thought of this very obvious next step, and that they hadn't.

'Well, no,' said Aileen. 'He was extremely well up in it. He's the man the council use.'

'Fine, but don't you want someone else to take a look?' said Natasha. She took out her phone and started tapping away at it.

'What are you doing, pet?'

'Googling subsidence,' said Doon with what looked like a smile.

'So we need another surveyor – a structural engineer,' said Natasha, after a few minutes pecking at her phone.

'I might be able to get someone to take a look after you've gone back to London,' said Aileen. 'But nobody will come out this side of Christmas.'

'Well, we don't know till we ask. Here's someone in Wicklow town . . . he's got thirteen five-star reviews. Will I text him?' said Natasha.

'Um, sure,' said Aileen, feeling bewildered at the speed at which Natasha was moving.

'It says here that seventy per cent of subsidence is caused by trees being planted too close to the house,' said Natasha. 'Did your guy say what was causing it, Mum?'

'Um, no,' said Aileen, aware that she was just repeating herself like an automaton. 'He didn't. Other than the fact that we're built on a hill, I suppose. Yes, I think that was it.'

'We do have a great big thirty-foot tree right outside too,' said Doon. 'Maybe that's the problem? In which case, we might have to prune it – or fell it.'

'What?' said Natasha. 'Doon, are you serious?'

'Well, only if that's what's causing it. There's no point repairing it if it's going to happen again. We'd have to tackle the root cause surely.'

'By chopping down Monkey? How can you just sound so calm about it?'

Aileen shushed them, distracted. The monkey puzzle tree – Monkey – was part of the family. It was where the girls learned to climb; most children found it too prickly, but Doon and Natasha had never minded it.

Doon had read the entire Anne of Green Gables series in its branches. Dan had hung a swing on the lowest limb, and they had used it for years, until the ropes became threadbare and the seat rotted and it had to come down. Natasha had cried over it for days, even though she was thirteen and old enough to know better. But Monkey had remained: a refuge that Natasha was known to still use even in her twenties, climbing to its highest branches and ignoring the green prickles to enjoy the view that stretched as far as the sea. No wonder she looked so shocked at Doon's suggestion. Aileen decided to change the subject before the two of them came to blows over it.

'Doon is just trying to think of solutions,' Aileen said to Natasha. 'Look, it was a great idea to get a second opinion; let's do that.'

'Yes,' said Natasha. She tapped rapidly at her phone, then put it down. 'I've messaged him now – so let's see. He might take a different view to the other one. Or he might even say there's no issue at all.'

'I think that's pretty unlikely,' said Doon.

'Oh yeah? And where did you study structural engineering?' Natasha shot back.

'Girls! Stop it,' Aileen said again.

They were quiet. Then Natasha said, 'All I'm saying is – something might turn up.'

'Let's wait and see. But listen, girls. No matter what happens, we will manage. Maybe this new surveyor – thanks for suggesting that, Natasha – will have better news for us. It might be that the problem's not as bad as the other one thought. Or that it will be a simpler job to repair it.'

'Yes,' said Natasha. 'Either way, let's not just give up before we've even tried.'

Doon opened her mouth, but Aileen gave her a look; she couldn't deal with any more ructions. And she felt energized by Natasha's optimism. She should have thought of a second opinion sooner. And Natasha was right. It was too soon to give up; they had faced harder trials, after all. 'We will figure it out indeed,' said Aileen. 'Now, who's for a cup of tea?'

4

Awaking the next morning in her attic room, Natasha had a moment of pure happiness before she remembered it all. Ben going back to Lucy and the house falling down. Meaning that they had to raise the money to fix it, or her mother would have to sell.

It was impossible. It couldn't be. Her mum could no more sell the house than she could sell one of her own children. Nobody else could live here; nobody else could understand Ballyclare. Natasha's eyes roved around the attic room which had been hers since childhood. There was the low window that peeped out over the front garden at the woods beyond. There were the creaky oak floorboards and the slightly crooked whitewashed walls. Her posters were still up – Pre-Raphaelite art and *Eternal Sunshine of the Spotless Mind*. The double wardrobe still held her deb's dress and countless other museum pieces like her body-con dresses, gladiator sandals and maxi skirts.

In the corner of the room was her most prized possession: the antique doll's house bought by her father over twenty years before. He had given it to Doon initially, but when Doon turned ten – just over a year after Dan left – she had given it to Natasha without explanation. 'Are you too old for it now?' Natasha asked, in awe of Doon's double figures. 'No, I just don't want it any more,' was all she would say.

Natasha thought she was crazy, and still did. The house was perfect. Each room was a whole world, with endless intricate details from the patterns on the carpets to the tiny paintings, all masterpieces in miniature. The curtains could be drawn and the doors and cupboards opened and shut. It was just a pity it was too small for them all to live in.

Natasha sighed, wishing she could confide in Ben about this new worry. On a normal day their messaging was non-stop, but this wasn't a normal day, as he was presumably still with Lucy. Or was he? For the first time Natasha considered the possibility that maybe they weren't back together. And even if they were, Ben was still her friend, and Natasha could still tell him what was happening. *It's only weird if you make it weird*, said a voice in her head that she recognized as Doon's.

She sent Ben a message. Hope things went well with L, she forced herself to write. Bad news here – it looks like the house has subsidence, which will cost ££££ that we don't have, so Mum might have to sell. Stressful. Are you free to chat at all?

She pressed send and waited for a minute before she realized she had to distract herself now. She just wished she knew what had actually happened with Lucy. Unable to stop herself, she went to his Instagram page, and scrolled through his followers to find Lucy's profile. Her grid was a hall of mirrors of model-type selfies, all pout and eyelashes. Her skin was better than Natasha's, her hair was better, her figure was a million times better, her make-up was flawless; she looked like a model. Perhaps she even *was* a model or baby influencer? She clicked through to Lucy's stories and found exactly what she didn't want: a selfie of her and Ben taken the night before, with a brimming-eyes emoji and the caption *This one*.

It hit her like a physical pain. Natasha clicked away and closed her phone before she remembered that Lucy would see that she had watched her story. Well, too bad. It was the least of her worries really.

In all the tumult of last night, she had forgotten to charge her phone and it was as precariously low as her bank balance, so she scrabbled in her bag for her charger. And drew out Charlie Cuffe's business card.

It was certainly a swanky-looking card printed on stiff, expensive paper. It was hard to square it with the boy she had known, who threw water balloons from the back row and set out to measure the height of each teacher on the blackboard while their backs were turned. But he was doing well enough now presumably. It would be nice to see him. Natasha tapped the number into her phone and composed a text. Hey, Charlie. Tasha McDonnell here. How's tricks? Will I see you in Keogh's tonight? It was the traditional get-together night for the people from their year in school: Christmas Eve Eve, so that Christmas Day itself could be hangover-free.

She inched herself out of bed, feeling how freezing

the room was despite Aileen cranking up the heating to maximum. She put on an old woolly jumper, a cardigan and two pairs of socks over her pyjamas, and hurried out of her room down towards the warmth of the kitchen. Doon's bedroom was half open and she could see that Doon was still asleep, one bare leg sticking out of the bed. Doon was famous for her amazing gift of sleep, conking out anywhere and sleeping through anything. In contrast to Natasha's room, as lovingly preserved as a shrine, Doon's room was as blank and neutral as the other two guest rooms.

Looking at her sister, Natasha reflected on how Doon was a walking reminder of how she, Natasha, would look in a parallel universe if she ate nothing but salads and carrot sticks. They were the exact same height, but Doon was slender and athletic while Natasha was built on more generous lines. It wasn't even as if Doon made any efforts in that direction, bar the running, or gave any thought to her weight or what she ate. She was just one of those people who said things like 'I forgot to have lunch', which Natasha simply couldn't understand. She was capable of forgetting many things, but lunch wasn't one of them.

A message pinged on her phone; it was from Charlie.

Deffo. Think there will be a good crowd. See you then! Xx

That was nice. Not that she had any romantic interest in Charlie obviously. But he was fun, and she had to distract herself somehow from endlessly obsessing over Ben.

Downstairs, Natasha passed the door to the study,

which had once been Aileen's studio. Aileen taught art at the local secondary school; she was one of their best-loved teachers, famous for hippyish practices like making the students meditate for five minutes before their lessons. Natasha peeked inside, wondering if her mum was painting at all. She had started up again a few years ago, but she seemed to lose heart and had abandoned a few canvases halfway through. The studio was crammed with teaching materials, including various pieces of furniture that her Transition Year students were supposed to be working on as part of a furniture-restoration module. Aileen had taken pity on the most unloved and bockety tables and chairs, and Natasha knew that she would do most of the work on them, restoring them to a satiny finish that the students would never have managed alone.

She padded into the kitchen, feeling herself relaxing and soaking in each beloved detail. Of all the rooms in the house, this was her favourite, the place she thought of when she imagined home. The air still smelled of peat smoke, as it always did, mingled with the faint scents of yesterday's cooking. Being there calmed her jagged nerves. She was home. Aileen had done the biggest of big shops, with all the favourite treats like Kimberley biscuits and After Eights, but there was no soda bread, so she decided to bake some.

She rummaged in the cupboards, finding pinhead oatmeal, brown flour, baking soda, salt and sugar. No buttermilk, so she added lemon juice to the milk and let it sit. On a whim, she decided to add some treacle too. The loaf came together quickly and she kneaded it competently, feeling the calm that descended on her whenever she baked. A final sprinkle of oats and she marked the loaf with a cross, before sliding it into the range, exactly as she had been doing since she was eight. What a pity she had never taken to anything else in life as easily as she had to cooking and baking. Not that it translated to a career. She had had a stint in a restaurant kitchen, but that had ended, literally, in tears – hers – with the head chef, yelling, just like in a movie, *'Get this girl out of my kitchen!'* She set the old kitchen timer and started cleaning up. After ten minutes, her phone pinged with a text.

Ben? No. It was the surveyor. She hadn't expected a reply so soon, especially so close to Christmas. Yet here he was; obviously an early bird. Thanks for your enquiry. It's short notice, but I am in the area this morning and can call by around eleven if that's convenient?

She replied slowly on autopilot. Yes, sure.

This was all happening too fast. This time yesterday she was coming home for Christmas with Ben. And now some random guy was going to come by and see how quickly her house was falling down. Then the doorbell went, and she said 'Oh God' aloud. It was only ten o'clock. But what if this was the surveyor already, an hour early? She hurried along the corridor into the hall, reflecting that if it was him, this was typical; the visitors you dreaded were always prompt.

A man whom she took to be the surveyor stood outside, very neatly and warmly dressed in a dark blue North Face down jacket over a neat flannel shirt, with a black beanie on his dark head. He was younger than she'd expected, and quite handsome in a pale, serious way, with thin-rimmed glasses and high cheekbones. He also looked a little familiar, though she couldn't think why.

'Hi. Is Mrs McDonnell home?' he asked. He had an American accent, which seemed odd.

'No, she's gone out for a walk. But I'm Natasha. Are you the surveyor?'

'What?' he said. 'Ah, no, I'm not. But I had an appointment with her. My name is Gabe – Gabriel Foley.'

'Um, OK?' she said. Thrown by his accent, she wondered for a moment if he was a Mormon missionary. Except why would a Mormon have an appointment?

'With Aileen? Is it about the house?'

'Yes, it is,' he said. 'I emailed her a couple weeks ago. I'm here because of the family connection?'

'Not the subsidence?' said Natasha, totally confused now.

'What? No. What subsidence?'

Natasha drew her dressing gown round her tightly. 'I don't – It's freezing, you'd better come inside. Oh, look, there she is now.' She was relieved to see her mum coming up the lane in her padded coat and welly boots.

'Mrs McDonnell, hi,' said the newcomer, turning

round to see her. 'I'm Gabe Foley. We've been in touch by email . . .'

'Oh my God,' said Aileen, standing stock still and clasping her hand to her head. 'Yes! Yes! I'm so sorry – it completely slipped my mind. Oh no, I'm mortified. Come on in. This is my daughter Natasha. She's just come home for Christmas, so I'm a bit distracted.'

'I'll go and get dressed,' said Natasha, but neither of them seemed to hear her; as they proceeded down the hall towards the kitchen, she could hear Gabe exclaiming over the house and Aileen continuing to apologize for her forgetfulness and introducing him to Doon, who was obviously up by now. So, not the surveyor, not a Mormon missionary, but an American on some kind of local pilgrimage. She got dressed quickly in thermals, grey jeans and a black polo neck, thinking that Ballyclare was the place to be this morning.

Trudging downstairs, she found Doon and Aileen in the kitchen, both listening raptly to their new visitor tell them his life story by the sounds of it.

'So I've been teaching at UCD since September, in the art history department. And I really wanted to come visit this house – because of the family connection. So I'm here in Rathowen for Christmas. I'm renting a place in the village.'

'Mum,' said Natasha, 'sorry to interrupt, but the surveyor has said he can come around eleven this morning.'

'So soon? OK, grand,' said Aileen.

'I'm sorry, have I come at a bad time?' said Gabe.

'No, no,' said Aileen. 'We are just having some structural issues looked at. These old houses, you know. But you were saying about the family connection? Tell Natasha.'

The newcomer glanced at Natasha, and with a faint blush he said, 'My great-grandfather grew up in this house.'

'No way,' said Natasha, mildly interested. 'Was he one of the Redmonds?'

'Who were the Redmonds again?' asked Doon.

'They were here in the early 1900s,' said Aileen. 'John Redmond was a doctor and he used to do the rounds with a horse and cart, so they say. But where do you come in, Gabe? You're not a Redmond, are you? They had no children.'

'No, I'm not. Well, it's quite a story. There was a servant here at that time, whose name was Mary Foley. She had a baby, though she wasn't married. And Mrs Redmond, the doctor's wife, let him live here and basically helped raise him. And when he was eighteen she gave him his passage to America. And that was my great-grandfather, Tom Foley.'

'Isn't that wonderful?' said Aileen. 'What a story. She was a lucky woman, wasn't she, your great-great granny?'

'Lucky, to have her only son head off to the States forever?' said Natasha.

'Well, when you think what else could have happened,'

said Aileen. 'Normally she would have been put into a workhouse and the baby taken away. Good for Mrs Redmond. They must have been great women, the two of them.'

'So how did you discover all this?' asked Doon.

'Well, you probably know the census from 1911 was recently made available online,' Gabe began, before elaborating on the ins and outs of his research, both online and in archives. Natasha, half listening, remembered her bread in the oven; she might miss flights but she never let a loaf burn. She turned off the timer with a minute to go, and took it out – perfect – and tapped the bottom expertly: nice and hollow. She put it on a wire rack to cool and put the butter on the table, along with salt and pepper.

'Who's for scrambled eggs?' she asked, and her mum and sister put up their hands. 'And yourself?' she asked Gabe.

'Wow,' he said, looking dazzled. 'Are you sure? I really don't want to impose . . .'

'No, you're grand,' she said, cracking eggs into the bowl and whisking them briskly.

'This is such a treat. I didn't ever think I'd be able to see inside the house my great-grandfather lived in. Let alone be given breakfast. Thank you again,' he added, as Natasha served up the food.

'So are you guys any relation to the Redmonds?' he asked.

Aileen said, smiling, 'I'm afraid we're just blow-ins.

My late husband and I bought the place in the early nineties. It was a wreck then, and the Redmonds were long gone.'

'But how did you find out about it, Gabe?' said Doon. 'The house, I mean?'

'I read about it in my great-grandfather's letters – that was how I found Ballyclare, and then the census told me "the doctor" had to be Dr Redmond. By the way, I'm pretty sure Dr Redmond was the one who called the house Ballyclare. Because that was his mother's home town in County Antrim.'

'Oh, really? What a find!' said Aileen. 'I'm sure you must be right; it's a strange name for a house because "Bally" you know means town. I've always wondered about it, and nobody seemed to know. Isn't that fascinating, Tasha?'

'Yes, it is,' Natasha said; it was interesting, but she felt faintly resentful that it was a stranger who had discovered it. Especially when Gabe proceeded to give them chapter and verse on all the previous owners of the house going back to the early 1800s, including the Victorian owner who had slapped a porch on the front of the house.

Gabe continued, 'I noticed you have a monkey puzzle tree outside – that might be his contribution too, because he was interested in exotic trees. He was friendly with Samuel Hayes – you know, the owner of Avondale, who planted all the trees?' He glanced at Natasha, who said 'mm-hmm', though actually she had no clue who Samuel Whatsit was.

'Oh, I'm sure that's true! How fascinating. Isn't it, girls?' Aileen was loving all this, and Natasha could see why, but wasn't it also kind of annoying that this guy had made himself such an expert on *their* house? He was reminding her of someone, but she couldn't think who. Someone she really liked . . . someone she felt hurt by . . .

'I'm glad you think so – I found it fascinating but often that's just me,' Gabe admitted.

Natasha gave a start. She knew who he reminded her of now. Ben. He looked a bit like him, but it wasn't just that. He was sensitive, smart, interested in history; he was sitting at the table exactly as she had imagined Ben sitting, deep in chat with her mother.

'So where are you from in the States, Gabe?' Aileen was asking.

'From Massachusetts. A town called Hingham.'

'Natasha spent a summer in Massachusetts,' said Aileen, nodding at her daughter. 'In Cape Cod.'

'Oh, nice,' said Gabe. 'What were you doing there?'

Natasha gave the briefest of replies, not wanting to encourage Aileen's heavy-handed attempt to make her bond with their visitor. Now Doon was talking about the book *Brooklyn* by Colm Tóibín, which was also about emigration. 'It's really good; have you read it?' she asked Gabe.

'Sorry, no,' he said apologetically. 'I'm not great with books written after, like, 1990. But I'll make a note of it,' he added, writing it down in his Moleskine notebook – the same brand that Ben used.

Natasha gasped aloud, and the other three glanced at her.

'Sorry,' she said, doing a fake cough. 'Went down the wrong way.'

It was uncanny; not just the notebook but the reluctance to read newer books, exactly like Ben. This guy was just a new version of Ben, sent by the universe to torment her again. Well, she wasn't going to make the same mistake twice and get sucked in to his orbit.

Now they were talking about the various areas in Wicklow that had been used for filming.

'*Braveheart*, really? I thought that was filmed in Scotland.'

'No, no, it was in Wicklow. I can't remember which locations exactly . . . Natasha's the person to ask. She knows this area like the back of her hand.'

Aileen looked at her with a 'go on' expression, and Natasha again gave the briefest possible reply. She could see Aileen had taken a great shine to Gabe; no doubt she would soon be offering him another cup of tea and a guided tour of Wicklow to boot. But Natasha wasn't getting involved or playing hostess to him any more in any way. The only man she was interested in, right now, was the surveyor who would, she hoped, turn up at any moment and tell them how to save their house.

5

Doon watched Gabe as he tried to eat and praise the food at the same time, amused at how polite and enthusiastic he sounded. He had been quite shy initially, when she and Aileen first sat down with him, but the family story was obviously a big deal to him and telling it had made him forget his self-consciousness. He was attractive in a quiet, serious way; he also *looked* like a historian, though Doon couldn't have said why except for the glasses. Now he was praising the food as though he was in a Michelin-starred restaurant.

'Natasha is an excellent cook,' said Aileen. 'In fact, Tashie, I don't know why you don't make a living out of it.'

'Well, I wasn't cut out for restaurant life,' said Natasha.

'You could do something different,' said Aileen. 'Like open a B & B.'

Aileen and Natasha looked at each other.

'I mean, you're right – we could,' said Natasha, slowly.

Doon immediately scented danger. How had she not seen this coming? Natasha and Aileen were both partial to those books in which some woman was dumped by a heartless boyfriend and started up a cupcake bakery/hat shop/antique crockery shop and within weeks was doing a roaring trade despite no previous retail or even business experience. But they couldn't possibly think that they could turn this house into a B & B, could they? Aileen would be charm itself with the guests, but Doon couldn't imagine her dealing with the admin, staffing and marketing, let alone fixing the blocked toilets in the middle of the night and all the other things guests would expect.

'Of course we'd still need the money for the repairs up front,' said Natasha.

'That's true,' said Aileen. 'Well, let's see what this other fellow has to say.'

'That should be him now,' said Natasha, turning her head at the sound of tyres on the gravel outside.

'I should get out of your hair,' said Gabe, standing up.

'No, no! Come and take a look too. You can give us a second opinion on the second opinion,' said Aileen with her cheerful laugh. They all trooped into the hall to put on their coats, Doon marvelling at how Aileen was managing to make this potentially depressing situation – a professional assessment of whether the house was falling down – into something that felt somehow exciting.

The surveyor was a thin dark guy in a fleece, who parked his car neatly beside Doon's and got out, looking slightly bemused at the size of the group waiting for him.

'Who is the, um . . . homeowner?' he asked.

'I am!' said Aileen. 'I'm Aileen – good to meet you – and these are my daughters Natasha and Doon and our friend Gabe. And this is Ballyclare.'

The surveyor glanced up at the house, and Doon found herself looking at it properly for the first time in a long time. It was Georgian, square and white, its windows and doors beautifully proportioned, the front porch with its red door adorned with the beautiful fir wreath that Aileen had made herself by hand. The sky behind it was leaden, promising snow, and the house looked like what it was: a welcoming haven, with roaring turf fires and cosy places to sit and shelter from the chill outside. Home. Doon hadn't always been happy here, but that wasn't the house's fault. She prayed briefly that the surveyor would somehow bring them better news than the last guy.

'Mike, is it? Are you local at all?' said Aileen, all smiles and obviously ready for the customary ten-minute chat about roads, neighbours and any bit of news, before settling down to business.

'Not really, I'm based in Wicklow town. Can we begin?' said the surveyor.

Mike was all business, getting straight to work without even a quick cup of tea. Instead he surveyed and photographed cracks, and took readings with a spirit level, and deployed an infra-red measuring implement.

'You definitely have subsidence,' he said eventually.

'The only question is how fast it's moving, and what's causing it. There could be a number of culprits but my money is on that tree. It should never have been planted so close to the house.' He pointed outside at Monkey.

'So if we removed it – would the problem be solved?' said Doon.

'It should prevent further sinking if that's the cause. But the damage has already been done, so you're still looking at potentially rebuilding the foundations.'

'How much will that cost?' said Aileen. 'Ballpark,' she added, as Mike demurred.

'I'm not a builder, so I can't quote you exactly, but my best guess would be somewhere in the region of three hundred to three hundred and twenty – thereabouts? Thousand, yes.'

'Oh God,' said Aileen.

Doon shot her a concerned look. She had obviously been hoping for a more optimistic view from this guy, but here he was quoting a hundred thousand more.

'What would happen if you did nothing?' said Gabe. 'Sorry – do you mind me asking?' he said to Aileen, who made a 'not at all' movement.

'As I said, that all depends on how quickly the damage is progressing. Which you can't tell before going in and digging up the ground. But in general, first you'll find that doors and windows stop opening properly.'

'That's already happening,' said Aileen, looking pale. 'I didn't realize – I thought it was the damp.'

'Then cracks start getting bigger. Then, worst-case

scenario, you could get a ceiling coming down. That might be in ten years or five, or sooner – again, it's hard to tell. And the weather is not helping, with the soil getting warmer year on year.'

Doon watched Aileen and began to feel worried; she was crumpling visibly. 'Mum, do you want a cup of tea? I'll make us all tea,' she said.

Doon fully expected Aileen to tell her no, or to say she would make it, but instead Aileen said, 'A glass of water, please.'

Doon hurried to the kitchen, feeling very concerned. Things must be bad if Aileen was drinking water; young at heart she was but she was not of the hydration generation and rarely touched the stuff except on the hottest of hot days.

She let the tap run and topped up the glass with some ice. She couldn't blame Aileen for feeling faint. Three hundred thousand. It was a horrifying sum. Doon wished that she had gone into banking or something similar and had that kind of money to give or lend her mother. But her nest egg, God dammit, was all being splurged on that stupid wedding. *The wedding*, she corrected herself. It was going to cost twenty thousand, ten thousand each, a sum that made Doon feel sick every time she thought of it.

And then she had an idea. Was this possibly even a sign or a blessing in disguise? It was the perfect excuse – not an excuse but a reason – to downsize the wedding. Not to cancel it, of course, but to make it what she longed for: a simple ceremony with the two of them and a handful of family or friends.

She would talk to Ciarán again. He would understand. They had met four years ago in a marathon-training group, and she could remember her first sight of him: a sweat-soaked back in a green Mayo county T-shirt, above a pair of black shorts, strong legs pumping away. Doon found the sight very motivating. He had been in the faster group, but when she shaved an extra five minutes off her time, she moved up into his. And he had practically saved her life during one of their practice runs, a nightmarish race up Three Rock Mountain in the driving rain. The way up was brutal enough, but on their way down Doon had lost the will to even try to jog, even though night was falling. Several runners floated past her without even seeing her, but Ciarán stopped and talked her down the mountain like a Sherpa, keeping up a stream of chat that hypnotized her legs into working again.

'You're strong; you've got this,' he kept saying. 'You can do it. Grand job. Just focus on getting to that next hillock. And the next one . . .'

Before long she had reached the bottom, and was changing into dry clothes, almost weeping in gratitude at the feeling of being on the flat again. In Lamb Doyle's pub afterwards, she bought him a pint.

'I'd still be on the mountain if it wasn't for you,' she admitted. 'You ruined your own time, I'm sorry.'

'Not at all . . . No man left behind, that's my motto. Or woman.' He stuck out a hand. 'Ciarán.'

'Doon,' she said, cringing slightly as she always did when she gave her odd name. It wasn't a typically Irish name at all; it was Scottish, she believed. But *dún* was the Irish for a fortress and literally meant 'close' or 'shut'. She dreaded introducing herself because people either said 'Doom?' or else she got a hearty laugh and the crack '*Dún an doras!*' – shut the door. But Ciarán passed the test; he just nodded and said, 'Good to meet you.'

He joined her circle of friends and the night flew by. Doon couldn't even remember when their friendship had turned into romance. There was a drunken kiss at the running club Christmas party, then drinks and the cinema, but she couldn't remember which came first; he was just always there. Around the same time Ciarán's best friend Setanta started going out with her best friend Amy. Before long their social lives were fully entwined, the two couples going out regularly together. This worried Doon initially. What if things didn't work out between her and Ciarán; how on earth would they disentangle their social lives? She watched him for all the red flags she had found in previous men – cancelled plans, mixed messages, drinking, future faking, porn addiction – surely he would have one, if not all?

There was nothing. Ciarán always texted when he said he would, remembered birthdays and planned dates. He was a deputy head teacher in a local Irish-language secondary school, who cared deeply about the kids, many of whom were from deprived families, and he went the extra mile for them, cheering them on during GAA practices and giving them extra classes after school. He was the eldest son of a big traditional family, the kind Doon had always dreamed of. After a year of dating, Doon met them all at a giant christening party in Castlebar, County Mayo. They were delightful and welcomed her with open arms. She remembered Ciarán's sister, Síle, pulling her into the family photo that was being taken outside the church.

'Oh no, it should be family just,' said Doon, demurring.

'You're grand,' said Síle with a secret smile, and Doon saw Ciarán's mother, who was very reserved, give a nod and move up slightly to accommodate Doon on the steps of the church. She took her place and felt Ciarán's hand clasp hers. Her smile for the camera was radiant. Shortly afterwards, Ciarán celebrated when Doon bought her tiny one-bedroom cottage in the run-down area near the running club, both of them knowing that she would probably sell it, and that they would move in together. And on New Year's Day, almost a full year ago, Ciarán had proposed at the top of Three Rock mountain, where they had first met. The ring had three diamonds in a platinum band.

'Three diamonds – for three years together,' Ciarán said, smiling down at her. 'And hopefully many more.'

Doon didn't love diamonds, but the sentiment was priceless. Looking at the ring on her finger, she thought she had never been happier. And she still felt that way – it was just the stress of the wedding. But maybe now there was a solution?

When she got back outside with the water, she was relieved to see that Aileen had recovered herself and was questioning Mike on practicalities.

'Would we really have to take down the tree? To prevent more damage?' she asked. Doon saw Natasha welling up, and she felt a lump in her own throat; she was surprised that Aileen could talk so calmly about axing Monkey. But her mum was made of sterner stuff than that.

'I can't say for sure until you go down into the foundations but it's very likely,' said Mike.

'But isn't it true that – may I?' Gabe asked Aileen. At her nod he continued, 'Isn't it also true that you can try other things? Like, you can put a sheet of plastic down to separate the roots from the house's foundations.'

'Yes, you could – though that's a lot of bother, versus just taking down the tree.' He stood back. 'It's a bit of a monster, isn't it? It must block a lot of light. You'd be as well to get rid of it, I would have thought.'

They all stiffened and Doon knew what they were all thinking: that Mike was not a kindred spirit and he would never be allowed to get his hands on the tree. She was grateful to Gabe for speaking up. Now Aileen was asking him, again, about the price of the works.

'Of course builders are in short supply. I'll send you some recommendations if you like. But that would be

65

my ballpark guess – three hundred thousand or possibly more.'

With these gloomy words, he gathered up all his stuff and beetled back to the car, resisting all Aileen's offers of a cup of tea and saying that he would email his invoice. They all watched him drive off, Doon marvelling at how he had managed to deliver so much bad news in barely a quarter of an hour. Not only would it cost more money than the last man said, their beloved tree might have to come down as well – unless they found a builder who could carry out Gabe's suggestion.

'Not much bedside manner,' Aileen remarked, obviously aiming for an airy tone but not quite managing it.

'I hope you didn't mind me getting involved,' said Gabe.

'Not at all,' said Aileen. 'You were great to speak up for the tree – it's good to know we don't necessarily have to chop it down.'

'Well . . . I should go,' said Gabe.

'No, come inside. Let's have a cup of tea first.'

They all trooped back inside, Aileen talking away to Gabe, and Doon was grateful for his presence, remembering how visitors and strangers always energized their mother. She made tea while the others chatted, Gabe offering sensible suggestions about not making any decisions until they had had builders in to take a look. Aileen agreed this was a good idea, Natasha talked about local builders she knew, and Doon bit her tongue to stop herself asking where on earth they all thought the money to pay the builders was going to come from.

'I did also wonder if you would be eligible for any kind of grants with the repairs . . . if it's a building of historical interest?' Gabe said, sipping his tea.

'Well, we haven't been eligible before, even when we did work on the house initially.' Aileen looked gloomy. 'That's the problem, you see,' she admitted to Gabe. 'We simply don't have the funds at the moment. We were hoping the estimate might be a bit lower. But this chap who just came is saying even more than the man I had out. It's such a huge sum, and I don't know where we're going to get it from.'

Doon was surprised at Aileen, normally so private, being so candid with this unknown visitor, but she supposed that was the point. He was just a stranger passing through; who could he tell?

'Of course, yes.' Gabe looked awkward. 'Do you have anything you could sell? Any paintings or other stuff like that?' he said, then immediately looked embarrassed.

'A kidney each?' Doon suggested, aiming to break the tension, and she was relieved that everyone smiled.

'Well, there is supposed to be gold in the hills,' said Natasha. 'Remember that, Doon?'

Doon smiled briefly at Natasha, wondering how to change the subject. She didn't want Gabe hearing about the summer their dad developed an obsession about exactly this, taking them panning for gold every day for weeks. She was surprised Natasha even remembered, because she was four going on five then; it was the summer he left.

Gabe looked amused, obviously thinking she was joking.

'No, there is gold in Wicklow,' Aileen told him. 'There was a gold rush even, back in the day.'

'Hey,' said Natasha. She stood up. 'Look!'

They all turned to where she was looking, out of the window, towards the mountain. The sky outside had darkened further; it was now a deep pewter shade and little flakes were coming down.

'But the forecast said nothing!' said Aileen.

Doon stared outside, marvelling at the sight and hoping that Ciarán would be OK on his long drive home to his family. She must ring him and tell him about this development with the house; she had no idea why she hadn't done so yet, except that she didn't want him to worry.

'I think it's a sign,' said Natasha.

'Of what?' said Doon.

'That it's going to be OK,' said Natasha. 'It will be hard, but we will raise the money somehow. Don't you think so, Mum?'

Doon looked at her mother. Surely Aileen, who had so much more life experience than any of them, would understand that it was too difficult? A bank loan or remortgaging was the only possible option, but why would the bank lend such a sum to a single person on the brink of retirement? Ballyclare would have to be sold; and the sooner they all got their heads around it, the better.

But Aileen seemed to be drawing conviction from her youngest daughter. 'I'm hoping so, Tasha. At least we will certainly give it our very best try.'

Aileen and Natasha were beaming at each other with that shared enthusiasm that Doon knew so well. Gabe interrupted their moment by saying, 'Would you mind if I took a few pictures of the house before the snow gets heavier – from out front?'

'Yes, of course,' said Aileen, distracted, and Doon said, 'Do you want us to take one of you?'

Gabe said, 'No, no – I don't need to be in it. Thanks.'

He left the room and Doon was about to suggest they take a moment to think about the whole issue of the building costs, when Natasha said, 'Doon, come outside with me – let's see if the snow is sticking.' She raced out of the kitchen door, picking her coat up off the back of her chair, leaving Doon to follow in her wake and wonder why she was the only person in her family with any relation to reality.

6

Left alone in the kitchen, Aileen watched the snow drift down outside, covering the heads of the two girls, who were arguing away. She could guess what was happening; Doon was telling Natasha that there was no way they could raise the money and Natasha was telling her they could. Maybe Doon would be proved right. But one thing she knew: this was their home. And even if she wasn't going to be successful in the end at saving it for them, she was certainly going to try, by asking the bank for a loan for a start, or a new mortgage. Or even by trying to sell her paintings again. She was so grateful to Natasha for her optimism. You needed the Doons of the world, of course, to keep you anchored to reality. But as life ground you down and you got older and more fearful, you needed the Natashas to remind you of when you were young and ready for any challenge.

A creak behind her told her Gabe had re-entered the room. He had taken off his hiking boots now, she noticed – a well brought up young man.

'Did you get your pictures?' she asked.

'Yeah, I did. The snow gave a nice effect actually.' He showed her on the screen, and she admired it, oddly touched to see that he had used a real camera instead of a phone. The pictures were good too; he had an eye for composition.

'Would you like to take any more pictures of the inside?' she asked, smiling at him. 'This room for instance? I'm sure your relative spent a lot of time here if his mother was the housekeeper.'

He was obviously about to say no, but the next minute he admitted, 'Actually, yes – that would be great.'

He took several more photos, and then put down his camera. 'It probably looks a lot different now?'

'Not really,' said Aileen. 'The kitchen was in quite good nick when we arrived, compared to the rest of the place. And the range – the cooker here – it's had lots of repairs, but it is original. So that's where your great-grandad would have had his porridge stirred up and his tea made. The table we bought, though.'

Gabe didn't gush, or ooh and aah; he just looked around silently. But he was clearly moved, and Aileen felt moved too. This house, the lives it had seen. No human being would ever see so much.

'Let me show you the rest of the downstairs,' she added. She took him around the dining room, the study and then the drawing room, feeling glad that he was seeing it all decked out for Christmas. Gabe declined the chance to take more photos, but he noticed all the details, from the sash windows with their shutters and window seats to the marble fireplaces – luckily too heavy for thieves to move, though they had tried, Aileen told him, showing him the painted-over cracks at the edges where someone had used a crowbar. But he was most struck by the plasterwork in the two main reception rooms.

'Look at that,' he said, gazing up at the cornices and ceiling rose in the drawing room, all delicately adorned with scrolls, leaves and blossoms.

'Yes, it is lovely, isn't it?' she said. 'When we came, all of that was sort of muffled with layers of paint, if you can picture that. All blobby. I thought it was just crude plasterwork. But Dan, my husband, he knew what would be underneath. He worked away on it for weeks – applying pastes and acids to it – and the detail all came out.'

Gabe nodded, and she could see that he understood the significance of the memory.

'He must have had a real talent for that kind of thing,' he said.

'Yes, he really did. He could see things I couldn't.' Aileen smiled. 'It made a terrible mess at the time, and the smell was dreadful, but it was all worth it.'

'That's for sure.' He looked up again at the ceiling, and Aileen thought that he did have an Irish look about him, with the dark hair and pale colouring.

'So have you traced any of your relatives?' she asked. 'I don't know of any Foleys in the village, I'm afraid.'

'No, I haven't. I know Mary Foley moved to Dublin after the Redmonds died and the house was sold. But I don't know what happened to her after that, or if she had any more children.'

73

'Oh, that's a pity.'

'I know. I'll keep looking, though.' He glanced out of the window, where the snow was falling more thickly now. 'I should go,' he said reluctantly.

'Can I give you a lift?' she offered.

'No, no – please. You've already been so kind. And I like walking in the snow.'

They went out to the porch together. Aileen would normally have called the girls to say goodbye to him, but she decided not to just in case they were still in the middle of an argy-bargy. It was like having teenagers again.

'By the way, how did I not know that there was a gold rush here?' Gabe was saying, as he sat down to put his hiking boots back on. 'When was that?'

'I believe it was the late 1700s,' Aileen said. 'One or two locals got lucky and then word got out, and hundreds of people descended on the rivers – using sieves and pots and pans and whatever else. Then they called in the militia. And since then it's been mined on and off, but they've never found the mother lode. Croghan Kinsella is called the Gold Mountain, you know, so who knows, it might be there.' She added, joking, 'Perhaps you'll get lucky and strike gold.'

'I already have. I feel lucky to have met you,' he said.

'You're very kind.' She thought how lovely his manners were.

'I hope things work out with the house.'

'I'm sure they will,' she said, hoping this was true.

He said, 'In fact, on that subject, I know this is probably jumping the gun, but – if you were interested . . .'

She looked at him, wondering what this was about.

'My parents have talked about buying a place in Ireland. So if you ever did decide to sell –I hope you'd let us know, because we would be interested.'

'Hey, thanks a million,' said Natasha in chilly tones. She and Doon had just appeared in the corridor behind them at precisely the wrong time. 'But it's not for sale.'

She looked at the other two. 'Is it?'

'No, no,' said Aileen.

'Well . . .' said Doon.

'Doon!' Natasha said, indignant.

Gabe said, 'I know. I just meant – if you ever did want to sell. That's all. It would keep it in the family,' he added, making everything worse.

'Oh, well, when you put it that way!' said Natasha, deeply sarcastic.

'But wouldn't they mind that it's falling down?' asked Doon.

'I mean, I'd need to talk to them first,' he said seriously. 'Given the subsidence. But my dad works in property, actually he owns a building firm, so he might not mind a project. They would probably want to rent it out too, in case that's interesting to you guys . . .'

'So we'd be your tenants, in other words?' said Natasha icily. 'Lucky us.'

Finally the penny seemed to drop. 'Oh,' he said, glancing at Aileen. 'No. Forget it. It was just an idea.'

'No, it's a great idea,' said Natasha. 'You know so much more about the house than we do – you should definitely keep it in the family. Your family.'

'*Natasha*,' said Aileen.

Working herself up further, Natasha added, 'Enjoy your tour of Wicklow. Sure, why not pick up another few houses while you're here? You might as well.'

Natasha whirled off down the passage towards the kitchen. Aileen was tempted to drag her back to apologize. If she slammed that door now, she would definitely do it. But the door was closed with angry care. Still, words would be had. She knew Natasha was upset, and Gabe had been tactless, but that was so unnecessary.

'I'm so sorry, Gabe,' she said. 'We're all a bit upset about the house, but that was dreadful. Please excuse her.'

'No, I'm the one who should be sorry,' he said, looking down. 'Should I go and apologize?'

'No, no. Don't worry. Just leave her,' said Aileen.

Doon, who was still there, said, 'She'll cool down in ten minutes.'

'Exactly. It's really OK – don't give it a second's thought.' Aileen felt sorry for him; after the lovely visit, he was clearly absolutely mortified by having dropped his clanger. She wasn't offended, though. He was so young – just Natasha's age. And he was a long way from home. She went to open the door, then paused.

'So where will you be over the Christmas?' she asked.

'Well, here. I'm house-sitting in the village, as I said.'

'No, I meant what are you doing for Christmas – for the day itself?'

Gabe said, 'I don't have specific plans. I thought I might take a walk – watch a movie?'

Aileen thought this sounded dismal. A nice young man like this, alone for Christmas? That was out of the question.

'You must come here for Christmas dinner,' she said on impulse. 'Isn't that right, Doon?'

'Of course,' Doon said. 'That would be really nice.'

'But wouldn't I be intruding?' Gabe said. 'Especially after . . .'

'Not at all,' said Aileen. 'We will look forward to it. Honestly, don't worry about Natasha. Come around one and we'll eat around two. And you can stay over if you don't want to walk back in the dark – we've plenty of room.'

Gabe still looked unsure, but a nod from Doon seemed to reassure him.

'Well, if you're sure – I'd love to,' said Gabe. 'What can I bring?'

'Just yourself,' said Aileen. 'Great, that's settled. Now I hope you won't be drenched going home. Are you sure you're OK to walk?' she added, seeing that the flakes were still coming down thick and fast.

Gabe smiled. 'I'm from Massachusetts. I can handle this, I think.'

He held up a hand in farewell and then set off down the lane, putting up the hood of his high-tech coat.

77

They both watched as he walked briskly towards the main road, his feet crunching on the light snow. Doon closed the door carefully, giving a shiver, and grabbed another fleece from the coat rack.

'You don't mind me inviting him, do you?' Aileen asked, though she knew Doon never minded things like that.

'Of course not, Mum; he seems nice.'

'Right, I'm going to talk to your sister,' Aileen said, and went off down the corridor. She was doing angry tidying up in the kitchen, but Aileen could tell from her posture that she was embarrassed now too. Aileen said nothing, just leaned against the table.

'I'm sorry, Mum,' said Natasha resentfully. 'But wasn't it outrageous? He was offering to buy our house like it was a – a – a shamrock keyring at the airport.'

Aileen continued to say nothing, just waited.

'OK, OK,' said Natasha. 'I'll tell him I'm sorry if I ever see him again. Which hopefully I won't.'

'Don't be so sure,' said Doon, coming inside and pouring herself more tea.

'What? No! Mum!' Natasha said. 'You didn't ask him for Christmas, did you? Oh, God, why?'

Aileen fought the impulse to tell her to act her age. 'He's a stranger with nowhere to go,' she said briskly. 'Now, look. Both of you. We're not going to worry about the house for the rest of the Christmas. We're going to enjoy ourselves. And in the New Year I'll talk to the bank, and I'm sure we can find a solution.'

'Really, Mum?' Natasha asked. 'You think we can?'

'Yes, really,' said Aileen. She was very far from being sure, but she wasn't going to show them how worried she was. She would let them have this Christmas at least. 'And meanwhile we've got a Christmas tree to buy!'

'I want a shower first,' said Doon.

'I'm going for a walk,' said Natasha.

'Fine,' said Aileen, wishing that she had just bought the tree herself.

7

Natasha walked slowly round the side of the house, passing a hand over Monkey's trunk before climbing the path that led uphill from the garden towards the woods. Her feet crunched lightly on the scattering of snow, but the flakes themselves had stopped. Normally it was impossible to feel sad while it was snowing, but she was horribly ashamed of her outburst just now, and gloomy about the entire debacle of this Christmas. Instead of having Ben here to enjoy a normal Christmas, she had just embarrassed herself by losing her rag with a complete stranger – who would now be joining them for festive good times. Aileen had probably only invited him to make up for her rudeness. Now they were stuck with him, when she had really wanted it to be just the three of them for once – since it might, in fact, be the last time.

She turned back on the edge of the woods to look down at the view, which was unsurpassed all around. You could see the Wicklow mountains spread out to the south, and then to the east was Dublin bay, with the city itself smudged up the northern horizon. And there was Ballyclare, white against the green fields and gardens with their dusting of snow. It looked as serene as ever, but inside she could imagine the cracks spreading and the foundations crumbling. Her house was falling down, and she hadn't even talked to Ben about it.

She picked up her phone, and her heart leaped to see that he had replied to her text this morning, asking if he was free to talk. His reply said, Sorry to hear it. Bit tied up but can ring you after Christmas?

The tone was so different it was like a message from a different person. Normally when they were apart he messaged her constantly. His ban on new things didn't extend to his phone, which was rarely far from his right hand. She flipped through their chat, to the last three things he had sent her: a long article about Wes Anderson, a video of a cat on a skateboard and a photo of the Salisbury pub on St Martin's Lane with its beautiful ornate lighting and mirrors. He sent her so many things they even had a shared hashtag: STATOY – Saw This And Thought Of You. It was a far cry from 'bit tied up'.

She cringed at the thought of how he must have tried to word his message politely and let her down gently. It was obvious that he was busy with Lucy and didn't want to talk now that he was in the couple bubble. But they were still friends, surely? He had told her, more than once, that nobody else 'got him' in the same way that she did. That she was the only person he could stay up all night talking to. And she felt the same. She had other friends in London, wide circles of acquaintances and a few good girlfriends, but in the past six months Ben had gone from a colleague she worked with most days in the cinema to the person she was closest to. Their friendship was so intense, more intense than any female friendship she'd had. It was – she realized now – the kind of friendship you could only really have when the two of you were single.

And that was what hurt the most. It wasn't just her dashed hopes for romance; it was the fear of losing him as a friend. She tried to imagine it: no more messaging, no more late-night walks all over London, no more screenings together with endless discussions afterwards over noodles in Chinatown. She felt a tear brimming and then another one; she started stumbling downhill with the hills and fields blurring before her eyes.

She wished she had someone she could talk to, but she didn't want to upset her mother, who was already dealing with the stress of the house. Perhaps she would phone her friend Billie and see if she was up for a walk – unless she was working, of course, in her job at the local hotel. The one person she couldn't confide in was Doon. They just didn't have the close relationship that her other friends with sisters had. A perfect example was over the wedding. Natasha hadn't even known Doon was getting married until she saw it on Facebook. Not only that, she had to read a gushing comment from Doon's best friend Amy saying she was 'so excited' to be maid of honour – all before she had even had a text from her sister. She was fairly certain that Doon wouldn't even have asked her to be a brides-maid had Aileen not asked her to. Natasha had tried not to be petty about it, but it still hurt. It stung so much, in fact, that she had walked almost all the way home before she realized that it was a full five minutes since she had thought about Ben or the house. Well, there was a silver lining for you.

Natasha almost found herself laughing, but the thought of the subsidence made her depressed again. She wasn't an idiot; she knew that it would cost a colos-sal sum to fix it, and she didn't know how they would ever pay back a bank loan of that size. But she wouldn't show her mother that she was worried; she would make sure she had a good Christmas at least. And something, surely, would turn up; it had to.

She thought of her mother mentioning the gold rush at breakfast. And then a memory came to her, one of the few she had of her father. They were paddling in a cold stream – maybe near Powerscourt? Or some-where else, the Gold Mines River itself? He was picking up a lump of rock from the water and showing her the sparkle in the sun. She couldn't have been more than four. But she could hear him saying, 'There's something here all right. I'll put it to one side – it might be good to have one day.' Or had he said something about getting it valued? Or was she imagining it completely? She would have to ask Doon, but a new feeling of hope came to her, as she walked through the field back down towards the house.

Then she thought once more of the American guy and his crass offer to buy the house and felt herself getting annoyed all over again. It was so unfair; here they were worried sick over the money but he could just suggest it like an impulse eBay purchase. Well, he had another think coming, or was it 'thing'? Either way, it wasn't going to happen.

8

'Come on, girls. This tree won't buy itself!' said Aileen, marching out of the house towards Doon's car. Doon followed, smiling at Aileen's haste when actually she had been waiting for ten minutes while Natasha and Aileen rushed around finding hats, phones and lip balms. She had successfully got them all into the car when Aileen had suddenly said she had forgotten something and went back into the house, emerging later with a packed Dunnes Stores bag for life that she stowed away in the boot in a mysterious fashion. Doon thought it was probably old junk that she wanted to give away without Natasha finding out; she got sentimental over any old piece of tat that had once belonged to the house, pleading for a reprieve for even old dishcloths or broken milk jugs which Doon would have put on the skip.

There was no discussion needed as to where they would buy the tree: it would be from Fenton's Christmas Tree Farm, as it was every year. Laura Fenton, nee Cuffe, was a great friend of her mum's, and also the aunt of her long-ago ex David Cuffe. The fact was that you couldn't escape that family around here. Happily David had emigrated to Australia eight years ago and now worked in Sydney as a marine biologist. He came back only every few years and never at Christmas, which suited Doon perfectly; the moon would have been better, but Sydney would do.

Doon was a careful driver but she was fast, much faster than Aileen, and her car was fast too. She had gone shopping for something to drive a few years ago with every intention of getting a nice sensible Golf or Volvo, but she had fallen in love with a second-hand Maserati Biturbo with 100,000 kilometres on the clock. They made the trip in no time at all, entering Fenton's Christmas Tree Farm with a positive skid.

'Check out Santa,' said Natasha, nodding at a sign showing John Fenton dressed as Santa Claus, and they all laughed; John, it was agreed, was no slouch when it came to publicity. Even though most people had their trees well bought by now, people were obviously still attracted to the farm for the shopping and festive atmosphere, and the place was rammed.

The car park was almost full, but Doon sidled neatly into an awkward space that Aileen or Natasha would have taken ten minutes to get into. They walked up to the entrance yard, which now featured various stalls selling Christmassy decorations and food trucks selling hot dogs and gingerbread, as well as coffees, hot chocolates and mulled wine.

'Whose idea was it to set all this up, remind me?' asked Natasha, looking around with interest at the place, which seemed to get busier by the year.

'John had the idea for the tree farm. But it was Laura

who thought of all the bells and whistles,' said Aileen. 'Did you see all the licence plates? They're from all over Leinster. They come up for the tree and make a day of it.' Doon saw that the place was staffed by various strapping local lads in Santa hats. And at dusk fairy lights would come on, making a little Christmas market in the midst of the Wicklow hills.

Doon bought them all hot chocolates, while Natasha made an impulse buy of some lemon shortbread from one of the little stalls. Then they set off down one of the tree lanes lined by twelve-foot Norway spruces. The snow had stopped, but the light dusting from earlier enhanced their colour and their cool green botanic scent. Doon trailed her finger along the branches as she passed, enjoying the spiky feel of the pine needles. Aileen was looking out for exactly the right shape and size, while Natasha was inhaling the scent.

'One of these would be perfect for the drawing room . . . and then how about one of those little dotey ones for the kitchen?' said Natasha, pointing to a row of smaller trees.

'I'm afraid one tree is plenty this year,' said Aileen. 'It's probably more than we should be spending at all. And not one of the twelve-footers – six foot is more than enough.'

'What?' said Natasha. 'Mum, no. We always have two. And a six-foot tree would be tiny in the room; that's just too sad.'

'I think you have a different idea than most of what's "too sad",' Doon suggested.

'Don't be so preachy, Doon. I'm just saying. What difference will one more tree make?'

'How about this one?' said Aileen, stopping beside a handsome eight-foot fir. 'It's not one of the whoppers, but it's a nice shape.'

'It's lovely, Mum,' said Doon, wondering how she could get away with paying for the tree without Aileen objecting. 'How much are they? I can't see. Excuse me?' she said to a nearby broad back with a high-vis vest. 'Can you tell us how much this one is?'

Then they all exclaimed, for the familiar face under the Santa hat belonged to Charlie Cuffe.

'Charlie, what are you doing here? Have you had a career change?' Natasha laughed, giving him a hug.

'No, I'm moonlighting,' he said, his eyes twinkling. Under his high-vis vest he wore a red and black plaid trucker's jacket with a Sherpa lining. Doon blinked, because for a second the resemblance to David was so strong – they had the same smile – but Charlie's short-cropped dark hair and twinkling dark eyes were different to David's fair mop and blue eyes. 'Good to see you, Mrs McD. Hey, Doon,' he added, smiling at her. She smiled back briefly, thinking that she would always see him as David's thirteen-year-old little brother.

'Have you gone into the Christmas tree biz?' asked Natasha.

'Well, temporarily – it's all hands on deck here,' he

said. 'It's a quiet week for property, but people can't get enough trees. Are you here for one yourselves? This one? It's ninety, but we can do you a deal. It's got a lovely shape, and no needles dropping.'

'It's beautiful,' said Aileen. 'There's nothing like a real tree. I think the smell is the best thing about it.'

'You're exactly right,' Charlie said. 'Actually, if you like the scent, have you considered a balsam fir? We've got some over here – let me show you.'

He hefted his chainsaw easily to his shoulder, and the three of them followed him down another green avenue, where, sure enough, the scent did seem to be more intense.

'These ones are just gorgeous,' he said. He pulled off his glove and tore a few needles from one branch, crushing them in his hand. 'Smell that – that's the smell of Christmas if you ask me.'

Natasha and Aileen did so, breathing in deeply; Doon hesitated before giving it a quick sniff. It was beautiful; deep and cool and resinous.

'That is lovely, Charlie,' said Aileen. 'How much is it?'

'It's ninety-five euro. But for you ladies, seventy.'

'Thank you, Charlie. You're very good. We'll take it.'

They stood well back while Charlie revved the chainsaw and felled the tree, before wrapping it up in white mesh and then lifting it effortlessly on his shoulder.

'Can you manage?' said Aileen in a typical mum way, making Doon smile to herself. Charlie was obviously having the time of his life, not to mention he was built like a Viking.

'No bother at all,' he said, rotating around towards the exit. 'I'll bring this to the till for you. All part of the service,' he assured Aileen.

'So are you here full-time this week?' Natasha asked, as they all walked along.

'Yes, and I did a few nights last week too. We're on high alert because of the gangs.'

'Gangs?' said Natasha, sounding shocked.

'Yep, actual bad guys, up from the big smoke . . . They stole two grands' worth from us last Christmas, do you not remember? So a few of the lads are keeping a watch out of an evening. Any of them try anything, they'll get a buzz from my saw.'

'God, please tell me you're not serious,' said Natasha.

Charlie laughed. 'Not about the chainsaw. But I am putting in some hours here of an evening, me and Bella.'

Doon wondered why he was inflicting his vigilantism on his girlfriend, but all became clear when he added, 'She's got a bark that would wake half of Wicklow.'

They had arrived back at the yard by now. Charlie said, 'So, seventy euro, please. Cash or card?'

'Let me give you some cash,' said Aileen, opening her bag.

'No, let me get this, Mum,' said Doon. 'Please. Here's my card.'

'No! Doon, you're crazy. Ignore her, Charlie. Here you go.'

Doon was embarrassed, thinking they were putting Charlie in a tricky position, but he just said with a grin, 'Card payments are preferred, Mrs McD. Sorry, I'm going to go with Doon.' He then hoisted the tree on to the roof of Doon's car and helped her click it on to the rack with the spider cords she had stored neatly in the boot.

'Nice wheels,' he said, looking at her in some surprise; he obviously didn't figure her for a sporty car. 'Well, cheers, ladies. Thanks for shopping with us – enjoy the tree.' He gave them all a thumbs-up and then pointed at Natasha. 'See you tonight at Keogh's.'

'Definitely,' said Natasha. With one of the impulsive gestures that were part of her charm she reached up to throw her arms round Charlie's neck. 'Thanks for doing us a deal on the tree, Charlie. You're a pal.'

'No worries at all.' He smiled down at Natasha, and Doon felt a spooky feeling of déjà vu. David and Charlie were very different, but they both had the kind of charm that should come with a health warning. Doon looked at Natasha, who was still smiling and blushing as she got into the car, and thought that maybe this was a silver lining; she couldn't be that heartbroken over Ben if Charlie Cuffe was able to make her smile like that. It was a pity that they couldn't ask him now about putting the house on the market. She would have to let Aileen talk to the bank first about borrowing the money for the repairs. The chances of them saying yes were slim to non-existent in Doon's opinion, but they would face that music in January.

9

Aileen was pleased to see how busy the tree farm was; she was delighted for Laura and her husband, who had turned a small sideline into a real seasonal money-spinner. It was a nice reminder that you could find new opportunities at any time of life – or so she hoped anyway.

'Could we drop into the village on the way home?' she asked, as they drove off.

'Yes, I need to get a few bits,' said Natasha.

Doon said, 'Yes, sure. I need to get all your presents actually. I haven't got anything for anyone.'

'Are you serious?' Natasha said.

'Of course not. I just wanted to give you a fright.'

'Ha, ha, hilarious,' said Natasha, withering.

'Girls,' said Aileen, wondering at how they could turn the simplest thing into a wrangle. She clutched the Dunnes Stores bag at her feet, feeling butterflies in her stomach.

By the time they arrived at the village it was lunch-time, and the streets were thronged with festive shoppers doing a few last-minute messages like Aileen and Natasha, or just soaking up the atmosphere. They crawled the streets slowly, despairing of a parking space, until Aileen remembered a spot.

'Park up by the Rathowen Arms,' she instructed Doon.

'Don't the owners always give out when people do that?'

'Changed ownership,' said Aileen. 'It's a Cuffe now. I forget which one. Frank maybe.'

'My God, that family is like the Corleones,' said Doon. 'That Dublin gang doesn't know what it's messing with.'

They parked as instructed and got out, Natasha checking the tree was securely stowed. But none of them even considered the idea that it would be taken – this was their village; nobody could walk away with their balsam fir without running the gauntlet of a dozen eyewitnesses.

Rathowen was made up of three roads, two running uphill and one downhill, that converged at a higgledy-piggledy triangular green, now whited out with snow. Aileen watched as Natasha looked around, gazing lovingly at all her favourite haunts; Daisy's coffee shop with its wooden spoons hanging in the window, the Macroom Gallery with its displays of local art, and the little goldsmith's where you could see jewellers at work at their tables. The windows were cheerful with colourful displays and tinsel and artificial snow now coated with the real thing. In the middle of the snow-mantled green a twenty-foot tree stood decked in silver bells and golden garlands. Natasha sighed at how lovely it was, and took a few photos while Doon and Aileen watched her indulgently. Then one of Aileen's Transition Year pupils stopped for a chat, which was inevitable; she couldn't set foot in the village without meeting a pupil past or present.

'All right, girls. I'll see you later,' Aileen said, when the girl had finally left. 'Say in an hour?'

'OK,' said Natasha. 'We'll meet you then, in the hotel bar.'

'OK so,' said Aileen. She crossed the road to walk round the green and then slipped up the high lane, feeling almost furtive, until she reached the door of the Macroom Gallery. Two days ago she had phoned the owner, Maria Quinlan, to ask if she would like to look at any of Aileen's paintings, and Maria had asked her to come in and show them to her.

Maria was a former pupil of Aileen's and Aileen had to admit that she didn't relish the idea of having Maria assess her after six years of it being the other way around. It was a long time ago, however; Maria must be Doon's age now. She greeted Aileen with every appearance of delight, beckoning her into the back office and offering her a cup of tea while her assistant, a lovely German girl married to a local guy, manned the till. The gallery was packed with last-minute Christmas browsers, and Aileen wondered why she'd suggested calling around at such a busy time. Could it be that she wanted some last-minute stock? Aileen could only dare to hope. Not that she could sell a painting for the price of the repairs, but every little would help.

'Well,' said Maria after the requisite ten-minute chat about their families and Christmas plans, 'I'd love to see your pieces if you have any ready to show?'

'Of course.' Aileen pulled out three canvases, twelve-by-twenty-inch landscapes: views of the Glencullen Valley, the Turquoise Café and the Glenmalure Lodge. They were classic in subject matter, but Aileen had tried to bring something new to them.

'These are great actually,' said Maria, sounding surprised.

Aileen had to smile to herself; what had she expected?

'The light is beautiful. I'm not sure, though, that it's the right fit for us . . . Our customers tend to be looking for something cutting edge, and these look more . . . classic. Mainstream, I suppose.'

'I see!' said Aileen, trying not to show how deeply insulted she was. This was a gift shop for God's sake, and the artwork here was hardly cutting edge. But Maria had some insult still to add to injury.

'And these days, we can't just rely on passing trade . . . A lot of our customers are finding art through social media. So all our artists would be on Instagram, for instance.'

'I'm on Instagram,' said Aileen. And she felt amused as Maria did a visible double-take, looking as startled as if a dinosaur had pulled out an iPhone. Admittedly her Instagram account was mostly used for following Doon and Natasha and posting the occasional picture of the countryside and of Bobbin the robin. But still, how insulting that Maria obviously considered her a digital cavewoman.

'I'll give you a follow,' said Maria generously. 'And do keep sending me new works if you have them . . . I just don't know if these current pieces are quite up our street.'

'Of course,' said Aileen, smiling widely.

She felt like asking Maria whether if most of her artists were advertising their wares via Instagram, what was the point of the gallery? But there was no use in going there. One thing about living in such a small community was that you couldn't afford to fall out with anyone, ever. And there was no point. Maria was just trying to make a living, like all of them.

The visit ended pleasantly, with wishes for a happy Christmas all round, but Aileen still couldn't help feeling downcast as she stepped outside the gallery into the frosty street. She felt irrelevant and old. She had once been a regular seller to the gallery, but that was over twenty years ago. After that she had been too busy with teaching and the kids. She had tried in recent years but she had lost her confidence, or her eye, or both. There were already countless paintings of Wicklow's beauties; did she need to add another? Now she had an answer, or this gallery's answer anyway.

She turned towards the hotel, thinking she would get there early to get a table, but she had barely gone a few paces before she heard a voice behind her calling her name. Not her married name, though – her maiden name.

'Aileen!' said a man's voice. 'Aileen Byrne?'

She turned round slowly, feeling the years fall away at the sight of a face she hadn't seen in – could it be thirty years? Surely not. But it was him. He looked the same, just a little craggier and with deeper lines around his smile. But his eyes were the same, his hair, now grey, was swept off his face in the same way, and his shoulders as broad. Still, even, the same kind of clothing that he used to wear when they were students – a dark overcoat with the collar turned up and a tartan scarf.

'CJ! My God! How are you?' she said, and they embraced.

'I'm delighted that you remember me,' he said with a smile. 'How long has it been? Let's not even count. How are you?'

'I'm very well,' she smiled, trying to remember where she had seen him last. A party in someone's student digs in Rathmines, celebrating the end of their exams. He had been studying law in the same class as Dan. His name was Conor Jameson, but they had called him CJ for obvious reasons, and also because of his ambitions to be Chief Justice. Until, in their final year, his girlfriend Maeve got pregnant by mistake. Maeve had the baby, and she and CJ finished their degrees, but he didn't go on to the Bar. She remembered that at the party he had left early to go home to Maeve and the baby – who must be grown up by now. What was her name?

'Where are you living now? Is this home?' she asked, after catching him up on her life in its barest outlines: Doon, Natasha and the house.

'Aoife – my daughter – has bought a house here, about five miles away. I'm spending Christmas with her and her family. I drove her in here to do some last-minute shopping.'

'Of course,' she marvelled. That was it: Aoife. She remembered Maeve showing her off, a crumpled red bundle, in the college bar. That bundle was now a homeowner with a family, incredible as it seemed.

'How is Maeve?' she asked.

'She's well . . . She's living in Galway now, has two more kids of twenty and twenty-two. We split up quite soon after we graduated, you know.'

'Oh, I see. Sorry to hear it,' said Aileen, thinking that it was reassuring in a way to know that she wasn't the only one whose life hadn't quite turned out as planned.

'Well, you know . . . these things happen. It was a long time ago. I've actually been living in New York for the past ten – or, gosh, it must be fifteen – years. Brooklyn.'

'No!' said Aileen. 'Very glamorous. So are you just home for the Christmas?'

'No, no, I'm moving back – I've just bought a place in Greystones. I'm needed for babysitting, you see. Two and four,' he added, when she asked his grand-children's ages.

'How lovely. I'm sorry I didn't know any of this.'

'You don't keep in touch with the old crowd.'

'Not really.'

They didn't mention Dan, though she knew his presence was vivid between them. Feeling suddenly awkward, Aileen looked at her watch discreetly, not wanting to be late for the girls.

'Well, it would be lovely to catch up further,' said CJ. 'I don't suppose you would be free for lunch? Maybe on the twenty-sixth?'

'On Stephen's Day?' Aileen said in surprise. 'I'm not sure – that might be a family day.'

CJ laughed. 'Of course. Living in the States so long, you forget how long the Christmases go on for here. Back there, it was over in a New York minute, as they say. Aoife used to come and stay with me every other year until she got married. We used to go ice-skating on the day itself. She loved it.'

Aileen was intrigued by this glimpse into his family's set-up. It was astonishing to think how much time had passed – several lifetimes, it felt like.

'Anyway,' CJ was saying, 'that's no problem if Stephen's Day is family time. I'll be back in Rathowen another time, no doubt.'

'No, that's all right. I can meet you on the twenty-sixth – that would be lovely,' she said. 'You can just text me or call me to say when and where.' She reeled off her mobile number, glancing up the road for the girls, and feeling vaguely illicit.

He entered the number, checked it with her again, and patted the coat pocket where he had put his mobile phone. 'I'll look forward to it very much.'

IO

Natasha had seen the Christmas lights in Bond Street, Regent Street and Mayfair, but to her mind nothing was as pretty as Rathowen. Everything was exactly as it should be, down to the random encounter with one of Aileen's fangirls. She smiled to herself, thinking that she had forgotten this: how going anywhere with Aileen in Rathowen was like walking around with a celebrity. Aileen was the best kind of teacher – not the one who would frown or tell on you if she saw you smoking or with a can in the street, but the kind that cared about you and encouraged you when you were feeling small. Natasha thought how lovely it must be for her to be so rooted in the community here, which then led her to a gloomier thought, that it would make it even harder for her if she had to leave. But she wouldn't. They would come up with a plan of some sort.

Remembering how her mother had scurried off, Natasha wondered where she had gone to. She hoped she hadn't given away any old clothes to charity without showing them to Natasha first. Aileen had so many garments from the 1980s and 1990s, she could open a vintage shop. That was a thought actually. Maybe there would be some priceless vintage item that could save them all? But unless it was one of Princess Diana's bridesmaid's dresses, it was hard to imagine what single garment could raise 300,000 euro.

This reminded Natasha of what she wanted to ask her sister. As they wandered towards the pharmacy, where Natasha wanted to check out scented candles, she decided to bring it up casually. 'Doon,' she said, 'this might sound mad, but – you know the gold panning? That we were talking about this morning?'

'What about it?' said Doon briefly.

'Well, do you remember Dad saying he had found a nugget? I just thought of it this morning. He said he would put it away somewhere safe.'

'Oh, Tashie,' said Doon wearily. 'He was always saying stuff like that. Just like when he said he had won the sweepstakes or got us tickets to *The Late Late Show* even. It was just his illness. None of it was real.'

Natasha sighed, recognizing that this was probably true. But really, did Doon have to be so downbeat about everything? Would it kill her to say 'maybe' once in a while – just so they could dream?

Doon seemed to recognize that she was being a buzzkill, because her next words were conciliatory.

'Charlie seemed very pleased to see you,' she said. 'You don't fancy him, do you?'

Natasha laughed. 'God, no, I've known him forever. Also, I know you think I'm totally naive but I do realize that he's a major player.'

'We should ask his advice at some point about selling the house,' Doon said. 'In that the subsidence itself might make it hard to sell. I can't believe I didn't think of it before.'

'But, Doon, we're not looking at selling. Mum's going to go and talk to the bank . . .' But Natasha could hear how tenuous that sounded. 'Something will come up,' was the best she could come up with.

'I don't think it will,' said Doon simply.

Natasha said nothing, but she wondered how their mother, the eternal optimist, had managed to produce someone as pessimistic as Doon. Had their father been similarly glass-half-empty? It was hard to say what he would have been like outside of his condition, with its extremes of wild excitement and darker periods. She remembered going to his room – she couldn't have been more than four – and asking if he wanted to come and watch cartoons with her.

'It's *The Simpsons* – that's a grown-up cartoon so it will cheer you up,' she had said.

'Nothing will cheer me up, pet,' said her father, and his tone chilled her to the bone even then. Her mother or Doon must have appeared at that point, because all she remembered was someone hushing her and taking her away, and the door closing on the darkened room where her father lay in bed.

They were at the pharmacy now; Doon opened the door and a little bell announced them. They didn't recognize the girl behind the counter – she must just be here for the Christmas rush, probably from Wicklow town or Enniskerry.

'A candle, sure,' she said, when Natasha asked. 'What kind of fragrances does she like – woody, floral, earthy, oriental?'

'Her favourite smell is . . . Christmas really. A Christmas tree, or baking, or clove oranges.'

The girl produced one in a handsome green glass jar engraved with gold. 'Limited edition, for Christmas only – scented with cinnamon, orange and cloves.'

'That's gorgeous,' breathed Natasha. 'It smells absolutely divine. How much is it?'

'Sixty-two euro,' said the girl, and Natasha said, 'Oh. OK! Let me think about it.'

They went outside, Natasha's shoulders drooping. 'Sixty-two for a candle! That's daylight robbery.'

'It's pretty standard, I would have thought?' Doon said. 'And the exchange rate's in your favour, don't forget.'

Natasha wanted to smack her. Would it kill her to just empathize for once at a mad price for a candle? Or to remember that, surprise, cinema staff didn't earn as much as data analysts? Not for the first time she felt like a loser, and wished she was the kind of person suited to a proper job like Doon's. Now she couldn't even afford a fancy candle for her mother – let alone help her with the cost of the repairs.

'Never mind. I don't expect you to understand,' Natasha said.

Doon didn't respond, which made Natasha feel bad as they walked to the corner shop. What was it that made their relationship so unsatisfactory? She felt like Doon treated her like an acquaintance, or an old school friend maybe, someone you checked in with twice a year but didn't really think about the rest of the time. She was always the one who made the effort. Why couldn't they be like the sisters in films, sharing all their troubles and joys? She hadn't even told Doon about the crappy response from Ben; anyone else would have heard all about it by now.

They passed a shop window with a banner saying *Peace on earth; goodwill to all men.* She reflected on the message and decided to try to make peace. She said, 'I didn't mean that. I just ... I wish I was a millionaire banker or lawyer, and then I could just have what we need as small change.'

'But none of us have that kind of money,' said Doon. She paused and added, 'Of course I could downsize the wedding just to a tiny thing. That would be ten grand towards it anyway.'

'You can't downsize the wedding!' Natasha said, shocked. 'I mean, it's your wedding! We want you to have it. And what would Ciarán say? You're joking, right?'

'Yes, I'm joking,' Doon said briefly. 'Of course I'm not going to.'

'Phew,' said Natasha. 'Don't even suggest it. We'd hate you to have to do that. Mum is so looking forward to it – it's going to be a happy occasion, and we need that now.' She squeezed Doon's arm, wanting to reassure her. 'Anyway, the cost of the wedding would be just a drop in the ocean. So don't worry. You're worth it!'

They walked on in silence. A group of carol singers, raising money for the St Vincent de Paul Society, had assembled at one end of the green under the Christmas tree and were singing 'Silent Night'. Natasha found herself thinking wildly of busking, to earn money. A pity she couldn't play an instrument. What about putting on a show – some kind of fringe theatre production? But she knew enough about fringe theatre to know she'd earn more as a webcam girl. She wasn't that desperate – yet.

Interrupting her thoughts, Doon said, 'Look, I've got another quick errand that I want to do by myself. I'll see you back at the hotel with Mum, OK?'

'OK,' said Natasha, wondering why it was that Doon would never tell her anything, before cheering herself up with the thought that this way she could nip into the Spar and buy a scratch card without Doon's judgy commentary on how that was a waste of money.

Doon had been cautiously optimistic that Natasha – romantic and unconventional – would be the right person to talk to about downsizing the wedding. But no, she was just as set on the big day as everyone else. And if Natasha was so shocked at the idea, Doon could only imagine what Ciarán would say. Doon's heart had sunk into her boots and stayed there – all through their late lunch beside the fire in the Rathowen Arms (toasted brie and cranberry sandwiches for Aileen and Natasha, mulligatawny soup for Doon) and coffees afterwards, and even after they got home, during what should have been the cosiest time of day: decorating the tree.

This was a much-loved ritual. First the three of them had to carry the thing inside, taking care not to knock anything over, then they brought it into the drawing room to its usual place in the bay window, and heaved it upright like three sailors lifting a mast. In years gone by Aileen had stayed loyal to the traditional bucket full of sand. But at Doon's insistence, they had moved to the more modern tripod stand, which still needed all three of them to set up, with two to hold the tree and one to check if it was crooked. The decorations lived in a wooden crate in the attic and came out like old friends every year.

'You know, Doon,' said Aileen at one point, 'this time next year, you will be decorating your own tree, with Ciarán. Won't that be lovely?'

'Yes,' said Doon, nodding. This at least was something she was genuinely looking forward to: moving in together. Ciarán owned a house in Fairview, on the north side of Dublin Bay, bought for him by his family when he went up to Dublin for university. He currently had two housemates but the plan was for them to vacate the month before the wedding, so that Doon could move in afterwards. Doon wasn't religious, but Ciarán was, as well as being very old-fashioned in some ways. He had made a persuasive case for delaying cohabitation up until they were actually married.

'Otherwise,' he said, 'it's like you get all the downsides of being married – snoring, arguments over the bins – without the security. Do you know what I mean?'

'I think so,' said Doon thoughtfully. She was a big fan of security, as well as boundaries and clarity, and she liked the idea of complete separation of the married and cohabiting state. And it wasn't just a practical notion. Ciarán was also very romantic about it, talking about carrying her over the threshold after their honeymoon.

'You could still come up to Fenton's to get the tree,' Aileen continued, still talking about Doon's first married Christmas.

'Actually, Ciarán has an artificial one,' said Doon.

'Oh God,' said Natasha in tones of despair.

'What?' Doon said defensively. 'It's more practical.'

'It's not that,' said Natasha. She was holding the fairy lights, which were an impenetrable spider's nest of tangles. 'It's just these lights. We'll never sort them out. And my scratch card was worth nothing. It's all a mess.'

It clearly wasn't all about the lights or the scratch card; if Doon had to guess, it was about the house, and probably Ben. Doon tried to think of something positive to say, but the moment had passed. Aileen had already changed the subject and they were getting to grips with the tangle of lights. Doon found herself wondering, suddenly, whether she and Natasha would be closer if Aileen didn't always know what to do or say at moments like these, while Doon was left hanging around the edges.

Tired of all this uncharacteristic introspection, Doon decided to play to her strengths with an offer of practical help. 'Anyone for a cup of tea?'

'Oh, that would be just the thing,' said Aileen, and Natasha put a thumb up.

Doon walked down the corridor, sensing each familiar creak in the golden floorboards, running her hand along the dado rail, trying to picture the reality of what it would be like next year if the house was actually sold. Would she and Ciarán host Christmas? She supposed they would, strange though it would be. It was a semi-detached house in Fairview with four bedrooms. It was true that it didn't exactly have the charm of Ballyclare, but it had plenty of room for Aileen and Natasha, and Ciarán could cook. She was a dreadful cook herself. She remembered how she had managed to set a cookbook on fire the first time she tried to make him dinner, and they both spent the evening fishing shards of blackened paper out of the coq au vin. She had been mortified, but Ciarán had laughed and told her memories were made of this; and he was quite right. She smiled now.

She was glad that the prospect of living with Ciarán was still something she could look forward to. It was just this blasted wedding. She realized, as the kettle boiled, that even if it wasn't going to make a dent in the cost of building works, she still badly wanted to change it to a smaller affair. She wished she could confide in her mother and sister about it, but they were too preoccupied with the house crisis; plus, as Natasha had said, they were looking forward to the wedding – how could she take that away from them? She needed to talk to Ciarán about it, of course, but she wanted another perspective first to see just how unreasonable she was being. While the kettle boiled, she got out her phone and texted Amy, her oldest friend and her bridesmaid.

Hey, are you around for a drink tonight or tomorrow? Would love to chat about something. Xx

She put down the phone and turned her attention to making tea, feeling reassured that at least she could talk to Amy. They had been friends since they were ten, when Aileen had made friends with Amy's mother Susan, another single mum. Doon, with her father rarely around, had immediately felt a kinship with Amy, whose parents were separated. Amy understood what it was like to feel responsible for your mother and to silently envy the other girls whose fathers picked them up from swimming or dance practice.

Amy was a reliable texter and Doon wasn't surprised that the kettle had barely finished boiling when she got a reply back:

> Sure thing! We can look at some bridesmaid dress ideas online ☺ Will I ask Mags and Emer along too? Say, 8 p.m. tonight at Keogh's?

Doon bit back her disappointment. She knew Amy was busy, of course; she had a full-time job in a bank in Wicklow town and was studying for a postgraduate degree in economics at the same time. So it made sense that she wanted to meet several friends at once; it was the sort of efficiency that Doon herself admired. But she had badly wanted to see her friend alone for once.

Doon knew what she should write in reply. She even typed it out: Actually, I could do with a chat. Just us two OK?

Her finger hovered over the send button, then she pressed delete, for so many reasons. Number one, there was no chance of them having a private chat anywhere in Rathowen this close to Christmas – someone would be bound to see them and want to join them.

Unless they both drove somewhere further afield, and that would make it too much of a big deal. And more importantly, even if they could meet in some underground car park, Doon suddenly knew the main reason she couldn't confide in Amy – who was dying to get married but whose boyfriend Setanta was less keen. They were stuck in a miserable limbo where Amy wanted to get married but wouldn't suggest it, hoping that Setanta would come through with a big proposal. Sure, Amy would try to be sympathetic, but it would be very hard for her to have patience for hearing about Doon's doubts over a big wedding. It was doubly awkward because she and Amy, and Setanta and Ciarán, were such a foursome, getting together almost every week or two.

So instead she wrote out, Sure thing. See you then. Xx It would be fine. It was just cold feet. It would all be fine.

Then a new thought occurred to her, so blindingly obvious she couldn't believe that she hadn't thought of it before. If she was moving in with Ciarán as planned, after the wedding – then she could sell her flat. They had initially planned that she would keep it and rent it out, but there was nothing stopping her from selling it. The price of it would probably almost pay for the works. It was the perfect solution. So why did she feel so nervous at the idea?

The kettle had boiled. She made tea and plonked all three mugs on a tray, knowing that Aileen would be pained that she hadn't decanted the milk into a jug, but who had time for that? Entering the drawing room, she saw her mother and sister beaming at her with pleased faces in the light of the tree, which was now twinkling from its crown to its lowest branches with what seemed like a thousand lights and ornaments, ranging from tiny wooden angels to huge, fragile glass baubles.

'Looks fab,' she said, putting down the tray. 'Will we do a selfie?'

Aileen agreed to the selfie, under duress, but then insisted on the traditional picture of both girls beside the tree, beaming, just like they did when they were little. Doon breathed in the scent; Charlie had been right. It was special. And it did strike her then how sad this was: that this could be the last time they decorated a tree at Ballyclare. She felt guilty again, as she thought that the sale of her flat could be the solution to all their woes. It was a big step, though, and would mean she would be deeply indebted to Ciarán, which didn't sit right with her. She had worked hard to buy that flat; she had been saving for it almost literally since she was twelve, starting with her confirmation money. Well, she would think about it carefully; and talk to him, of course. Right after they had discussed the size of the wedding.

'Are you going to Keogh's later, Natasha?' said Aileen. 'Make sure to have some dinner before you go. There's leftover fish pie, or you could have some smoked salmon and brown bread, or, let me see . . .'

'That's loads of options, thanks, Mum,' said Natasha with a laugh. 'Stop, or I'll eat them all.'

'I'm going too actually. I'll give you a lift,' said Doon.

'Are you? Amazing,' said Natasha, her face brightening at the thought of a lift rather than a half-hour walk along winding country lanes. Doon envied her ability to cheer herself up so easily, and resolved to try to emulate her, starting with tonight.

12

Three hours later, dinner consumed, the girls left for the pub, Aileen closing the door behind them with a slight but definite sigh of relief. It was lovely to have them home obviously, but it was also intense. She hoped the pub trip would be a bonding experience – they seemed very snappy with each other lately. No doubt it was due to the upset over the house, and hopefully the night out would take their minds off it. She went to the kitchen and cut herself three slices of Wicklow Bán brie and got some quince jam she had bought at the farmers' market and a slice of Natasha's home-made bread. She would consume all this by the light of the tree, while listening to one of her old CDs of the Vienna Boys' Choir. Heaven.

It was also a nice opportunity to think over her day, which had been eventful. Meeting CJ for a start. She hadn't thought of him in years and years, and to bump into him in Rathowen was an incredible coincidence. How long had it been since she had seen any of that crowd? Decades. She cast her mind back to the person she had been at that time, and the freezing-cold night in January 1983, when she had first met Dan.

Aileen was then in her second year at University

College Dublin, studying French and history with the idea of becoming a teacher. Not that her dream, at that point, was to become a teacher, but the idea of going to art school wouldn't even have occurred to her. Even to go to university was a huge deal; she was the first in her family to do so. Aileen cycled to the campus in Belfield in the mornings from her home in Crumlin, a suburb in the west of the city. She had the sense that other students were having a more exciting time, especially those up from the country who lived in digs. But Aileen, like the other Dubliners, lived at home and even on the occasions where she went to the mildest of evening socials, she was expected to be home by midnight at the very latest.

The winter of her first year was the coldest in living memory – the coldest, in fact, since she had been born in 1963. The house was cold; the library was cold. The snow fell deep on the ground in November and stayed there for months. Cycling became impossible, so she got the bus until she ran out of money and, not wanting to ask her mother for more, got the bike back out and cycled slowly in the slush. She had hoped that the second year would be both milder and more fun, but it was much the same, just with less snow. Cycling her bike home one January evening, her toes and feet freezing, she reflected that her college days were meant to be the most exciting in her life. It was a depressing thought.

'Phone call for you,' said her father that evening, as she sat shivering in front of the twelve-bar heater in the sitting room. Aileen turned in alarm; she hadn't remembered giving anyone her phone number. The phone itself wasn't new, but it was watched anxiously by both her parents, who seemed convinced that it would somehow cost money to receive a phone call or use electricity anyway. Her father, a nervous character at the best of times, jumped every time it rang. He had been a Garda until some incident – Aileen had never found out what – had caused him to retire and to work instead as a security guard in one of the banks in town.

'Don't tie it up,' her sister Nuala hissed on her way upstairs. 'I'm waiting for a call.'

Aileen raised her eyebrows and nodded, feeling vaguely guilty as ever at the sight of Nuala, who was plenty bright and could have gone to university herself, were it not for the fact that they couldn't afford her fees on top of Aileen's and so she was now drawing the dole while trying to find work.

'Hiya!' It took a second for Aileen to recognize the voice of Mairead, her friend from college. 'What are you doing this evening?'

'Oh, I'm just home for my tea.'

'No you're not.' She lowered her voice. 'You're coming to the theatre with me. The UCD Players are putting on *Julius Caesar*. I'm doing the make-up and I can get us into the after-party.'

'Oh.' Aileen twisted the cord of the telephone round her fingers before remembering that this was strictly forbidden. 'I can't. It's late, and it's freezing outside.'

'A few nips of gin will cure that,' said Mairead. 'Come on, you only live once. It starts at eight. I can meet you at the Blob at seven forty-five and we'll go in together.'

'I'll have to ask. Can I call you back?'

'Hardly, I'm at a payphone! Look, I'll wait at the Blob. I'll give you five minutes. Don't miss it. You're always saying you wish you could have more fun – now's your chance.'

She hung up the phone, leaving Aileen staring at the receiver. Her father was huddled over his *Evening Herald*, ash growing on his cigarette. She took the three paces into the kitchen where her mother, dressed in her flowery house coat, was frying liver and onions at the stove. The smell made her feel sick; the walls seemed to be closing in on her.

'Mam, is it OK if I go out this evening?'

Why am I even asking? Aileen thought. I'm twenty years old. But her mother's face looked as anxious as if she had requested a mission to Mars. Going to university was a concession she had made to give her daughter a better chance in life. But she obviously saw it as a path fraught with dangers. The summer before, a young nurse had been murdered in the Phoenix Park and the whole city was still in shock. But even if they didn't murder you, Aileen's mother had made it clear that men could present dangers that were just as deadly. Contraception was only available to married couples on the production of a marriage certificate. Aileen had protested that none of the squirrelly students were appealing to her, but her mother was unconvinced.

'Who with?' Aileen's mother said.

'My friend Mairead. From Knock.' Aileen hoped the mention of her friend's home town, a pilgrimage spot, would lend an air of authenticity if not holiness to the whole endeavour. 'She's got tickets to a play in college.' She added, inspired, 'It's Shakespeare.'

'Well . . .' What with Shakespeare and Knock, there was obviously nothing that could be said against it, except admonitions against the weather and the importance of dressing warmly and generally being 'careful'. Aileen flew upstairs and changed into her slouchy leather boots from Switzer's, now thankfully dry after getting soaked in the slush a few days before, though they were still a bit marked. She slid into a long wool tube skirt and changed her blouse and mohair jumper for fresh versions. She looked hickey but it would have to do. No time to do her make-up and she didn't want her mother commenting on it anyway, so she put her precious Rimmel lipstick and her new blue eyeshadow in her bag. She would apply them later in the bathroom at UCD.

'Be careful,' her father said.

'Da, I'm always careful.'

'So was poor Bridie Gargan,' said her father, referring to the young woman who had been murdered the previous summer.

Aileen kissed his cheek and slunk out of the door,

feeling utterly depressed. What a production over a simple night out. You would think they lived in a war zone, instead of a modern country in the twentieth century. Although was Ireland really a modern country? It sounded like one of the topical questions that she saw advertised on the noticeboards of the debating society, not that she often had the chance to attend them and find out for herself.

An hour's bus ride later, she was at the abstract statue known as the Blob, ready to meet Mairead, having done her face quickly in the ladies' toilets. Despite her lipstick, she still looked washed out, her face the colour of the slushy snow outside; *too much library and not enough sunlight*, she had thought, as she dabbed despairingly at her lips with her Heather Shimmer lipstick.

'You look fantastic!' said Mairead, who looked far better than her, in skintight black leggings and a red shirt slashed almost to her tiny waist. Mairead was studying arts too, except she liked to say her focus was the 'art of living' before she had to return home to Mayo to get a job. She lived the life of Riley in a hall of residence in Rathmines, and earned money on the side by cutting and styling the hair of all her fellow students, as well as doing stage make-up for the college drama society.

'I don't at all,' said Aileen. 'I'm washed out.'

'Soon fix that,' said Mairead. She got out her make-up bag, which was the size of Aileen's entire handbag, and lathered two stripes of blusher on to Aileen's cheekbones, going right up into her hairline.

'Oh,' said Aileen, looking at herself in alarm in Mairead's compact mirror.

'Now you look twenty – instead of fifteen,' said Mairead. 'Come on, it's about to start.'

The play was being held in the student theatre; Aileen had never been there and felt a pleasant sense of novelty as the audience filed in to their seats. She didn't know the play and had only a hazy notion of the plot of *Julius Caesar*, but it didn't matter. She let the poetry wash over her and enjoyed the set and costumes. The set with its columns and blue skies, the white togas and green laurel crowns made her think of sunny Mediterranean climes. She reached for her sketchbook, surreptitiously opened it and started drawing: a quick landscape and a suggestion of the figures milling around. Oh, how wonderful it would be to travel. But she didn't even have a passport.

The actor playing Mark Antony stepped forward to give his big speech over Caesar's body; this scene she knew. Aileen stared, her pen stilled. His dark curls were brushed forward under his laurel crown; his arm showed strong against the white toga. But it wasn't just his looks that caught her attention but his speaking voice: low, resonant and commanding. The others sounded like students playing a part; he sounded like a soldier.

'Who's he?' she asked Mairead in a low voice.

'Mark Antony?' she chuckled back. 'His name's Dan. Join the queue.'

Aileen looked surreptitiously in the programme. *Daniel McDonnell.* The surname seemed Scottish or Northern Irish, but he spoke like a Dubliner – a posh one. For the rest of the production, she tried not to stare but she couldn't resist a few more sketches, trying to capture the smooth lines of his profile. Mairead was eyeing her, so she put the sketchbook away, but she kept watching him. As he spoke his lines, shivers went down her spine.

'For the evil that men do lives after them. The good is oft interred with their bones . . .'

At the end she joined in the applause, but she was rolling her eyes at herself. To have her head turned by a handsome man in a play, what a dope. No doubt he had a girlfriend or a million girls after him. But she was glad she'd seen him. And she had enjoyed sketching.

'That was great, thanks, Mairead. I'd better head home now,' she said as they filed out.

'Are you mad? I can get us into the after-party. Come for one,' pleaded Mairead. Aileen glanced at the clock; she could stay for half an hour.

The party was being held in one of the smaller lecture halls down the corridor from the theatre. A keg of Guinness stood on a desk and someone was pouring perfect pints into glasses that had obviously been supplied by the brewery itself. The air was thick with smoke and chat; the cast were all there, some in normal clothes and some still in togas and laurel wreaths. Aileen was relieved to be with Mairead, who seemed to know everyone.

'Aileen, this is CJ,' she said gesturing to a tall young man with brown hair and freckles. Aileen recognized him as Julius Caesar.

'You were very good,' she said, shaking his hand. 'The play was excellent. I'm glad you're not really stabbed to death.'

CJ laughed and Aileen thought what a friendly, open face he had.

'You want to keep an eye on this lot. Infamy, infamy, they've all got it in for me! I'm glad you liked it. What are you studying and why haven't I met you before?'

'Oh, I'm doing arts. I'm in my second year,' said Aileen. She felt prickles on the back of her neck and knew, without looking around, that Mark Antony – or Daniel McDonnell – was in the room. She chatted easily to CJ, who turned out to be the boyfriend of Calpurnia in real life, until a presence beside her made her turn her head. It was Daniel.

'Hello,' he said, looking down at her.

'This is Aileen,' said CJ. 'She's studying arts. Aileen, this is Daniel McDonnell, aka Mark Antony.'

'Dan – please,' he said in that low, resonant voice. He had changed out of his toga into a dark tweed jacket, a white shirt and jeans. His eyes weren't brown as she'd thought, but a deep dark blue.

Aileen managed to stammer out a greeting. She hardly heard what CJ was saying until he repeated it twice.

'I think you should join our crew,' CJ repeated patiently over the noise.

'I can't act to save my life,' she said.

'Have you ever tried?' said Dan.

She shook her head. CJ had turned to talk to someone else and she half expected Dan to follow but he stayed gazing down at her. The effect of him, close up, was dizzying. He still had traces of stage make-up, pan-stick and eyeliner making him look like one of the New Romantics. 'I don't want to,' she found herself saying. 'Standing on a stage, everyone looking at me – that's my worst nightmare.'

He laughed. 'What do you enjoy doing then?'

'Drawing,' she said, surprised that he had asked.

'Yeah? Show me.'

'What, here?' She looked around the sea of bodies around them, wreathed in smoke and waving pint glasses.

'Yes, it's a bit rowdy,' Dan said. He lit a cigarette, offering her one first; she shook her head. 'Where are you from?'

'Crumlin,' she said, lifting her chin slightly.

'Where's that – is it Connaught?' he asked with interest.

'Are you serious? It's in Dublin,' she said, staring at him in amazement. 'It's about an hour away by bus. Out past Harold's Cross,' she added.

He laughed, but she was relieved that he looked a little embarrassed. 'So it is in the west.'

'Yes,' she said, smiling slyly at him. 'Just not as far west as you thought.'

They both laughed, and her heart warmed to him as she saw a trace of pink along his cheekbones. Oh, how handsome he was. Any moment now, surely some beautiful actress would claim him or he would make an excuse to leave. And yet, miraculously, here he still was.

'So, Aileen from Crumlin,' he said, 'you're studying arts. And you like drawing. What are you planning to do after college? What are your wildest dreams?'

'My wildest dreams?' she said. 'I don't have any really. I'm probably going to go into teaching.' She felt how utterly dull she must sound. But she really hadn't considered the question before.

'That's it?' he said. 'But what if you could do anything. Anything at all?'

She swallowed. 'I was just thinking, looking at the sets, I'd love to travel. I'd love to go somewhere hot and sunny and Mediterranean. Greece or Spain or Italy.'

'Do it,' said Dan.

She smiled, thinking it wasn't so simple. 'What do you want to do after college?' she asked.

'So many things,' he said. 'I want to travel the world. Swim the Hellespont. I want to find a beautiful old ruined house in the country and restore it. And I want to see some of your drawings.'

She was laughing now. He was so charming; she didn't want to admit that she didn't know the Hellespont from a hole in the wall.

'I'll be impressed if you do even one of those,' she said. The room was emptying out; she looked across for Mairead, who made a huge thumbs-up at her before shooting over to her side.

'Are you coming? There's a gang going to Leeson Street.'

'Leeson Street? Oh God. I can't,' said Aileen. She had only the haziest idea of what Leeson Street was like, except that it had nightclubs and would definitely be expensive.

'Of course you can,' said Dan. 'I'm going. Or I am if you are.'

Mairead gave her a look that spoke volumes.

'I can't,' she said. 'I have to get the bus home.'

Someone had turned on a record player and rigged up a disco light; one of the actresses started dancing, and others joined in.

'Ah!' said Dan. 'No need to go to Leeson Street. They've brought Leeson Street to us. May I?' He held out a hand to Aileen. Mairead's eyes were like saucers.

'I really can't.' She looked at her watch.

'Tell you what, Cinderella,' he said. 'One dance, and then I'll take you home.'

'Have you a car?' asked Mairead.

'I have a magic carpet,' said Dan. 'May I?'

She was out of excuses; she melted into his arms. Most men saw a slow dance as an excuse to cop a feel but he held her at the perfect distance: close but not too close. Despite this, she felt like she'd been plugged into mains electricity. He kept his eyes on her the entire time.

'I really have to go,' she said at the end of the song. She would have given anything to stay, but it was ten past eleven. 'I'll barely make the last bus.'

'I said I'll take you.' He put on his coat and looped a striped college scarf round his neck. Barely able to believe it, she followed him out of the room.

'Shouldn't we say goodbye?' she asked, as they hurried down a deserted corridor.

'We'll take French leave,' he said.

They were outside, in the freezing cold, before she realized she didn't know how he intended to take her home. A taxi? Or maybe he had a car? That would be luxury; she couldn't expect it. They hurried along, beside the artificial lake set in its concrete surroundings, and towards a car park where he stopped beside a motorbike.

'Oh my God,' she said.

'Have you ever ridden one of these before? OK, here you go.' He put his helmet over her head, and carefully moved her hair out from under her collar, before zipping up her coat.

'Now – sit behind me and hold on tight.'

'How will I be able to give you directions? You won't hear a thing.'

'Good point. You said it's out west? You can squeeze my left shoulder when I need to go left, and right when I need to go right?'

'OK. What about straight on?'

'Both shoulders, of course.'

She slid her arms carefully round his middle, and they were off. She had expected to be terrified but she wasn't; she was freezing cold but it didn't matter. Her tube skirt had ridden up completely; she had to cling on to him like a limpet. The rough feel of his wool coat on her cheek, his body next to hers, the wind on her face; she was flying. She remembered just in time to stop him round the corner from her house; the talk, if the neighbours heard him, would last for months.

'Here,' she yelled in his ear, squeezing his shoulder. 'Thank you,' she said breathlessly, climbing off. The ground swam beneath her. She reached out a hand to steady herself on him. He took it, and then bent his head over it and kissed her hand though her woollen glove. She took off the helmet slowly and gave it back to him. And then, thinking that this was all a dream anyway and she might as well, she bent her head and kissed him. Time stood still. They were locked together in this moment that she never wanted to end. But eventually she had to.

'Is this your house?'

'God, no. I'm round the corner. I can't have you waking up the neighbours.' Already she could see a couple of lights turning on; no doubt she would be spotted by someone.

'Will you meet me tomorrow?' he said. 'At the lake. At twelve.'

She nodded wordlessly. She would meet him anywhere, go anywhere with him.

'And bring some of your drawings. I want to see them.'

He revved up the engine, shattering the quiet of the street. She turned round, barely able to put one foot in front of the other, until she realized she was walking the wrong way. She remembered the song they had danced to: 'More Than This'. There could be nothing more than this. Meeting Dan had changed everything and there would be no going back.

It was midnight. Aileen smiled and sighed. That was a lifetime ago – a literal lifetime in Dan's case. She could never have predicted what that night would lead to: weeks of dating, opposition from both their families, then a whirlwind wedding. Then a house and a family, two beautiful girls; and then it started to go wrong.

She had often wondered if things would have been better for him if he had never met or married her. Maybe the demands of family had exacerbated his illness and sent him on his downward spiral? But she had spent enough evenings agonizing over what happened to Dan. She would put it aside and make herself go to bed before the small hours and get some sleep before the girls came home.

13

Natasha had been thrilled at the prospect of getting a lift, not least because it meant she could wear her favourite boots, high-heeled Victorian style, instead of carrying them in a tote bag as she had planned. They went beautifully with the big black velvet circle skirt that had once belonged to Aileen, which she had teamed with a low-cut magenta top with a wrapover front. She had left her hair wild and curly and added some sparkly bronze eyeliner. But as they had driven off, she had looked at Doon in her jeans and Christmas jumper and wondered if she had maybe overdone it a tad.

'Am I OK? Not too eccentric?' she had asked.

If she'd been fishing for compliments, she was in the wrong pond; Doon just glanced at her briefly and said, 'Not really.'

Thanks, Doon, thought Natasha, feeling worried and a little envious. Despite having made little or no effort, her sister looked miles better than she did, her legs endless in her jeans. But Natasha felt she did have a certain reputation for eccentric dressing to uphold; it would probably be disappointing if she turned up in normal clothes, especially the night before Christmas Eve. This was the traditional Big Night Out in Rathowen, everybody having discovered that Christmas Day was no day for a hangover.

Her thoughts turned back to Ben again, wondering what he was doing in London, before she wrenched them away. She had regained a little bit of perspective since her meltdown that morning. He would send a better reply to her message soon, she was sure. Or they would speak after Christmas. It was understandable that he'd be busy; it didn't mean they weren't friends any more.

'Who are you meeting again?' Doon asked Natasha.

'Just everyone I suppose,' said Natasha, cheering up at the thought. 'Moya ... Síomha ... Billie ... and Charlie, of course.' She smiled again at the thought of him all dressed up in his woodcutter's gear.

Doon said, 'You're sure you're not into Charlie?'

'Doon, not this again. Why are you obsessed with this? Is it because of David –' She broke off.

'I'm not obsessed,' Doon replied, almost snapping.

Natasha said nothing, knowing from experience that David Cuffe was a topic not to be mentioned. She wasn't sure of the last time they had even spoken his name. Natasha had been thirteen going on fourteen at the time they went out, and thought Doon was so lucky to have a gorgeous seventeen-year-old boyfriend, who picked her up in a car and took her to Brittas Bay on the weekend, where the Cuffes had a caravan. Those caravan trips were a source of endless conflict with Aileen, who would only let Doon go if the Cuffes senior were there, or if there was a 'group' – which Natasha thought showed how naive Aileen was. Since when did a group ever prevent something from happening? But then things had ended with David, and Natasha had found the change in Doon quite frightening. She had taken to her bed for three full days – unheard of – with Aileen leaving trays of food outside for her. It had reminded Natasha of their father. Her terror had been matched by her relief when Doon finally came out and resumed her normal activities. Surely Doon was over him by now – it was a lifetime ago – so why was she still touchy on the topic? Maybe it was just a sense of humiliation, which Natasha could understand. Certainly there was no point in asking her.

'Here we are again,' said Doon, parking back in what Natasha now thought of as 'their' spot in the hotel car park.

'Cheers, big ears,' she said. 'Don't feel you have to stay to drive me home,' she added, thinking she should make a token gesture of independence. 'I'm sure someone will be heading back my way.'

If she had been expecting Doon to protest, she had the wrong sister in mind. 'OK,' said Doon.

Natasha was a bit startled; she was used to Doon being the designated driver. But it was fine. She was back in her happy place, and she was going to enjoy herself and forget about the house, and Ben.

*

137

Keogh's was the oldest pub in the village, and for most of its inhabitants it was *the* pub. Stepping into it, two days before Christmas, was like stepping into a time machine. The place was decorated as it was every year since Natasha and Doon had both worked there as teenagers, with probably the same old-fashioned multi-coloured lights. Each old-timey pub mirror advertising Guinness or Murphy's was crowned in holly and tinsel. No Christmas music, though, unless you counted a sing-song during the illicit lock-ins of days gone by. Just the hum of conversation, the clink of glasses, and in quieter moments the soft roar of the turf fires. Nothing had changed in Keogh's and hopefully nothing ever would.

The same went for the clientele. Within seconds Natasha had spotted three of her old school friends, the father of one of the families she used to babysit for, and – mortifyingly – a farmer who had once caught her and a boyfriend parked on his land. Luckily he was deep in his pint and crossword, ignoring the festive crowd who surged behind him.

'There's my crew,' said Doon. 'Catch you later.' And she went off to sit with her friends, while Natasha made her way to her gang to be greeted with a hero's welcome.

'She's back! Yay, Tashie!' said Moya Downes, one of her best friends from primary school. Stunning Síomha Lyons, the prettiest girl in Wicklow, was sitting beside her; there was Arthur Doyle and his boyfriend; her college friend Jayne Finucane who had briefly shared a flat with her in London – too many friends to name, all related to her through connections as intricate as a spider's web. Natasha felt the love of her home life encircle her like a hug. She was also deeply grateful that she hadn't trailed Ben's arrival to any of them, so she didn't have to answer any awkward questions.

'Who's for a drink?' she said, rubbing her hands. A cheer went up and she waved a hand to the lounge girl on duty to beckon her over.

'I'll get this one!' said Moya once their drinks arrived.

'No, I will!' she said. After all, Moya was unemployed and living at home – or she had been last time Natasha had checked. Whereas Natasha at least had a job. And if it wasn't enough to save her mother's house, it was still enough to get in a few drinks for Christmas.

'How's London, how are you, how was your flight, how's your mam?' asked Moya. Natasha beamed.

'All good. All great,' she said, clinking her glass against everyone's. 'Oh God,' she added, as she saw a curly head in the distance.

Gabe. He was sitting in a far corner, glasses on, reading a book. Oh great. Of all the pubs in Rathowen – three of them to be fair, if you counted the hotel bar – he had to come to hers.

'What?' said Arthur.

'Nothing,' said Natasha, turning her head away from Gabe. She had planned on saying something to him to smooth things over when she saw him at their house on

139

Christmas Day, but this was so awkward. It wasn't even a case of a guilty conscience; she was just embarrassed.

'Who are you staring at? That American guy? He's house-sitting Billie's uncle's house on Glenview Road,' said Síomha Lyons. 'He was at the farmers' market on Sunday. I sold him some apricot jam and some bread. Extra crusty.'

Natasha sighed. 'He's coming to us for Christmas dinner.'

'Hey, lucky you,' said Síomha. 'I think he's really cute. Kind of Clark Kent with the glasses on.'

'Do you think so? I don't see it,' said Arthur. 'Why is he having Christmas dinner with you, Tasha?'

'Mum felt sorry for him and invited him – you know she can't resist waifs or strays,' said Natasha.

'Well, go and show him some Irish hospitality! Ask him to join us,' said Síomha, sitting up and adjusting her low neckline.

Natasha pleaded briefly but peer pressure was against her; it was the proper hospitable way of Rathowen, not to mention Síomha wanted to chat him up.

She walked over to Gabe, trying to hide her mortification. 'Hi,' she said awkwardly.

'Oh, hi,' he said, looking startled and closing his book. It was a copy of *Brooklyn*, the book Doon had recommended earlier. This was also like Ben; if you recommended a book to him, he would read it. And sitting in a pub reading by himself was also very Ben. But he wasn't Ben, and she had an apology to make to him.

She said quickly, 'I'm sorry about this morning. I was a bit touchy on the topic of the house, and I lost the run of myself there.'

'Oh. No, not at all. It was a really insensitive thing for me to say. Especially after you all showed me such hospitality. I am sorry too, honestly.'

'It's OK. Let's just forget about it.' Feeling relieved, Natasha was about to make her escape when she remembered the second part of her mission. 'I'm actually over there with some friends, if you wanted to join us?' she said. 'Some old school friends. You can meet some locals,' she added, hoping that didn't sound sarcastic.

She followed his gaze behind her to where her friends were sitting. Arthur and Moya were shrieking with laughter while looking at something on Arthur's phone, Síomha and Jayne were singing Mariah Carey, and everyone else was in the middle of a screamingly loud conversation. The table in front of them contained about twenty pint glasses in various states of emptiness.

Gabe said, 'Actually, I'm good for now. Thanks, though.'

'Oh! Right,' she said, trying to hide her surprise. 'Of course. As you were.'

She turned on her heel, her face flaming. 'He's good for now, he says,' she said briefly, when she sat down, which made the others burst out laughing.

'Seriously?' said Síomha, looking insulted.

'Burn,' Arthur said sympathetically. 'Not to worry, girls. Honestly, he looks a bit of a cold fish. Why is he here if he just wants to read his book?'

Natasha said nothing but her cheeks were still hot. After she had made the effort to go over and apologize, it felt like a slap in the face. He obviously thought she and her friends were too uncouth or something and preferred to sulk in his corner with his book and soda water. Well, it was his loss.

'Where's Charlie?' she asked, to change the subject. 'He said he'd be here. We bought a tree off him earlier.'

'He's at the bar. Why do you guys always buy your tree so late?' said Moya. 'We've had ours for weeks now.'

'Tradition,' said Natasha happily. She realized she was glad not to have Gabe join them; she would have much better craic not having to make small talk with him. She would focus on her friends and enjoy her Rathowen Christmas Eve Eve as if it might be her last one – which it wouldn't be; she would make sure of that.

14

Doon was waiting at the bar, thinking about David Cuffe.

She was surprised that Natasha even remembered that romance from when Doon was sixteen, which probably looked like a non-event from the outside. There hadn't been any soap opera style drama. Just a few months of delirious happiness when they started dating just after Easter. 'Dating' was the wrong word maybe; mainly what she remembered was the kissing. Kissing for what seemed like hours parked in David's Nissan Micra in various car parks in secluded woods and glens all over Wicklow. He was seventeen and had a full driver's licence; to Doon this made him like James Bond.

They didn't just park in cars; they did other things too. Climbing the Sugarloaf mountain, David holding her as they looked out to sea. Swimming at Brittas Bay, where his family had a caravan. And then finally, going all the way with him in said caravan, armed with a twenty pack of Durex and a month's supply of the pill. She had expected it to hurt but it hadn't; it had been gorgeous, stronger and headier than any Class A drug she could imagine. What had hurt was him dumping her in August, because he was going off to university and didn't want to be tied down. Doon had never experienced pain like it. Not even the pain of her father leaving had equalled it, because this felt so personal. Dan had left all three of them, her and Natasha and Aileen, but David had only left her.

What Natasha didn't know, and hopefully never would, was what Doon did after David broke up with her. She sent letters to his house, which went unanswered, as did her calls and texts to him. So then she phoned the house and spoke to his mother Carmel, a brisk no-nonsense person who obviously thought Doon was out of her mind. 'I'll pass the message on, dear – again,' she said when Doon called for the second time. Doon vowed not to call ever again, but she cracked on the day after her seventeenth birthday. She had been convinced that surely today David would contact her, but no – he didn't text her and didn't return her call. So the next day she rang his house and got a very disgruntled Carmel Cuffe. 'Please stop calling, would you? Or I'll have to speak to your mother. Or the police.'

Doon had hung up the phone, out of her mind with shame and misery. She had gone down to the drawing room and got out a nearly full bottle of gin, while listening to 'Fix You' by Coldplay and *The Very Best of Sheryl Crow*. She had drunk almost half of it, with splashes of 7UP, when Aileen found her, and rushed her to St Columcille's Hospital in Loughlinstown where she had to have her stomach pumped. The next time she saw David, at Christmas as it happened, he spotted her coming and walked to the other side of the street to avoid her. She felt publicly humiliated, and somehow it brought the trauma of her father's loss back. For years she had nightmares where she was walking naked down the main street in Rathowen or chasing after David there. Sometimes she would see the missing posters that had been put up for her father; sometimes they had David's face on them. It was a therapist's field day, of course. Even now she still felt her toes curl with shame whenever she thought about David and his family. And she had not drunk a drop of alcohol since.

But that was years ago. She knew, rationally, that David and his mother and whoever else they told had probably forgotten about it. She had even managed two minutes of small talk with David himself last year at a school friend's wedding. Either way, Doon needed to forget about him and focus her thoughts on her own issues: namely, how to deal with her wedding cold feet.

'Doon?' said Mikey the barman, startling her from her thoughts. She got out her card and tapped his machine, realizing she had been miles away and years ago. *Present moment, Doon*, she told herself.

'Cheers, Mikey,' she said, and brought her round over to where her friends were waiting: Emer Noonan, her cousin Maggie Noonan and Doon's best friend Amy Ryan.

'Oh, Doon, what are you like? You shouldn't have bought a round. You're not drinking.' Amy shook her head mock sternly while taking the white wine Doon offered her.

Doon felt grateful, as ever, for Amy, who was really her link to her Rathowen social life, keeping her in the loop with those who would probably otherwise have drifted away from her. It was really because of the Amy connection that Doon had received an invitation to Emer's wedding, which would be two weeks before her own. It was going to be a huge affair with two hundred people in a castle in Sligo and a honeymoon in New York.

'We're just talking about Eem's honeymoon,' Amy said to Doon. 'She's booked the Sex and the City tour.'

'Oh. Will Mark enjoy that?' Doon asked, and the other two laughed even though Doon hadn't been joking. Of course there was going to be lots of wedding talk since Emer was mid-planning; she hoped that wasn't a drag for Amy given her troubles with Setanta, but she seemed chipper.

'Mark is a total Carrie,' said Emer. 'Where are you and Ciarán going, Doon?'

'We haven't actually booked it yet,' Doon said, feeling guilty; Ciarán had sent her several links to places but she hadn't been able to focus on them yet. 'We'll have to sit down in the New Year and figure it out.'

'Mark planned ours as soon as we were engaged. He's more of a Miranda actually,' said Emer thoughtfully. 'Which I suppose makes me a Steve.'

'No, no, you're a Charlotte,' said Maggie. 'You're a Carrie, Amy. And, Doon, you're definitely a Miranda.'

'Fine by me,' said Doon, flicking a glance at Amy, who made a 'sorry' face; Maggie could be a bit of a Bunny MacDougal, aka a pain in the neck, but she was Emer's cousin and such was life, so Doon made a 'don't worry' face back.

'Anyway,' said Amy. 'Now that you're here, Doon. I have a bit of news . . .'

The other two women exchanged glances and smiles; clearly they already knew what this was about.

'Are you . . . ?' said Doon.

Amy slowly drew up her left hand and wriggled her fingers. 'Yes. Setanta asked me last week. We're engaged!'

The shrieks from the three of them turned heads even in the noisy pub; Doon slid from her stool and hugged Amy tightly. 'I'm delighted for you,' Doon said in her ear. She truly, truly was. She knew how important this was to Amy and she was glad that she and Setanta had figured it out.

'When did he propose?' Doon asked.

'Ah, last weekend, when we climbed Lugnaquilla. The ring was his grandmother's; he had it reset.' Amy held out her hand and they all exclaimed at the pretty solitaire set in platinum. Doon thought how lovely it was that Setanta had done it well before Christmas, so that Amy could enjoy the whole festive season even more.

'Have you thought about when and where and who?' said Emer.

'I don't know! I want to fly off to Vegas!' Amy laughed

and knocked back her white wine, as Emer said they should get a bottle of champagne.

'After New Year's, I'm off the sauce and back on the diet,' said Emer. 'The last dress alteration is in March, so I've only got three months – two really. I'm spinning twice a week. I'm like Lance Armstrong.'

'If you really want to drop the pounds, though, Emer, cardio alone won't do it,' Maggie lectured. 'You've got to add in the strength training.'

The conversation moved to dresses and fittings, and Doon found her mind wandering. She was so happy for Amy, though – even if it did mean more wedding talk.

'I'll get a bottle of champers in,' she said, getting off her stool. 'No, really,' she said, squeezing Amy's shoulder.

'You're a star, Doon,' said Amy, smiling. She added in a low voice, 'I wanted to tell you before the others, sorry. But Emer came to my place and saw the ring before I had a chance to take it off – you know how it is.'

'All good,' said Doon and meant it. She was relieved, though, that the others had found out by chance, rather than it being proof that they were closer to Amy than she was. Suddenly an uncomfortable thought came to her. Was this how Natasha had felt when she had found out about Doon's engagement from Facebook?

The queue at the bar was elbow deep, but Doon welcomed the chance to take a breath and marshal her thoughts. Mikey had given her the near invisible bat signal saying that he had seen her and he would get to her when he could. There was nobody faster than an Irish barman, and Mikey was the fastest pour in Wicklow. He had been a new hire when Doon had had her first job in this very pub aged fifteen, and had remained unfailingly kind while she got flustered over orders and mislaid her 'float' of spare change.

'Hello again,' he said now with a nod. 'What can I get you?'

'Bottle of champagne, please, Mikey,' said Doon.

'Easy, tiger,' said a voice beside her. 'Is that all for you?'

She turned round to find that Charlie Cuffe had materialized at her elbow. He had shed his gilet and was wearing a pale blue shirt and faded jeans. *Nicely ironed shirt*, she noticed irrelevantly; Doon never ironed anything, but she appreciated those who did.

'No, we're celebrating. And four glasses please, Mikey,' she said, noticing that Mikey was simultaneously pouring Charlie's pint; the guy had four hands seemingly as well as telepathic powers.

'What's the celebration? Oh, you're engaged,' said Charlie, looking down at her left hand.

'Not me. I mean, I am, but we're celebrating my friend,' said Doon. 'Thanks, Mikey. Keep the change,' she said, tucking a fifty under an empty glass.

'Would you like a hand with those glasses?' said Charlie.

She shook her head, loading them on to a tray.

'Wedding season is coming. Brace yourself,' said Charlie.

'I know,' said Doon. She found herself adding, 'Honestly, I sometimes wish someone would crack down on it all, the way some parishes did on Holy Communions.'

'Oh yes,' said Charlie. 'At my niece's Communion recently, one kid had a tiara that lit up and played "Congratulations" when her dad pushed a button.'

Doon raised her eyebrows and nodded, thinking this must be his oldest brother Mark's little girl, whom she vaguely still thought of as a baby. 'Yes, well. None of that. No fake tan, no stretch limos, no releasing doves. Just a plain white dress and five guests each – that's what everyone should have.'

He smiled. 'Are you always so . . . practical?' he said.

Here was where someone else would have some witty banter, but Doon didn't have the banter or chat gene.

'Yes,' she said.

She was about to leave but was also distracted by tracing the resemblance to David in his face. He was dark eyed where David's were blue. But their eyes were the same shape, slightly creased at the corner, and they had the same straight brows. Similar hair; good hair, it had to be said. But Charlie's mouth was different. Wider? No, just fuller.

'Well, good for you. It's a good way to be,' he said.

'Oh. Thanks.' Doon recognized that she had probably been unfair to him. He wasn't a terrible person, just a young guy who looked a bit like his older brother. She didn't really have many memories of Charlie from back then; she hadn't spent much time at the house. And thank God for that really.

'Well, enjoy your evening,' she said, and she made her way back to her friends. She had just realized something. Amy's engagement meant, hopefully, that the whole topic would be less sensitive. So Doon could confide in her after all.

Doon sat down beside Amy and poured them all champagne, even a quarter glass for herself to toast the big occasion. 'To Amy and Setanta,' she said, smiling.

'Cheers!' said the others.

The four flutes clinked together; Doon took a sip and immediately felt her stomach heave. She put the glass down. There was no point in even trying to join in; ever since that night of the bottle of gin, her drinking days were over.

'So!' said Amy, turning to her while the other two chatted. 'What did you want to chat about? Was it bridesmaids' dresses? I wanted to show you these.'

She tapped at her phone and showed Doon multiple pictures of the same chiffon dress, sea-foam green with a dropped ruffled hem and cap sleeves. It was very pretty; Amy had great taste.

'I thought Natasha might like it too, it's got sleeves you see, and, look, it comes in this darker green too – that might suit her. And in case you don't want to be matchy-matchy. Yes?'

'Oh yes!' said Doon, trying to sound as if matchy-matchiness was what was keeping her awake at night. 'Yes, it looks great. Perfect. Thanks.'

'Fab! I'll send you the link,' said Amy, pressing buttons. 'Let's try it on anyway; we can send it back if it's no good. And Natasha can try it on too while she's here. How long is she home for?'

'I'm not sure – a week? Ten days?' Doon swallowed. Seeing a way in, she decided to seize her moment. 'Amy, I was going to say,' she said, as quietly as she could in the noisy pub.

'Uh-huh?'

'Well, there's a problem with my mum's house.' Doon caught Amy up as briefly as she could on the subsidence, the need for repairs and the likely outcome – in her opinion anyway – of Aileen selling.

'Oh God, that's desperate. So stressful. I'm really sorry, Doon. If she does have to sell I hope she gets a good price for it.'

'Thanks. I know. But one thing I did think of was – is it right for me to be having this big expensive do, while my mum's house is falling down? I was thinking of saying to Ciarán –' she glanced at the other two to check they weren't listening – 'that maybe we could scale things down. Not cancel the wedding obviously, but just go for a smaller venue.'

Amy stared at her. 'But you can't do that!'

'But what if I want to?' said Doon. She added, in her lowest possible voice, 'What if I don't really want a big do – and I'm just going along with it?' She gazed at Amy imploringly, hoping that she would get it.

'But you've sent the invitations. You've got over a hundred people who are all booked to come. So no matter what you do, you'll still have to cater for them. Is it just that you don't want a big do?'

Doon nodded.

'Well, I'm sure that's normal . . . but you have to honour the invitations. Can you imagine the conniptions if you guys tried to cut the list down to eighty or whatever? Families have fallen out over less.'

'Uh-huh,' said Doon tonelessly.

'Unless – is it really just the size of the thing? It's not cold feet about getting married, is it?' Amy was obviously trying to look sympathetic, but Doon sensed a bit of anxiety or was it just impatience?

She shook her head vigorously, as much to reassure herself as Amy. 'Oh no. No.'

'That's all right then. Look, don't be worrying yourself,' said Amy. She rubbed Doon's hand. 'You'll be grand. I'll be there beside you, don't forget!'

'Yes, of course,' said Doon. What more was there to say? She had tried, and she had got exactly the reaction she had expected. If she really tried to do this – scale down the wedding, let alone cancel it – the consequences would be appalling. She had made her bed and now she must lie in it. And it was a bed that millions of people would want! What was wrong with her?

'And, Doon, you'll be my bridesmaid, won't you?' said Amy.

'Of course I will,' said Doon, stretching her lips out into a smile.

The crowd was at a peak now, everyone full of the joys of the season. The girls were deep into the bottle of champagne, chatting hilariously. Doon sipped her tonic water and wondered what was so wrong with her, why she could never just let go and relax the way others did.

'I'm just going to the loo,' she told Amy.

She went to the bathroom even though she didn't need it; she just wanted to think. She reapplied some lipstick and then walked back out, where the first person she spotted was Cara Clarke, who had been in her class in primary school. She had obviously just been to the bar and was making her way back to her table. Doon turned round, hoping the back of her head wouldn't be recognized.

She had just turned nine and was back to school for the first time since Dan had gone missing in August. She had approached Cara and a few other girls to join in their game of elastics. And Cara had said, 'This game is only for girls who have daddies.' She had turned her back on Doon, who stood frozen to the spot.

After a minute she had found her voice. 'I do have a daddy,' she whispered.

'Where is he then?' said Cara.

Doon had had no answer for that. The other girls

had resumed their game and Doon had spent the rest of that break time hiding in the toilet. Aileen, distracted by her own turmoil, didn't notice anything when she picked her up and Doon said nothing either. And gradually the whole incident was forgotten by the other girls. She and Cara even ended up on the same camogie team in secondary school and were ostensibly cordial again, but Doon would never forget that incident and had never forgiven her.

'Doon!' said Cara pleasantly.

Too late; she had been spotted.

'Cara,' she said as nicely as she could, turning round. 'Happy Christmas.'

'You here with Ciarán?' said Cara, and Doon shook her head, remembering that through some ill wind, Cara knew him through the teaching circuit. She was now a primary-school teacher herself – the irony of which was not lost on Doon.

'Well, thanks so much for the save the date!' said Cara. 'I just sent Ciarán my RSVP. It should be a fabulous day.'

Doon somehow managed to produce pleasantries on autopilot until Cara left, while meanwhile her mind was screaming. What the actual hell? She didn't even know that Ciarán had sent out invitations without asking her, let alone invited *her*. But of course he didn't actually know what had happened between them. Doon had never spoken of it; she hadn't told him much about her father's departure, in fact, except that it had been a painful time. And now that she came to think about it, he had said something about issuing a few more invites to some teacher friends, after a few of his relatives dropped out. She just thought they would have discussed it first. Well, there it was. Not only did she still have to go through with this giant three-ring circus of a wedding but watching her on the tightrope would be Cara Clarke.

Now she had to rejoin the girls and act normal when she was feeling completely fed up with this night out. She suddenly wished she was at home with Aileen, eating cheese and crackers in front of the fire. Perhaps she could say she had a headache and flee, but she would feel bad leaving Natasha without a lift. She had told her to make her own way home, of course, but when it came down to it she wouldn't leave her stranded. And yet hadn't she made her own way home more than once after working a late shift here? Doon wondered suddenly if the reason that Natasha acted younger was because she and Aileen expected and enabled it. Or was it just that Natasha needed more minding, and so her family minded her? Maybe a bit of both.

Turning round, she collided with Charlie Cuffe, who was still standing with some guys at the bar.

'Sorry,' she said, before noticing that he seemed very distracted.

'No, no. My fault.' He looked up from his phone, somewhat wild-eyed.

'Are you OK? Did something happen?' Doon asked, concerned.

'I've had a text from Jim up at the farm. The gang are back, he says.'

'The gang?' Doon repeated, not following.

'Criminals, thieves up from Dublin. They've a van parked outside. He's called the guards but they're miles away. I need to go up there right now but I'm three pints in so I can't drive. And there's not a taxi to be had.'

Doon made a split-second decision. 'I'll drive you,' she said.

'Seriously?' said Charlie.

'Yes, as long as Natasha is OK to get home.'

'One of our friends will drive her I'd say.' He looked relieved, but then he added, 'Just a lift, though, Doon; you don't need to stay around. It's too dangerous. If you're OK to drop me off then you can come straight back here to your friends.'

'Right.' Doon turned in the direction of her friends, wondering how best to explain her mission to them. But they had been joined by Cara. Another split-second decision was all she needed.

'You know what? Let's just get out of here,' she said to Charlie.

'You don't want to tell your friends?'

No, she didn't. She couldn't say why exactly except that she was sick of trying to explain herself. She would text Amy from the car and tell her something had come up. She shook her head. 'No, it's fine.'

'OK – well, will we head?' He spoke briefly to the guys behind him who lifted their pint and nodded to him, presumably knowing about his mission. Doon noticed one of them clocking her, and thought she saw a ghost of a nod or wink. Oh no. What if he hadn't actually told them about the raid on the farm, and they thought he had just got lucky? Knowing Rathowen, anyone who saw them leaving together would put two and two together and make five.

'Actually, hang on,' she said. 'I'll head out to my car. I'm parked at the Rathowen Arms. I'll see you there in five minutes?'

'OK.' He was obviously wondering why the cloak and dagger, but he didn't ask more questions, just disappeared in the direction of the pub's back exit.

She turned and walked out of the front without a backward glance.

15

Aileen had been in bed for an hour when she realized that this was going to be one of those nights, more frequent as she got older, when she just couldn't sleep. Whether it was the stress about the house, the extra glass of wine after dinner or the knowledge that the girls weren't home yet, she didn't know, but there it was. She got up and put on her felted slippers and her fleece dressing gown before going downstairs and putting on the kettle. She swallowed a melatonin tablet – brought back by Doon from a trip to the States – and curled herself up in the rocking chair, looking into the fire and thinking back to their first Christmas in the house, when she and Dan were young.

It was 1992, and Natasha was six months old. They had moved into the house in June – just weeks before Natasha's birth – and had spent the summer making the ground floor habitable. Dan would drive up to Dublin for work every morning as a solicitor in his father's firm in Ballsbridge. Aileen was on maternity leave from her teaching job. One of the rooms had been set aside as her studio, and during Natasha's naps she would dash downstairs to paint for as long as she could, leaving the door open so she could hear any wails from upstairs. At two thirty she strapped Natasha into her double buggy and walked half an hour down the country lanes to pick up Doon from her preschool in the village. Dan fretted about the walk and was always suggesting a second car but for Aileen it was the best part of the day: the fresh air, the changing seasons, the baby asleep in her pram or blinking at the sky while Aileen thought about her current painting and gathered ideas and impressions for more.

The only cloud on the horizon was what she thought of as Dan's ups and downs. He had always been prone to mood swings: periods where he stayed listless and low for days or even weeks at a time. These would be followed by bouts of wild energy, where he would be brimming with schemes and ideas, talking so fast that Aileen could barely understand him at times. Some of the ideas were obviously too wild to bear fruit, like his notion of taking a trip to Turkey in a minivan, to bring back sheepskin coats and other curios to sell at the Dandelion Market in Dublin. But some – like their purchase of the house, in fact – had worked out brilliantly. This Aileen found reassuring.

Once she had made the mistake of mentioning Dan's moods to his mother, as they sat in painful decorum at tea in their house in Waterloo Road. Doon, aged two, was whinging and clinging to her mother, seeming to know that she wasn't welcome in this huge house she had visited only three times in her whole life. It was immaculate aside from the three Persian cats who dropped their white hairs everywhere and looked accusingly at Aileen as a trespasser on their property.

'Dan's always been quite – up and down, hasn't he?' she said casually to his mother. They were during an 'up' phase; Dan was out of the room, having gone to the end of the garden to show his father what he was convinced was a rare wild orchid. Dan's father never seemed to know what to say to Aileen and would have gladly gone to see a dandelion if it meant escaping her company, but Dan was all wound up about this supposed orchid so they had gone off together to investigate.

'What do you mean "up and down"?' said Miriam, or Mrs McDonnell as Aileen still called her. She was all smiles every time Aileen met her but the smiles never seemed to reach her eyes, which travelled instead up and down Aileen's body and clothing. Aileen was wearing her best clothes: a big black shirt from Katharine Hamnett and a pair of brown check pedal pushers with stirrups. They had seemed so smart when she found them in a charity shop in Dublin, barely worn. But she knew that as far as Mrs McDonnell was concerned, Dan might as well have found her in a charity shop – and left her there.

'Well, just that,' said Aileen. 'Up one day and then – down the next. It's OK,' she added, aiming for composure while trying to steer Doon away from an inlaid side table and back towards the crayons and colouring book she had brought for her. 'I just wondered if you'd ever . . .' She was about to say 'worried' but changed it to 'noticed it'.

'Not at all,' said Mrs McDonnell. 'Just the artistic temperament. He's certainly always been very brilliant. Six As in his Leaving Cert, a first from UCD . . . the lead role in every college play, writing plays himself . . . a beautiful tenor voice like Frank Patterson. Who knows what he would have achieved really, had he not settled down *so* young. Ah, ah, ah.' She leaned forward and delicately picked up one of Doon's crayons from the carpet and dropped it back into her pencil case. 'We don't want another crayon trodden in here.'

'Well, he's not doing too badly,' said Aileen, firing up. She zipped up the bag of crayons, wondering why it was that the cats could scratch the furniture with impunity but a dropped crayon was a crisis. How on earth had Dan ever survived here as a child?

'Nobody said he was,' said Mrs McDonnell, the bright smile back in place.

Aileen tried to tell herself that Dan's parents were just a bit precious and protective of their only child; there was no harm in them. It was natural for them to be disappointed that he wasn't married to a solicitor's daughter and living near them in Dublin 4, instead of living in the wilds of west Dublin with an aspiring artist from Crumlin. Not what they had in mind. She wouldn't have minded even, had they remained chilly with her; it was their coldness towards Doon that she couldn't forgive.

'Well? Was it an orchid?' Mrs McDonnell asked, her head turned to the door.

Dan and his father stood there, Dan's face flushed with excitement and his father looking as sombre as ever. Mr McDonnell shook his head and said briefly, 'Just a little clover.'

Looking at them, Aileen suddenly knew that Dan's father had noticed the 'ups and downs', and that there was perhaps more to them than just 'artistic temperament'. She felt a chill settle in her chest, but then she noticed that Doon had unzipped the bag of crayons again and all thoughts of Dan were forgotten as she tried to come up with some way to entertain Doon in what amounted to a museum.

At least the chilly relations with Dan's family meant that there was no agonizing over where to spend Christmas; once they moved into Ballyclare, there was no question of going anywhere else. It was a magical place for the season. Dan cut big branches of fir and holly from their garden and nearly gave Aileen a heart attack by sneaking into one of the woods with a chainsaw to cut down a fir tree. Natasha was only a bundle, but Doon was old enough for the magic to be real, watching from her attic window for the first signs of Santa Claus in the sky. But it was during their first Christmas there that Dan's issues reached a crisis point.

It was Christmas Eve. Doon, age five, was in bed and finally out for the count, having been persuaded that Santa wouldn't appear until she was fast asleep. Baby Natasha, who was fretful with a cold, was downstairs dozing in her bouncer. Aileen was in the kitchen with her, waiting for Dan to come home, torn between anxiety and resentment. Dan had been on a high recently, driving all around the county to get last-minute presents for the girls. Aileen had been delighted when the gallery in Rathowen had taken three paintings, and she had had a call the day before to say that one of them was already sold. She had hoped that once the girls were in bed, she and Dan could open a bottle of champagne and celebrate her first sale and their first Christmas in the new house. But there was no sign of him.

She had just put another turf briquette on the fire when she heard the front door open and close, and let out the breath she didn't know she had been holding.

'Dan!' she called out quietly. 'I'm in here.'

He came inside, as tall and handsome as ever, bearing frost on his shoulders and a scent of outside with him – as well as the distinct smell of cigarette smoke, telling her he had been a pub. He had two huge packages in his hand, which he placed on the table.

'Where have you been, Dan? I was worried. Why didn't you call?'

'I did! You didn't answer. I left a message on the machine.'

She knew this wasn't true, but she didn't bother contesting it. She knew by the glitter in his eyes that he was on an upswing; the only question was what new schemes he was planning – or had already done. Wild spending was one sign she had learned to dread, along with elaborate plans for the house.

'Have a look.'

She opened the bigger box, and gasped aloud as she saw that it was a doll's house; it looked like an antique, perfectly furnished inside from the carpets and curtains to even miniature paintings. The style of the house was Georgian but it was so perfectly preserved it must be a reproduction.

'I got it for Doon – well, they can both play with it later. Do you think she will like it?'

'She will absolutely love it.' Aileen was filled with delight and remorse; here she was cursing him to the heavens when he had been planning this extraordinary surprise for their little girl. She had never seen the like of it; she could imagine it hadn't been cheap, but it was worth every penny. 'Where did you get it, Dan?'

'In a charity shop, would you believe! He wanted fifty quid for it, and I said fair enough. Wait till you see what else they had, though.' He pulled out another package and handed it over reverently to Aileen. She opened it, and pulled out an oil painting, a fairly dingy-looking family portrait that she thought was probably late nineteenth century.

'It's nice,' she said doubtfully, wondering why this had appealed to him. 'A present for the house, is it?'

Dan laughed. 'It's more than a present to the house. It's a present for the girls – it will set them up for life. Turn it over.'

She did so and saw a faded label with copperplate writing, *From the studio of Auguste Renoir*. Before she could stop herself, she laughed out loud. She wasn't great on art history, but the idea of this crude piece of work having been anywhere near Renoir's studio was a joke, though she admired the audacity of whoever wrote the label. They hadn't even bothered to put it in French.

'It says the studio. But I know that it's the real thing. Look at the rosy cheeks.'

Aileen looked again, trying to give him the benefit of the doubt, but all she could see was a bad painting; the ugly colours, blank faces and poor composition couldn't be further from the real thing. Even the frame was low quality.

'Danny, I'm sorry, I don't think so. Look at the hands – that's always a giveaway. These are so badly done; they look like chalk sticks.' She tried to laugh. 'Well, no harm done. Not many people have a Renoir knocking about the house.'

Dan shook his head. 'I know it. Look. It came from a sale, a big house, the knight of something – anyway that doesn't matter. The fellow told me . . .'

He was off, talking so quickly he could barely get his words out. Aileen felt suddenly weary. She had spent the evening getting the girls to sleep, wrapping presents, making dinner that she ate alone and then washing it up. Dan was still talking; she could barely focus until one phrase stood out.

'So I wrote him a cheque. Five grand. It seemed fair.'

'Dan,' she said in a whisper, 'did you say five grand?'

'Yes. Sure, look, it was a charity shop. You'd feel bad robbing them.'

Aileen tried to steady her breathing. Five thousand pounds: their entire savings. Gone. But it would be all right; it would. She would find them. She would get it back. She would tell them that her husband hadn't been in his right mind. Except that it wouldn't be a figure of speech, but the plain truth. A chill snaked down her body as she faced it at last. Something was wrong.

'Where was the shop?' she asked, when he finally paused for breath.

'Ah, Baggot Street, I think. Somewhere around there?'

'OK,' she said. 'Grand. Look, let's talk about it tomorrow. I need some sleep.'

'What? You're crazy. It's early – let's have a nightcap. What have we got to drink?'

She wanted to tell him to buzz off, taking his hideous painting with him, and get their money back. But it was clear that she couldn't. So instead, for the first time in their relationship, she found herself humouring him – as if he was a child or a crazy person.

'There's some champagne in the fridge.' She watched him open it, thinking that she hadn't even had a chance to tell him about the sale of her own painting.

The Christmas holidays had crawled by. Dan was up to ninety with the excitement, while Aileen tried to keep things normal for Doon. She went through the Golden Pages and phoned every charity shop she could find in the Baggot Street area; none of them remembered Dan or admitted it. Ten long days later, with Doon finally back in preschool, she waited till Dan had left the house to go to work and Natasha was down for her morning nap. Then she picked up the phone to his father at his solicitor's firm. She noticed the receptionist's surprise when she asked who was calling and Aileen said his daughter-in-law. She might not even know his son is married, she thought, even though they work together.

Mr McDonnell listened in silence, for which Aileen was grateful, as she told him what had happened.

'I can't ask the GP here,' she said. 'He's a good family doctor, but I don't know if he could even help us.'

'I'll make a phone call,' said Mr McDonnell. 'And I'll ring you back.'

'Not in the evening,' she said in a whisper. 'Please call while he's out.'

She was helped unexpectedly by Dan himself, who had now plunged down into a low mood, going straight to bed after work and getting up later and later, not leaving for the office until noon. Until one day he told her he couldn't face going in at all.

'I don't think I could even lift my hands to the wheel,' he said. He looked awful, not having shaved or washed in days.

'It's OK,' she said. 'I've got an appointment with you tomorrow at St Patrick's.'

'St Patrick's Hospital?' he repeated.

She nodded. She knew that he would understand what she meant: the psychiatric hospital near Heuston station. The next morning they dropped Doon off at preschool and then drove there in silence, Natasha strapped into the back seat. Aileen prayed that she would sleep during the appointment, or at least not cry. Dan didn't feel up to driving, so she drove all the way into Dublin's city centre. They passed the turn for Crumlin, where her parents lived; she wished she could have confided in them or maybe dropped Doon with them, but her father's health was going downhill with some kind of heart condition and her mother was wrapped up in his care. As they approached the hospital she saw a sign for Blackhall Place, where Dan had qualified as a solicitor, and felt a deep sense of sadness. But perhaps this was a good thing; they were finally going to get help.

The consultant they saw, Mr Maguire, was a college friend of Dan's father from the west of Ireland, with neat grey hair and a smooth manner. He asked Dan some general questions about his moods and well-being before suggesting that he go next door to get some observations taken.

'Observations?' said Dan.

'Just blood pressure and so on,' said Mr Maguire. When Dan had left the room he said, 'I don't necessarily need those but it gives us a chance to talk frankly. Let me ask you some questions.'

Aileen answered briefly and to the point. Depression

and hopelessness, yes. Periods of elation, yes. Rapid talking, not needing to eat or sleep, excessive spending. Yes, yes, yes.

'Alcohol?'

'Not really. He says it makes him feel sick.'

'That's very lucky. And during his "up" periods does he ever make – excessive demands in the bedroom?' the doctor asked, his ink pen pausing over his pad.

Aileen blushed scarlet. 'No,' she said, feeling mortified. How much worse could this get? Then Natasha started whimpering for a feed, which Aileen had hoped she would be able to avoid until after the appointment. She picked her up and tucked her under her shawl trying to avoid the doctor's startled gaze.

'That can be a symptom also,' he said, looking at the ceiling. 'There's a general tendency to wild romance as well, we could say – whirlwind weddings and the like. Would that be right?'

She nodded again, feeling her heart crumble inside her. Dan came back into the room and sat down beside Aileen. She held his hand and together they looked at the doctor.

'Dan, I'm going to be very candid with you. All your symptoms point to what we call manic depression. They have a new name for it now but the condition hasn't changed. Normally men like yourself would be diagnosed much younger, but it sounds as if you've had tendencies that way for some time, just not very pronounced.'

Aileen felt sick. 'Manic', such a harsh word. The psychiatrist was talking smoothly about the fact that the late onset of Dan's illness could be a good sign that it could be managed more easily.

'Managed?' she said, searching for a chink of light. 'How?'

'I'm going to write you a prescription for lithium. It's the gold standard for this kind of condition. We'll have to see how you respond to it, so it's very important that you take it religiously,' he added. He passed the script over to Dan, who looked at it for a long moment.

Aileen held her breath, wondering if he was going to protest or query the doctor's conclusion. But he just said seriously, 'I will.' Aileen remembered him saying the same words during their wedding ceremony, and thought she might cry.

After a long wait at the hospital pharmacy they walked out, both feeling shaky. Aileen was in such a state that she took a wrong turn and ended up on the quays. The traffic was appalling and she started to worry about getting back in time to pick up Doon. She suddenly realized how isolated they were in Wicklow. She knew the local mums to chat to but hadn't made friends. She had been so absorbed in doing up the house, painting, looking after Natasha – and coping with Dan's moods. Not moods, manic depression. Natasha started to cry in the back seat. Aileen felt the tears starting too, and soon they were pouring down her cheeks so fast she could hardly see the road ahead.

'It will be all right,' Dan said unexpectedly beside her. 'I'll take the medicine and everything will be fine.' He reached behind and held Natasha's foot. 'It's OK, chicken,' he told her, and miraculously she quietened down.

Aileen wiped her face and tried to smile, feeling a sad admiration at how quickly he had seemed to absorb and accept the news.

'Was he a friend of my dad's?' he said then. 'The doc. Did Dad make the appointment?'

Aileen held her breath. She didn't want to admit it, but there was no point in lying to him. 'He did,' she said briefly. 'I hope you don't mind.'

Dan shook his head. 'It's OK. I understand.'

She felt a new sense of relief; they had faced it together and now things would get better. But her mind kept playing on what the doctor had said, about Dan's wilder moods: his optimism and elation, his dashing nature that had swept her off her feet. She remembered how quickly they had fallen in love and how impetuous he had been in rushing her to the altar. It had all been so romantic. But how much of it had been Dan, and how much had been his illness?

16

It was nearly closing time at Keogh's, and Natasha had had a good night. Mostly, anyway. She had been so happy to see everyone, and to be among old friends who knew her so well and who reminded her that there was a whole world outside of Ben and London.

Natasha did get a slight shock to the system, though, as she started to hear updates on what all her friends were up to – and noticed big changes. This time last year, they had all been working in Joe jobs, as Aileen called them: entry-level positions in various big companies in Dublin, waiting tables in various cafes, nannying. But now! Arthur was working for one of the film studios, and not just as a runner but as an assistant AD. Síomha was freelancing for another studio, doing hair and make-up on actors whom Natasha would be totally star-struck to meet. And her friend Moya, who used to draw eyeliner on herself with permanent marker, was now some bigwig in the county council, helping to organize a new literary festival no less.

'God,' said Natasha, half joking, 'I don't know why I bothered going to London – it's all going on here, isn't it?'

She had intended it as a joke but realized, when she

was halfway through the sentence, how insulting that would sound – all the more so as it was, clearly, no more than the truth. Why was she trying to build a career in London when there was so much going on here? The sad fact was, she realized, that she was scared – scared of competing with her own peers and of the consequences of failure if things didn't work out here.

She shook herself, not wanting to let such gloomy thoughts spoil her Christmas drinks. She didn't want to have a sourpuss on her like Doon, who she'd seen earlier talking away to that nice Cara Clarke as if she had a gun to her head. Doon had everything – a great job, a place of her own, a devoted fiancé – and yet she never seemed happy; nobody knew why. Then she felt uneasy. Natasha was Doon's sister; shouldn't she know why? But it wasn't her fault that Doon told her nothing.

'Natasha! You're home! How's it going?' said a voice beside her and she turned with delight to see Billie Gallagher, one of her best friends from school, arriving late having finished her shift in a nearby hotel. 'Billie! I love your coat,' Natasha added, stroking her blue fake-fur arm.

'Oh, do you like it? Try it on. You could even have it honestly; it doesn't really suit me.' Natasha laughed because this was so characteristic of Billie, who would literally give you the shirt, or coat, off her back.

'No, no, keep it,' said Natasha, clinking her glass against Billie's. 'Happy Christmas! How are you? How's work?'

'It's good . . . I mean, the pay is good, I can't complain, but I am getting sick of it. It's quite impersonal. I might look for a small B & B instead for a change. Anyway. What about you?' said Billie. 'I thought you were meant to be bringing a friend over? I met your mum in the Spar last week and she said.'

Typical; this being Rathowen, it was bound to get out somehow. Natasha explained, as briefly and with as much dignity as she could, about Ben and his last-minute dash from the airport.

'But how did he even . . . ?'

'Security man. Phone call. Special exit.' Natasha hoped this would be the last time she'd have to tell this story. Since it was Billie, though, she added, 'I did really like him. And I hoped something might happen between us. But he turned out to be into this other girl.'

She almost wished she hadn't said anything, but Billie was the right person to tell; she shook her head and said she got it. 'It sounds like the two of you are perfect for each other and he just hasn't realized it yet. But they've broken up once, right? Which means it could happen again . . .'

'Well, I'm not sure,' Natasha admitted. 'He did talk about her a lot.'

'But to who? To you! You were the one he confided everything in. Hey! Do you know what it is, Tasha? It's textbook Taylor.' Billie started singing 'You Belong With Me' by Taylor Swift.

'Oh my God, you're right,' said Natasha. 'It is exactly

like that song. She doesn't get his stories like I do.' She sang a few bars, then looked around, briefly self-conscious, but singing on Christmas Eve Eve in Keogh's was not unheard of and few glances came their way.

'Do you remember when that came out – singing it on the golf course, in Third Year?' said Billie. 'It always made me think of Tommy O'Shea.'

'Yes. Oh my God, you're so right! She *is* the captain and I *am* on the bleachers!'

'Yes. I know this couple – my friend Maeve McDermott and this guy Fiachra – it was the same story for years and years: they were friends and she watched him pick all the wrong women . . . and then, as soon as she got a serious boyfriend, he realized how he felt. And she told him she felt the same. That's what you have to do obviously. I mean, have you even told him how you felt?'

'Well . . . no.'

'You didn't? Oh my God.' Billie's eyes grew rounder. 'Well, there's your mistake right there. You have to tell him, otherwise how is he supposed to know? And if he tells you he really is into this other woman – which I doubt – at least then you won't be wondering any more.'

'I suppose,' said Natasha, getting more and more fired up. 'I mean, you're right – I won't know if I never tell him, will I?'

'Absolutely not!'

'Cheers girls. Happy Christmas.' More rounds had descended on them by this point – Natasha was on to what might have been her third gin; it couldn't possibly be her fourth?

Some others joined them then, and Natasha tried to join in the conversation but she couldn't stop thinking about Ben. Should she get in touch with him and actually tell him how she felt? She could only imagine what Doon would say to that. Come to think of it, where was Doon? Her friends were there, but she had disappeared.

Natasha checked her phone and saw a text from her. Had to leave early. Don't wait up for me. See you tomorrow.

'Yes, I'm fine, thanks, enjoy the rest of your night,' muttered Natasha. 'Lovely to see you too. Great bonding time.'

'Natasha?'

She looked up to find someone standing over her – Gabe. He looked very sober beside everyone else.

'Oh, hi,' said Natasha. 'You decided to join us after all?'

'Yes, if that's still OK? I thought . . .' His voice trailed off. Natasha felt less than thrilled at the idea of having to make polite chat with him now at this point in the evening, but at least Síomha looked pleased, flipping her golden hair over her bare shoulder.

'Hello! I'm Síomha. Would you like me to say that again for you?' She held out a slim hand, and purred, '*Shee*ova.'

'Sheeova,' repeated Gabe, looking mesmerized as he shook her hand. 'Thank you.'

She was welcome to him, thought Natasha. 'I'm off to the loo,' she said, standing up.

Her journey to the ladies' toilet took twice as long as it should have, with hellos and chats at every turn. She looked at her reflection in the full-length mirror: flushed red because of the heat, with all her mascara smudged and the velvet skirt looking crumpled and odd, as if she was in fancy dress. She looked awful. She could see why Ben had chosen Lucy over her. But maybe that would change if he knew how she felt?

She sat down in the cubicle and pulled out her phone. She paged her way to Ben's messages, and started reading back on them as if they were a novel. They had exchanged literally hundreds of messages. It must mean something; it must. She typed a quick message to him. I have to tell you something. And before she could second-guess herself, she sent it. Then, in for a penny, she typed another one. I think we could have been something great. We still could be. And sent it. Finally she searched for the song Billie had been singing. 'You Belong With Me'. This was it; this was all her feelings in three minutes of pop music. She sent him a link to the song too, with the hashtag STATOY, thinking that there was no point in hiding anything any more.

As soon as she came back out, she realized that she was in a bad state. The room seemed to sway and swirl round and round, like the waltzer on the seafront at Bray when she used to go there in the summer. That was OK, though. She felt as if she was floating above everything; she was a little tipsy, but she had access to a kind of wisdom that wasn't available otherwise. She had absolutely done the right thing in contacting Ben.

Or had she?

Her seat at the table seemed to have disappeared along with her coat; she had done a few circles of the area before she realized that she was holding her coat and the table was no longer where it had been.

'Are you OK?' said yet another voice. Billie this time. 'Tashie, maybe we should get you home. Doon left, didn't she? Let's see.' Natasha felt mortified now; she could see that Billie was looking around, trying to find a good Samaritan that could carry her home. Which wasn't what was supposed to be happening; Natasha was meant to be leaving with Ben, in a haze of gracious waves and goodbyes to all his new friends, having dazzled the pub with his romantic good looks and gorgeous personality. Well, nothing like Christmas for surprises.

'I know,' said Billie. 'Let's ask Gabe. He's got a car and he wasn't drinking. He'll be happy to drive you.'

'What? No, no, no,' said Natasha, digging in her heels as Billie made to pull her along. 'I mean, I don't know him. How do you know he has a car?'

'He's house-sitting for my uncle,' Billie said. 'He's pretty sound. Come on. Let's just ask.'

Resistance was futile, so Natasha pinned her hopes on Gabe being deep in chat with Síomha and refusing to do it. But Síomha had disappeared and Billie was persuasive.

'Come on. She's not in a state to walk.'

'Sure,' said Gabe, looking at her dubiously. He didn't seem thrilled at this new responsibility, but Natasha didn't have brain space to worry about it. The reality of the message she had sent Ben earlier was sinking in.

'Billie,' Natasha told her urgently, as she was struggling to put on her coat, 'I told Ben. I sent him a message.'

'Did you? Good woman yourself!'

'I don't know. I don't think it was the right thing maybe.' Natasha blinked, as prickles of reality, like pins and needles, started to stab against her alcohol-numbed self.

'You never know – he might have another change of heart. Christmas isn't done with yet.'

'That's true,' said Natasha, but an uneasy feeling was building in her stomach, of either too many drinks or the shame hangover to end all shame hangovers.

17

Doon couldn't remember the last time she had done something unscheduled, let alone vaguely dangerous. Her life was so regimented: work, running club, Friday-night date with Ciarán, Sunday brunch with Ciarán, Amy and Setanta. They even went to the same restaurants most of the time: Paulie's Pizza on a Friday, Brother Hubbard on a Sunday. Yet here she was, driving to Fenton's Christmas Tree Farm at eleven at night, with Charlie Cuffe.

They had met at her car, as arranged. Five minutes after she had left the pub. Charlie had slunk up to the car, the collar of his coat turned up. He made a theatrical show of looking left and right before sliding into the passenger seat, and Doon smiled despite herself.

'I got tailed by a couple of cheap gumshoes, but I shook 'em off,' he said.

'Very funny. OK, let's go.' She powered up the engine and slung the car into a quick three-point turn.

'This is a fine car,' said Charlie, running his hand appreciatively along the dashboard. 'I had not pictured you driving something like this.'

'What did you picture?' asked Doon, turning left out of the car park.

'Hmm . . . maybe like a Volvo or a Saab.'

Doon understood; he thought she was boring, conventional and safety conscious. All of which was true, except tonight when she had obviously lost the run of herself. She tried to imagine what Ciarán would say if he knew she was driving to intercept a gang of Dublin criminals at a tree farm. Given how alarmed he had got once when she took a piece of toast out of the unplugged toaster with a plastic knife, she thought he probably wouldn't be best pleased. Which was another good reason for not wanting anybody to find out about this, along with her habitual paranoia about anyone remembering her obsession with David Cuffe.

She moved up to the speed limit, climbing the road towards the Christmas tree farm. She realized she was half expecting Charlie to tell her to be careful or sound her horn when she came up to corners, as Ciarán would have, but instead he seemed utterly relaxed, almost lounging in his seat and even – enjoying himself? He didn't seem at all worried about his impending brush with a gang of dangerous criminals. No doubt this kind of caper was par for the course for him as the finale to a night out.

Charlie seemed to read her mind. As they slid round a tight corner, he said, 'I would tell you to slow down, but I can see you know what you're doing.'

'Well, it's urgent, is it not? What are you planning on doing when you get there, by the way? Blast them all with a machine gun?'

'That would be great. Feckers. No, just scare them off by turning up, I suppose. Jimbo was terrified and high-tailed it off. Which is fair enough. But it's my farm. Or my family's farm anyway.'

'Where are they anyway? I mean, everyone else?'

'Well, my Auntie Laura and my Uncle John are in their seventies, and their kids both live in Dublin. My brother Mark's at home with two small children. And David's in Sydney. So that leaves me, I suppose, unless you think I should get my parents out?'

'No, no,' said Doon, though she privately thought Carmel Cuffe, Charlie's mother, would be a match for even the most hardened criminal.

Charlie paused. 'If you're worried, though – you know you can just drop me there and drive straight off. I don't want you staying while there's troublemakers around.'

'I'm not particularly worried,' said Doon. She couldn't imagine that thieves, however organized, would want any kind of open confrontation. And at least they wouldn't want to quiz her on wedding details or come up with crazy schemes to save the crumbling family house. 'After the week I've had, this doesn't bother me,' she found herself adding.

Nonetheless, she did get a real fright as she approached the tree farm and clocked the grey van parked in a lay-by near the entrance. Its lights were off but she could see three men clearly inside. She took a minute to memorize their registration number, while

Charlie leaned forward to zap the electric gates with his key fob. Then they rattled up the drive, the van staying parked behind them. Doon felt her heartbeat ratchet up a knot and she watched intently in the rear-view mirror until she saw the gates close again behind them.

'Why haven't they just jumped the fence or broken in? What are they waiting for?' she murmured, as she approached the yard.

'I don't know.'

She parked the car and turned to Charlie. 'I got the registration number. I'll read it to you, it's 145, K for Kilo, E for Echo . . .'

Charlie plugged in the rest of the registration number to his phone, looking amused. 'Excellent. I feel like you should have been a detective instead of whatever it is you do. What do you do exactly?'

Doon decided to give him the short answer. 'Data analytics. IT basically.'

'Is it like Chandler's job in *Friends*, which nobody understands?'

'More or less,' she said.

'So why did you learn the NATO alphabet? Was it just for fun?'

'I suppose . . . I just thought it was a useful life skill.'

Charlie laughed. 'I'm going to call you "D" for "Delta". Or just "Delta" for short,' he said. Then he opened the car door.

'What are you doing?' she asked, wondering if he was planning to go and square up to them.

'I'm turning on the lights,' he said. 'Make it look occupied, scare them off.'

'Mind yourself,' she said, but he was gone.

Peering out, she watched Charlie stride into one of the sheds and a second later the lights came on – little lanterns strung along on all four sides of the courtyard, making the place a miniature Narnia. Then Charlie re-emerged and got back into the car, while she watched for movement at the bottom of the lane.

'All quiet,' she said. 'I wonder what they'll do now.'

'No idea.' He glanced back down the lane, then turned back to Doon. 'So why has your week been so bad?'

'What?' she said, and he replied, 'You said that you had a terrible week. Or "after the week I've had". So I was just interested. You can tell me to mind my own business, of course.'

'Oh.' She looked out of the window, wondering how much to tell him. Obviously she had been indiscreet enough about the wedding already. Instead of getting into that, she explained briefly about the house and the subsidence. 'So we may have to sell. That's if we can even get a buyer.'

'Oh, you'd get a buyer all right,' said Charlie. 'You can always get a buyer if you price it right.'

'I mean, could someone get a mortgage if the house is falling down?'

'Probably, just for less money than you'd want, as I said. Or you'd get a cash buyer.'

'Right.' This hadn't properly occurred to her. The prospect that Aileen might have to sell, and at a loss, was very sad. She thought again of the 3,000 euros that her mother had given her towards the wedding costs. On a strange impulse she continued, 'Plus I'm planning a wedding and . . . that's stressful.'

'Is it?' he said. 'I mean, I believe you. I would find your typical wedding stressful but I thought maybe that was just me.'

'It's not just you. It's fine,' she added quickly. 'It's just hard when there are expectations and you feel you're going to disappoint people, no matter what you do.'

'Oh, don't you worry. I know all about disappointing people.' He smiled. 'You know my older brother David, don't you? In fact, didn't you . . . ?'

Doon was blushing so hard she was glad the car was dark. She said, 'A million years ago. Yes.' Wouldn't Charlie know all about this? But he was probably being polite by pretending to be not quite sure.

'Well, let's just say he's a hard act to follow. Even in Australia he casts quite the shadow. Christmas Day we're all meant to turn up at eight a.m. so we can Face-Time him together before his "Christmas is over". My mum sets an empty place for him at the table and puts his favourite champagne on ice, hoping every year that he'll surprise her and show up . . .'

'Seriously?'

Charlie laughed. 'No, not really. But we are supposed

to all do the FaceTime in the morning. I don't always make it, though. I do a swim at Brittas most years.'

Doon wondered what it must be like to just 'not make it' when family pressure like that was applied. 'Who else is coming?'

'Just Mark, my other bro, plus his wife Seona and my nieces Katie and Claire. They're seven and five, and they're my favourites out of the whole family, but don't tell anyone. I got them both rocket launchers, and a monster-building kit.'

'That must be nice, to just have to show up late and be fun Uncle Charlie.'

'Hey, I also make the Christmas pudding, I'll have you know. Yes, really,' he added, smiling down at her. 'I have Stirabout Sunday marked in my Google Calendar. The secret is having the right container. And I make my own brandy butter too.'

'Really,' she said, blinking slightly. She had not pictured him contributing anything to the feast beyond a six-pack of Heineken, but she was obviously still as bad as ever at reading people.

'What about you folks? Who's coming to Ballyclare for the Christmas?' he asked.

'Just me, my mum and Tasha. Oh, and a stray American.'

'Not your fella – your fiancé?'

'No, no. He's with his family, in Mayo. You know, there's this tradition that you should spend the last Christmas before your wedding with your own family – and then the first Christmas afterwards is with the bride's family. So that's what we're doing.'

'Really? I never heard that one. But I suppose I'm not very traditional.'

'Me neither,' said Doon.

'I feel like there are all these rules that other people know. I only know about getting your round in, and not nicking other people's lobster pots.'

Doon laughed. 'I don't think that's tradition, that's just not stealing.' But she was pleased to think that someone as popular as Charlie also found these social rules puzzling.

Charlie glanced again at the bottom of the lane. 'Speaking of – they're still there.'

She had almost forgotten the purpose of their visit, but she turned round and got a start to see the van still there, ominously waiting. She drummed her fingers on the steering wheel, wondering how exactly this standoff was going to end and when.

He was staring absently at her left hand on the steering wheel. 'Nice ring.'

'Oh, thanks.' She looked self-consciously at her engagement ring with its three diamonds. 'I don't know. I feel weird about diamonds because the industry is so dodgy. I would have liked something antique, but . . .' She suddenly heard herself. What the hell was wrong with her – criticizing her fiancé like this, even implicitly? She had to change the subject, pronto.

'Anyway. You've phoned the guards, yes?' she asked.

Charlie nodded. 'They're on their way supposedly.'

She nodded, thinking that in a strange way she was in no rush.

'Let's try something else,' he said.

Before she could say anything, he had jumped out of the car and headed for the yard, where he ducked back inside the same shed he had entered before. She stared after him, starting to get worried. What if he was hunting for some kind of weapon? She could imagine him digging out some dusty old shotgun and shooting himself in the leg with it, while enraging the gang who would probably kidnap them both for a ransom. At least, if she and Charlie were kidnapped, she wouldn't have to go through with the wedding. *Stop it*, she told herself.

Doon blinked as something caught her eye. Snow was drifting through the air, falling in waves before landing and settling on the cobbled ground. But only in the courtyard; the sky around was still black. Was she dreaming? There was Charlie, emerging from the shed, grinning, his broad shoulders filling up with the artificial snow. She looked around anxiously as he crossed the yard, but to her relief the grey van stayed closed while he got back inside.

'What do you think?' he asked.

'Oh, God,' said Doon, her heart racing. 'You scared me. I thought you were getting a shotgun or something.'

'Not at all. We don't have a gun. Though I do generally have a pair of pliers in my coat pocket, just in case I meet a sheep that's got stuck in some wire.'

She shook her head, trying to calm herself down. 'Why the snow?' she asked.

'It's a gimmick . . . one of the film studios had it going cheap so we bought a few kilos of it. We didn't know we were going to have the real thing.'

'No, I mean, why did you put it on right now?' she asked. It was one thing putting on lights to scare off some thieves, but did they really need full special effects?

He turned to look at her, leaning his head against the headrest.

'I just thought you might like it,' he said.

Doon looked back at him. She thought of Ciarán, who had introduced shower timers for his housemates and never put the heating on until the first Sunday in Advent.

She cleared her throat to speak. 'You're crazy,' she said.

'Look, they're off,' he said.

Startled, she turned to look out of the rear window and, sure enough, the van was driving away.

'The van's gone at least. They might have left some crooks behind, of course,' he said.

'Let's get out and take a look,' said Doon, and Charlie started laughing.

'Now who's crazy?'

Doon took a deep breath, and for some reason she thought briefly of what Natasha would say before her reason returned. 'Not me,' she said. 'But I don't see anyone – I think they've gone.'

'Wait – let me check.'

He touched her knee briefly and got out of the car. Outside, the artificial snow was still falling. She put her hand to her knee slowly, wondering why she could still feel the imprint of his hand. He was patrolling the courtyard again, the snow melting on his plaid shoulders. He gave her a thumbs-up. Without thinking, she slid out of the car and walked towards him. She had no idea why she was doing this; she just wanted some fresh air, she told herself.

'All clear. Nobody here but us chickens,' he said with that easy smile.

She stood close beside him, as they both surveyed the surrounding fields and woods, listening to the cold quiet. Then she almost jumped as a distant siren shattered the air.

Charlie said, 'That's the guards – better late than never.'

Doon stepped away from him instinctively as the blue and white car came up the lane, lights flashing. Danger. Danger. What was she *doing*? She was larking around in the middle of a tree farm, shadowed by gangs, with her ex-boyfriend's younger brother, all about to be witnessed by the police. She needed to immediately undo the past two hours or whatever it was and pretend it never happened. Starting with a quick getaway from here.

'Charlie,' she said.

He turned fully away from watching the approaching car, and looked down at her, in a way that made her head swim. It wasn't just his dark blue eyes; it was the fact that she could see that she had his full, instant, total attention, that nothing coming up the drive or down from the woods would deflect that.

'Yes, Delta?'

She opened her mouth to say all the sensible things, like *I should go* or *Please don't tell the guards I was here*. Who knew which guards it would be or who they would turn out to be related to? But what she said instead was: 'After they've gone – let me drive you home.'

18

Aileen had really tried to break herself of the habit of staying awake until the girls came home. But it was easier said than done, especially in the dead quiet of the countryside, where the slightest thump or step sounded like foxes ruining her garden or, unlikely but not impossible, burglars. It was one o'clock in the morning now. How the tables had turned. It used to be the girls who couldn't sleep at Christmas, while she sat downstairs praying for them to conk out so that she could do some last-minute wrapping or collapse in front of the TV. Aileen had had a text from Doon, but she looked out of the window all the same to check for her car, which was still missing. She got back into bed, sighing, and switched the radio on to RTE *Lyric Through the Night*. It didn't matter that the girls were both grown up; she would always feel anxious until they were home. Perhaps it was a legacy of the months and years she had spent watching out of that same window for Dan.

After Dan had started the course of lithium, things had seemed to settle down – initially at least. He got up, got dressed and went to work, came home for the girls' bedtime and kissed them goodnight. But within a year the highs and lows began to return, and one day Aileen discovered an unopened package of medicine in Dan's bedside drawer. When she asked him about it, as carefully as she could, she found out he hadn't been taking the lithium for months.

'It makes me feel – nothing. Numb,' he said.

There are worse things than feeling numb, she thought, but she held her tongue; of course she didn't know what it was really like for him. The gulf between them had never felt wider.

The dose was changed and then a new drug was tried, but every time she thought they were out of the woods a new crisis loomed. Aileen had planned to return to work as a teacher once Natasha started preschool, but she quickly realized that she couldn't; Dan's state was too unpredictable.

Three years went by in this way, until 10 August 1997, when she came home to find him gone.

It was a Sunday. They had all been to Mass in the village that morning. Then Aileen had dropped them home in the car and had driven up to Dublin to see her mother, who was still very low and lonely after her father had died of a heart attack the year before. She had wanted to take the girls, but they had complained so much at the idea that Aileen couldn't face the battle and said they could stay home. They had never really bonded with her mother any more than they had with Dan's parents, which made her feel sad. But she knew they would have a marvellous time with Dan, who was in good spirits that day. The forecast was for twenty degrees; there was talk of building a dam in the stream. Aileen could understand them wanting to stay and play in their sunny, beautiful garden, rather than driving to Crumlin and sit in her mother's small kitchen listening to dull adult talk.

Aileen had offered, many times, to pick her mother up and drive her back to Ballyclare for lunch, but her mother always made an excuse; it was too far, she got car-sick, she didn't want to be a trouble. She had never seemed comfortable in the house. There was always an undercurrent of resentment, as if Aileen had abandoned her mother for the life of Riley in a big house in the country. Curiously Nuala, who had gone all the way to Canada, didn't seem to come in for any of the same blame, and the visits were generally spent poring over the latest photos from Vancouver of Nuala and her baby boy Rory – 'a grandson at last'. She never asked about the girls.

All in all, the visit dragged, and Aileen felt both guilty and relieved to be driving back to Ballyclare, whizzing down the M50 eager to see the girls and Dan. He was planning on roasting a leg of lamb for dinner; Aileen had put a bottle of white wine in the fridge that morning and had made a pavlova with strawberries from the garden. When she arrived back, the girls were up in the monkey puzzle tree, scampering from branch to branch and squabbling over who got to sit in the swing Dan had made them. Aileen was happy to see them so joyful, but surprised that Dan wasn't watching them. Natasha was only five, and Doon was eight going on nine; they were ten feet up in a tree. Where was he?

'Hi, chicks,' she called up to the girls. 'How are you? Where's Daddy?'

Doon called down from the branches, 'We're not chicks; we're pirates.'

'Sorry, me hearties. Pirates, of course. Ahoy. Where's Daddy?'

'I don't know.' Doon inched back up the prickly branch to regain the swing while Natasha's back was turned.

Aileen made a mental note to get Dan to just put up a second swing. Then she went inside, thinking he must be somewhere in the house, but a quick search revealed it was empty. They only had the one car, and she had taken it. Where on earth could he be? The familiar dread crept over her, and she hurried down to check the stream, calling at the girls over her shoulder to be careful. There was nothing, of course. She stared into the water, unable to think what to do next. He had done so many strange things in recent years, but he had never just gone out like this without warning, leaving the girls.

'Where is Daddy?' asked Doon that evening, as Aileen finally got them sitting in front of fish fingers and chips, hastily cooked in between frantic phone calls to Dan's parents and the handful of friends who knew the score. She and Dan had been discussing whether to get mobile phones; how she wished she could have persuaded him. The leg of lamb was still uncooked in the fridge. She would have liked to open the wine but she didn't know what the evening held; she might need to stick the girls in the car and drive somewhere to pick Dan up.

'Do you know what, I'm not completely sure,' said Aileen, as lightly as she could. 'I think he must have forgotten to leave me a note – silly Daddy.' She couldn't think straight. It was so out of the blue; she hadn't spotted signs of either a high or a low. She could only assume that he would appear at any minute, with a tale of some auction he had dashed to attend or some antique he had tracked down on the other side of the county. But there was no sign until a week later, when a neighbour called to say she had seen him boarding the three o'clock bus to Dublin that Sunday afternoon – just at the time she got home. She must have missed him by minutes.

Even years later, Aileen couldn't bear to think of the weeks that followed, as the sticky summer faded into autumn. The mounting days of absence; the calls to local hospitals and then to the police. Their initial concern, and then the subtle change when she mentioned his illness, which seemed to convince them that this could only end in tragedy. Then the article in the local Saturday paper, which brought the whole thing out into the public gaze, making Aileen feel as if she had a target on her back every time she walked into Rathowen. The next day it was reported that Princess Diana had died, which made for a new tragedy to talk about, though it added to the general nightmarish feeling of that late summer. Aileen couldn't sleep at night, couldn't focus on anything at all except Dan's whereabouts and whether he was alive or dead. Could he be away on some adventure? Then he must be in an unimaginable state, not to think of putting her or the girls out of their misery. And if dead, how? He had talked in general terms about not wanting to go on, in his lowest moods, but she had never heard him express an actual desire to do harm to himself.

She went around in a fog, unable to connect the dots or find a way out of the limbo they were in. School resumed, and the girls went off to their first day without the traditional photo in front of the door; none of them had the heart for it. On 9 September, poor Doon's ninth birthday came and went, barely marked by a hastily arranged cake and candles. Aileen saw her watching the door, and her heart broke for her disappointment when Dan didn't reappear. She could have borne the pain for herself, but having to watch her daughters suffer was beyond endurance.

Another source of misery was the clash with Dan's parents, or more specifically his mother. She phoned Aileen almost daily asking for updates and she made missing posters and put them up in every village in Leinster, including one outside the girls' school, which Aileen wished she had asked her about first; it was upsetting for the girls, and it wasn't as if anyone in the school community needed telling. Aileen could understand her mother-in-law's frantic need for action – Dan was her only child – but sometimes she wished for softer parents-in-law, who could occasionally acknowledge that this nightmare was happening to Aileen and the girls too, or even offer to help by minding their grandchildren every now and then. At the bottom of it all, she felt, was an unspoken blame. *This happened on your watch*, she could feel Dan's mother telling her silently. And the worst of it all was that she agreed with them. Over and over it all she went, ruminating on what had gone wrong and how she could have prevented it, if she had only done something different.

It made for a sad Christmas that year – though Aileen felt that every Christmas from now on would be sad. The house was a different place without Dan. She was a different person. She woke up in sadness, went to bed in it, and the only thing that kept her putting one foot in front of the other was the girls. Aileen was back teaching again, but she hadn't painted since Dan had left. She was too tired – from getting up in the morning and getting them all to school, to picking them up after a day's work and doing homework, tea, bath and bed, and then chores and paperwork after they went to bed. Dan's departure had left her in an appalling legal limbo; having a missing husband was almost a full-time job in itself, requiring endless forms, meetings and phone calls with her Garda liaison officer, her solicitor, the bank, the county council. The only bright spot was that she had befriended another local mum, Susan Reilly, who was separated from her husband and worked full time in the local bank. They took turns to take each others' kids for the occasional afternoon, which was a great help.

'Us single mums have to stick together,' Susan had said cheerfully one day when dropping the girls back to Aileen's.

Aileen appreciated the support, but she felt there was a difference between them. She and Susan were both single mums now, true, but Susan had an ex-husband who paid child support and took the girls every second weekend and in emergencies. Whereas Aileen had nobody. There should be another word for mothers like her, she thought, who were completely alone. Her sister had emigrated to Canada just before her father's death; her mother was too nervous a driver to make it to Wicklow alone. Occasionally Mairead or other friends from college would make it down to visit her for the afternoon. But most of the time she didn't have time to even return phone calls; she was just trying to survive day to day. Finances were another worry, and the obvious solution became harder to ignore – sell Ballyclare.

In the years since she and Dan had bought the house, Wicklow, and Ireland in general, had experienced a property gold rush. Farmers with barely a hundred euro stashed under their pillows became millionaires seemingly overnight, thanks to the price of their land. Aileen read the property section in the paper every week and marvelled at the inexorable rise in prices. It was ironic, she thought, that of all Dan's get-rich schemes, the only one that had actually borne fruit was the one that he hadn't intended as such: buying the house. Now the house had outlasted him. Aileen was torn between feeling grateful for the roof over their heads, and resenting it for serenely surviving when its vital spirit was gone.

It was on that second Christmas Eve, in December 1998, that Aileen reached her lowest point. The girls were in bed asleep and she had just sat down in front of the fire to have a glass of wine, wishing for the next few days to pass quickly. Since Dan had gone, there were so many milestones that loomed horribly. The anniversary of his disappearance, of course, but also his birthday, the girls' birthdays, and, most of all, Christmas with its emphasis on family and togetherness. Aileen had racked her brains trying to think of ways to make the day less painful, but none of the options – including going to Dublin to spend it with Dan's parents – seemed likely to make it any better. She had invited her mother, but she was spending it with neighbours, and her sister Nuala was staying put in Canada. She was just wondering if it was safe to go to the drawing room and fill the girls' stockings when she heard little footsteps and Doon came in to the kitchen.

'Doonie! You should be asleep.' She held out her arms for her daughter. Doon folded herself in for a polite minute but then drew back, looking around the room. She reminded Aileen of a cat they had owned when she was Doon's age, one of two from a local litter. One had been killed by a car on the road and the survivor spent days nosing around corners of the house, expecting its brother to reappear. She felt Doon was similarly lost and hopeful at once. For the first time she wondered if it would be better for the girls if they moved – to a new place where they wouldn't be whispered about as the girls whose father went missing. And, maybe more importantly, not to be reminded of Dan's presence at every turn.

'Santa won't come till you're asleep, you know,' she said gently.

'It's OK, Mum,' Doon said. 'I know that it's really you. He uses the same wrapping paper.'

'Oh, Doon.' Ten was plenty old enough to have realized the truth about Santa but Aileen felt sad nonetheless. Another illusion gone.

Doon stood gazing into the fire with that oddly grown-up look on her face; Aileen, disoriented from tiredness, was almost inclined to offer her a cup of tea for a second before remembering that she was ten, not twenty. She was getting older, though.

'Are you feeling sad, honey?' she asked. 'It's OK if you are. I'm pretty sad too.'

Doon nodded, but she didn't seem inclined to say any more. Aileen realized that this was a rare opportunity to talk to her without Natasha present, and that maybe she should let Doon know about her idea of selling the house.

'I've been thinking,' she said. 'I know we love this house but it's pretty big for the three of us, isn't it? What would you think of the idea of selling Ballyclare – and moving somewhere smaller? Maybe in another village even – or in Dublin?'

Doon looked up, aghast. Her eyes were bright with tears and her voice trembled as she said, 'We can't do that! How will Daddy know where to find us?'

'Oh no. Doon! Don't cry.' Aileen kneeled in front of her daughter and pulled her into her arms, wondering how she could possibly have missed this. *She still thinks he's coming back.* Her mind raced as she tried to think how on earth she should handle this. Should she allow Doon to keep believing this? Or should she go to the other extreme and tell Doon that she was certain Dan was never coming back? She couldn't do that, though. Because technically Doon was right; yes, it was possible that Dan was alive somewhere. But Aileen knew, at this point, that he was most likely dead.

'He will come back, won't he?' Doon asked desperately.

Aileen drew a deep breath, praying that she would get this right. 'I don't think so, darling. I'm sorry. I'm so sorry, pet.' She let Doon cry, thinking that after all, perhaps this was what she needed.

'But you don't know. They haven't found him, so you don't know,' Doon said dully once the storm had subsided.

'We may never know for sure, but I think it's the

likeliest thing. Because he wouldn't be alive somewhere and not tell us. He wouldn't do that to us. And he could find us,' she added gently. 'We have the internet now, and all the papers and the guards and telephones and faxes. You don't need to worry about that part.'

Doon said nothing but started crying again. Aileen sighed, heartbroken that she hadn't known of Doon's hopes but relieved that at least she had been able to tell her what she felt was the truth. But it was clear to her that a move was no longer on the cards, or not for now. The girls had had enough upheaval; they needed to stay in the place they knew.

But what about her? How could she face living in this place that was meant to be her house of dreams with Dan? Once she had Doon back in bed and asleep again, she felt too miserable to sleep herself. For the first time she could imagine pouring herself another glass of wine and then another, until oblivion took her problems away just for the night or even a few hours.

Then her mobile phone buzzed with a text message. The mobile was a new purchase, her first, bought in order for the girls' school to be able to contact her at any time. Their landline number had been written on the first missing posters – a mistake, since it attracted nuisance calls and even malicious ones – so Aileen felt safer with the mobile, and had given her number to her Garda liaison officer.

The text said, Happy Christmas Eve, Aileen! Are you awake? For a wild moment and for the last time, she allowed herself to believe it was Dan. But he would hardly send her such a message. Then she saw it was Susan Reilly, her neighbour and fellow single mum. Susan had had a mobile since they were the size of shoeboxes, but Aileen, still faithful to landlines, hadn't got around to saving her number properly yet.

She replied, Awake and going round the bend.

Me too, came the reply. I'll pop by in ten minutes.

Aileen frantically cleared up some of the mess and the piles of tissues, and blew her nose and wiped her eyes, so that by the time she heard Susan's tyres on the gravel outside she was looking halfway human.

'How did you leave the kids?' she whispered, as she opened the kitchen door and ushered her in. By this point, Susan knew to come around the back; she was a back-door friend, Aileen thought, almost cheering up at the idea.

'Oh, Daithi's fifteen now – he can mind the littlies for a while. They're all asleep. They've been driving me demented, though. I had to leave the house. Playing up and asking why they can't drink Fanta at dinner like they do at their dad's. I thought maybe you'd be dreading the day too. So why don't we join forces tomorrow – we could come to you, or you to us? Whatever you prefer. I could stick my turkey and ham in the cool box. Not that they'll eat it anyway. I might as well grill some Birds Eye Potato Waffles and be done with it.'

Susan's sharp, pretty face, with its trendy glasses, suddenly looked like an angel's. Aileen was filled with unspeakable gratitude. This was exactly what they needed. Other people's noise and fun to distract them from the empty place at the table, which had cast such a terrible shadow last Christmas.

'That would be brilliant,' she said. 'You're a genius, Susan. Come to us in the morning as soon as you've done the presents and stockings.'

Susan looked pleased. 'Good woman. Look, I know we're not quite in the same boat. I do have Pat for all he messes me around. But I know what it's like to be alone with the kids all day; it's the pits. Now get yourself to bed – you look wrecked if you don't mind me saying so.'

Aileen went up to bed, feeling as if a snazzily dressed angel had descended and brushed its designer wings upon her house. She peeped in at Doon, who was sleeping peacefully, spreadeagled on her bed with one leg sticking out. She had been given a shred of hope, and it was enough to go on. She had a friend, and she had told Doon the truth. That would get them through this Christmas, and she would take the rest of the days one at a time.

19

Natasha walked out of the pub in Gabe's wake, her head down. Her Victorian boots were pinching; her head was starting to pound and her thoughts were circling around the messages she had sent Ben. What had she been thinking? Then she remembered; she could delete them. As Gabe led her towards his car, which was parked down the road near his house, she stabbed desperately at her phone to locate the messages and press 'Delete for everyone'. But then she saw the two ticks. He had already read them.

'Oh God,' she moaned softly. She pressed delete anyway but, of course, it was too late.

'Do you want to get in?' Gabe said.

Natasha obeyed automatically, hardly knowing what she was doing. The most embarrassing texts she had ever sent, and he had read them. She would have to walk into work in January and face him, having sent him heartfelt messages and a Taylor Swift song.

Gabe started the car and they drove off in silence.

'Did you have a good evening?' he asked, sounding as if he was making an effort.

'Um, yes, no – I don't know.' She supposed it had been a good evening – before she sent those texts. If only she had got to them a minute sooner. Not wanting to elaborate, she said, 'Would you like the radio on?'

'Sure,' said Gabe, and she pressed buttons, but what came out was a very familiar song.

'Oh, that's the CD – you can take that out,' he said quickly.

'No, it's good! I haven't heard this one in years.'

'You like the Waterboys?' he said.

'Well, who doesn't? Especially "Fisherman's Blues".'

'I had never heard of them until this week,' he said. 'John, whose house I'm staying in, had a bunch of CDs so I've been educating myself.'

She was glad that there was something he didn't already know all about.

'How come you're staying in John's place? How do you know him?'

'It was really lucky. I was telling one of my colleagues that I wanted to visit Rathowen and she said her cousin was from there – that's John, and he wanted someone to look after the place over Christmas. I couldn't believe it.'

Natasha thought it sounded like a fairly standard coincidence, but she appreciated Gabe's wonder and awe at the chance to have Christmas in Rathowen.

'He wouldn't even take any money for it. That's why I was in the pub. The house is pretty cold and I didn't want to keep the heating on – it's so expensive now.'

This sounded poignant. 'Why didn't you come and join us when I asked you to?'

'I was feeling shy. I'm quite a shy person.'

'Seriously?'

'Yes! I know, it's shocking. The history professor who's vacationing on his own, feeling shy of joining a group of loud strangers who've all known each other for years. Who would have thought it?'

'I see.' Her mouth twitched slightly. She supposed they must have seemed an intimidating bunch, all shrieking and laughing and drinking. And texting. Oh, God, that text: sent and received. She couldn't bear it.

'Also, I was still kind of embarrassed,' he said.

'About what?'

'What do you think? Suggesting my family buy your house. I cringe inside every time I think of it.' He paused. 'You know that kind of cringe?'

'Yes, I do,' she said, knowing all too well. 'But it's OK, honestly.' The gloomy thought came to her that they might be grateful to him for the offer one day. But then he said, 'Plus, I don't really think my parents would go for it. It was just a crazy impulsive idea. Which isn't normally like me.'

This she could well believe. He wasn't so bad, though. And if they were going to spend Christmas Day together, she might as well initiate some peace and goodwill.

'Where did you go today, anywhere nice?'

'Yeah, I went to Newgrange, to see the passage tombs there. It was pretty spectacular.'

'Oh, I see.' It seemed crazy to drive all the way up to

Meath when there was so much to see nearby, but she wouldn't rain on his Stone Age parade.

'Have you been there?' Gabe asked.

'Um, we had a school trip there, years ago.' She had actually missed that one, but she didn't feel like admitting it. 'What have you seen in Wicklow?' she asked instead.

'Well, not much . . . I've seen your house. And Avondale, and that's it.'

'Gosh. You've missed out.'

'How so? I mean, I know it's called the garden of Ireland . . .'

'Not just the garden! You've got the beaches – the whole coast is spectacular, from Bray down to Arklow. Then you've got the Wicklow Mountains – the highest ones in the East. Then, yes, you've got all the big houses and gardens, not just Avondale but Powerscourt, Russborough, Mount Usher . . . and the botanical gardens and forests and the bogs. Oh, and we have plenty of ruins if you like those. Monastic ruins at Glendalough, and tons of standing stones.' She paused to draw breath. 'It's the whole of Ireland in miniature,' she added.

He nodded. 'OK, wow. You should work for the tourist board here.'

'Maybe,' she said, thinking of her friends and their exciting new local jobs. 'But I live in London, so.'

She thought she might be in for a lecture on why she was crazy to ever have left Wicklow but instead he said,

'So I think your mom said she was from Dublin? And your dad?'

'Yes, he was from Dublin too. But he loved Wicklow. He was the one who found the house – and persuaded my mum to buy it and do it up.'

'Lucky for me that he did. Or I might have been visiting a wreck.'

They were nearly at the right turn for Ballyclare; she was about to say it, but he anticipated the turn and swung the car up the drive, his headlights picking out the front of the house with its porch and the wreath on the door.

'Well,' he said, parking in the drive. 'I'll see you . . . the day after tomorrow? No, it's tomorrow actually.'

'We will look forward to it. Thanks again for the lift,' she said.

'No problem. Goodnight.'

She got out of the car and closed it quietly – Doon always said she had a tendency to slam the door. Gabe put the car into reverse and drove off without a backward glance.

Walking slowly towards the house, she was almost relieved not to be obsessing over Ben for a minute, as if her brain had reached capacity and shut that section down. Instead she found herself thinking of her father for the first time in a long time and wondering how different things would be if he were still around. It seemed unlikely, from the little she knew of him, that he would be any more on top of insurance forms than her mother was. More probably she could imagine him hiring a JCB digger and saying that he would fix the subsidence himself.

As she let herself inside, she thought of the handful of memories she held of him, polished over and over like an old set of rosary beads. She didn't even know any more if they were real or not. Invention had certainly played a role. For years after he had left, she had woven various imaginary scenarios about his absence. He was away on a trip to the North Pole and would be back as soon as he had saved the polar bears. Or he was on a sea voyage to the Pacific and would send a postcard one day with a clue to his whereabouts that only Natasha could decipher. Or he was a spy on a secret mission that was vital to world peace (or at least the peace process in the North). Later, when she had outgrown those fantasies, she had felt embarrassed. Now she just felt sad for the little girl who had tried to make sense of a senseless situation. She had never even told Doon.

Not wanting to wake Aileen, she crept quietly into the kitchen and put a slice of bread in the toaster. It was sad, she thought, that she had so few concrete memories of her father. But she did remember the general air of excitement he had carried around with him, the sparkle he had brought to every situation. Her mother had taken care of the mundane details of their lives; her father had brought the magic.

Perhaps, in a small way, she could do the same. She

would draw a line under the whole Ben debacle and focus on what she could control. She could help by cooking the Christmas dinner, of course, but, more than that, she could try to infuse things with the air of fun and excitement that her dad used to bring. It wasn't too late to make this a magical Christmas.

She was about to bolt the door, which Aileen liked to do at night, when she remembered that Doon wasn't back yet. Where was she anyway? It was all very strange. She had swept out of the pub like a wanted criminal on the lam. But Doon would never do anything criminal; no doubt she had remembered a missing detail on her tax return or something. Doon would never do anything as reckless or stupid as Natasha had that evening, with her witless texts to Ben. Sighing, Natasha flung her coat over the bottom of the banister and stumbled upstairs to bed.

20

Doon opened her eyes. Her cheek was resting on an unfamiliar pillow; not a soft ditsy patterned pink one like the one at Ballyclare but a navy and blue striped one. She was in a huge wooden sleigh bed that seemed to occupy a whole mezzanine floor. Above her, sky-lights revealed branches heavy with snow, and a pink-tinged sky above. Peeking cautiously towards the downstairs area, she saw wood panelling everywhere, an iron pot-bellied stove and huge picture windows that seemed to contain a whole forest. There was no noise except the faint hiss of a coffee machine and even fainter birdsong outside. Sitting up cautiously, she registered that she was fully dressed. But she still clutched the navy duvet to herself when she heard footsteps coming up a spiral staircase and saw the tousled head of Charlie. Charlie Cuffe. Whose bedroom this was.

'Coffee?' he said. He looked a little self-conscious but still very pleased with himself. Oh God. What, in the name of all that was holy, had happened last night? She had her clothes on; that was something. But she remembered something. A kiss. Oh no, no, no.

'I wasn't sure how you took it, so I've put milk and sugar here on the side.'

Doon registered the milk jug – Aileen would be pleased – and the coffee: deep and fragrant in an earthenware mug that she was fairly certain was from the Considered by Helen James range at Dunnes Stores. The whole place was very Considered indeed. Somehow it wasn't the home she had expected cheeky chappie Charlie to have.

'What . . . happened last night?' she asked, taking the cup with a trembling hand.

A slightly wistful smile. 'Nothing, I promise.'

'It wasn't nothing,' said Doon. Now she remembered the kiss, two kisses, in fact: one outside the house and one inside on the sofa. Quite a long one, that one.

'I'm glad you think so,' he said. Seeing her flustered expression, he said more seriously, 'We came inside, we . . . sat on the sofa to warm up, I went out to get more firewood – and when I came back in you were dead to the world. I tried to wake you but you looked really peaceful.' Doon winced, believing him and not knowing whether to be relieved or disappointed by her eternal gift for sleep.

'But how did I get up here?'

'Oh, I carried you up. And I slept on the sofa.'

'You carried me?' She tried to picture this – it was a spiral staircase and couldn't have been easy.

'You're as light as a feather,' he said.

Hearing him say that that made her feel briefly dizzy, until she came to her senses. She was in Charlie Cuffe's house. Alone with him on the morning of Christmas

Eve. Christmas Eve! She checked the time. Eight thirty. The house would be stirring; she had to get home. She took a gulp of coffee – damn, it was good – and stood up.

'I'd better go . . . I'm sorry about last night.' She swung her legs out of bed and started looking around for her shoes.

'Your shoes are downstairs, by the front door,' he said. 'And there's nothing to be sorry for. Are you kidding? You helped me foil a raid. You saved next year's Christmas stock. You're a woman in a million, Doon McDonnell. Are you sure I can't give you some breakfast before you go?'

Doon shook her head and started inching down the spiral staircase, feeling as ropey as if she had been drinking all night. The place was beautiful, and she noticed all sorts of charming details; the black Labrador asleep on the sheepskin rug in front of the stove, the full bookshelves, the chess set on the coffee table and – was that a yoga mat? Yes, it was, in a basket along with a foam roller and various resistance bands. Was this Charlie's place or had he borrowed it from Gwyneth Paltrow or some other wellness guru?

'I didn't peg you for a yoga fan.'

'Yeah, I got into it after I banjaxed my knee playing tennis. Now I have quite a serious practice, as they say. I go to a really good class in Greystones once a week. I can give you the details. Or maybe we could go together some time.'

Was he on another planet? It was time for some clarity and, Doon's favourite thing, boundaries. 'Charlie,' she said. 'I can't go to yoga with you. Or anything. I'm engaged. I . . . I shouldn't have kissed you last night. I feel terrible about it. I am engaged to someone and we're very happy.' She realized, as she said it, that a lot of this wasn't true, but that didn't matter. The important part, the engagement, was correct.

'Are you really happy with him?' he said, and she nodded. She was trying to put on her coat while standing and also stepping into her boots.

He crossed the room and gave her his arm to steady herself. She took it, without knowing why, and next minute he had leaned down towards her. He said, in her ear, 'I don't believe you.' And then he kissed her. *Stop*, she told herself unconvincingly. But here was his arm round her and his hand in her hair and the dizzying magic that had surrounded her last night like the artificial snow. *Artificial*, she reminded herself sternly. Not real. Just hormones and Christmas madness and pre-wedding nerves. And the Cuffe black magic, as potent as ever.

'I can't,' she said, detaching herself. 'I really can't, and I shouldn't have. It was just a moment of madness.'

He stepped back and let her go. 'OK. Understood.'

She zipped up her coat and did a quick inventory. Bag, shoes, phone; she was ready to go without leaving a trace.

Charlie added, 'If you change your mind, though. I would really like to see you again.'

She said, 'I don't think that's a good idea. But would you still be willing to act for us – if it comes to selling the house?'

A new look came into his eyes. 'Sure. I'd help you out. Why wouldn't I? I'd get a good commission out of it, so I'd be mad not to.'

Doon felt simultaneously disappointed and glad to be back on a more sensible footing with him. 'I just wouldn't want any of this – business between us – to get in the way of you acting for us, if it came to that.'

He nodded. 'Understood.' He looked a little distant now; but Doon didn't have the bandwidth to worry about why.

Doon turned round to open the door; of course she couldn't figure it out and he stepped forward to help her.

'Thanks.' Trying not to sound too panicked, she asked, 'You won't tell anyone about this, will you?'

'Of course not. And don't worry – nobody will have seen you come or go. Part of the charm of the place.'

Doon nodded. 'Well, goodbye. Have a good Christmas.'

'Same to you and yours,' said Charlie crisply and closed the door.

Doon stood outside, as bewildered as she ever had felt in her life. Charlie's place really was a cabin in the woods. It had no real garden or even drive to speak of; it simply grew out of a clearing of fir trees, like a cabin in a fairy tale. How on earth had he got permission to build it like this in the middle of the forest? But of course he knew people and must have snuck something past the council, who were famously strict on planning permission. She got into the car and felt the comfort of sitting in the driver's seat, which at least felt familiar – even if inside she was in miserable turmoil. She realized she didn't know the way home. Nor was her phone any help; she had no signal at all. How could someone like Charlie exist in an internet black spot?

He must have Wi-Fi. She had managed to text Aileen last night, she remembered now – a quick holding one saying she would be staying at Amy's, thinking that would stop Aileen from worrying even if she didn't stay out all night. Oh, here was some signal; a new message. Oh God, it was from Ciarán.

How's it going, a stór? You've been very quiet. Hope all is well in Wicklow. Talk later? Xxx

Doon replied quickly. Yes, all good thanks. Just really busy here. Let's talk tonight xxxx She pressed send, thinking it would reach him as soon as she was back in civilization.

She didn't think she could feel worse, but then she saw a text from Amy.

Hey Doon. What happened to you last night? Hope your mam is OK. I'm here with Setanta and he's going to text Ciarán now to tell him we're engaged ;) Maybe we can make it a joint wedding! xxxxo

Oh, God. The interview with the Gardai last night came back to her; they had taken a statement from her. With a cold certainty she knew that word would soon get out and everybody would know that she had been up at the farm with Charlie. It didn't matter that there was a reasonable explanation; everyone would prefer the colourful one. She dreaded the questions, the amused comments and rumours. She pictured David crossing the road to avoid her; she heard Mrs Cuffe's voice saying, 'Please stop calling, would you?' And that wasn't even the worst of it. The worst of it was that it wasn't just a rumour; something had happened with her and Charlie. She had stayed the night at his place and kissed him twice. No, three times!

It was nearly nine o'clock and she had no idea how she was even going to get to Ballyclare, let alone how she would be able to face Ciarán when she saw him. Panic and terror threatened to overwhelm her. But then she talked herself down. *Stop being a wimp, Doon. You can do it.* This was her native county. She would drive down this crazy lane and once she got on the main road, she would follow her nose back home and forget that this entire episode ever happened.

21

Aileen woke up to find that it was half past nine. She couldn't remember the last time she had slept so late. She had been awake when Natasha crashed in and made toast before thumping up the stairs in her high-heeled boots and, presumably, passing out fully clothed on her bed. Doon had texted to say she was going to Amy's, which was strange but good. Aileen sometimes worried that Doon didn't have as fond memories as Natasha did of Rathowen, so she was glad of every local friendship she still had. She peeked out of the window to check for Doon's car and felt a swoop of relief when she saw it was there.

Doon was in the kitchen when Aileen came down fifteen minutes later. She was wearing leggings and a fleece, and putting a bowl of porridge into the micro-wave, as was her wont. Aileen felt that porridge in the microwave was a crime against nature, but Doon was too impatient to stir it on the stove. Aileen felt a surge of love at the thought that this was Doon's last Christ-mas under her roof as a single girl.

'Hi, my pet.' Aileen came over and kissed her cheek. 'How was last night? It must have been a good one if you had a sleepover at Amy's.'

Doon smiled but Aileen was dismayed to see huge circles under her eyes and also a suspicion of – was it redness? Doon never cried. She sat down at the table, saying nothing.

'Doonie, what's the matter?' Aileen had been about to make tea but she drew her dressing gown round her and sat down opposite Doon. 'Did something happen last night?'

'No,' said Doon, a bit too quickly in Aileen's opinion. 'I'm just tired, I suppose. And a bit stressed about the wedding. And the house obviously. And everything.'

'Stressed about the wedding? But what about it, love?' Aileen could see that a huge wedding in a hotel wasn't Doon's thing, but she had consistently professed not to care either way. And the great thing was that Ciarán's family were practically planning it all for her; she had nothing to do. Aileen felt deeply reassured that the clan had embraced Doon in a way that Dan's family had never embraced her. They would look after Doon. As would Ciarán, of course. He was a bit serious, but so was Doon. They were so well suited, and Ciarán was nothing if not reliable, which was what Doon needed.

Doon said nothing, and Aileen knew better than to press her. That would make her retreat into her shell; it always had. Instead she stayed quiet while she boiled the kettle and spread butter on a slice of soda bread. Then, just as she couldn't bear the suspense any longer, Doon replied, 'Just the planning of it. But it will be fine.'

Aileen nodded. She was watching Doon's face. She didn't look the way a young woman should on discussing her wedding. She looked positively green, and it wasn't as if you could blame it on alcohol. Aileen asked, as casually as she could, 'Doon, is there another reason you're worried about the wedding?'

Doon shook her head, but her face was the picture of misery. She was about to say something, when the kitchen door opened and Natasha came in, looking as green as Doon but much more cheerful. 'Morning, all,' she said, coming over and giving Aileen a hug. 'Happy Christmas Eve.'

'Same to you. Door closed, darling,' Aileen said for probably the millionth time, and Natasha closed the door. 'The teapot is wet,' she added.

Natasha poured herself a cup of tea, giving Doon a strange look. 'Where did you end up last night?' she said. 'You ran out of that pub like a bat out of hell.'

'I went to stay at Amy's,' said Doon in a tone that brooked no argument.

Natasha said, 'But she —' Then she stopped short. 'Oh yeah. So you did.'

'How did you get home?' Aileen asked Natasha, suddenly wondering about this.

'Oh. Our Christmas guest gave me a lift. Gabe.'

Now it was Aileen and Doon's turn to look surprised. 'That was nice of him,' said Aileen. 'Was he in the pub?'

Natasha shrugged. 'Yes, reading a book.'

Aileen nodded, but her thoughts went back to Doon. The Amy story was looking a bit suspicious now, but that wasn't even her first concern. She was pretty sure by now that despite her words, Doon was having doubts about the wedding. Aileen's heart went out to her. She knew how dutiful Doon was and how much it would take for her to go back on a promise, even if she wasn't sure about it. Aileen couldn't solve this for her but she could tell her that she should only marry Ciarán if she was madly in love with him.

And yet – doubt assailed her. She had married someone she was madly in love with, and it hadn't been exactly the fairy tale she had hoped. Not that she would wish her life with Dan away, but it wasn't exactly what she would want for Doon either.

'Oh my God,' Natasha was saying, checking her WhatsApp on her phone while eating cereal from the packet. 'Did you guys hear what happened at Fenton's Christmas Tree Farm last night? The gang came back, up from Dublin; the guards were called and all.'

'Oh, that's awful. I hope nobody was hurt?' said Aileen.

Doon had looked up sharply too, but she didn't seem as shocked or dismayed as Natasha.

'Don't think so. Charlie raced up there apparently and chased them off. God knows how, set his Labrador on them or something.'

'His poor mother,' said Aileen. 'Is he mad? He

shouldn't have gone near the place.' She shook her head. 'Hopefully they'll be gone for good now.'

'Yeah,' Doon said, adding blueberries to her porridge. 'Is there any brown sugar, Mum?'

'Yes there is, three kinds . . . in the press there. We do need lemons, though, and probably a few other bits.' Aileen reached for her notebook, feeling half daunted and half energized at the thought of all the planning still to do. 'If you help me in the kitchen, Tashie, can you do a few messages in the village, Doon?'

'Yeah sure.' Doon nodded, shovelling away porridge.

Aileen smiled; that had always been one of the great things about Doon. Ask her to run some errands, or do anything at all, and she just did it; no ifs and buts or delays. A great quality. Except when it was going to force her into something she deeply didn't want to do.

It was a beautiful bright day outside; from the window she could see the sky was as blue as a jay's wing and the sun gleamed on the snow-peaked mountains and on the slips of snow still on the fields. Aileen had been planning to forgo her morning walk as there was so much to do, but the glimpse of outside made her change her mind. Crisp winter weather like this was better than drinking champagne; she couldn't miss it.

'Oh, and will you go and get your Christmas stockings and put them out downstairs before you forget?' she said over her shoulder, as she put on her boots.

'Yay,' said Natasha.

'Mum, actually, I really don't want one this year,' said Doon. 'I forgot to tell you earlier, sorry. I just feel too old for it. Tasha can have mine.'

'Really, Doonie?' Aileen said mildly. She was about to say that of course that was fine, when Natasha's voice cut across her, outraged.

'Doon, are you mental? You have to have a stocking. It's Christmas.'

'Why should I have to if I don't actually want one?' Doon replied sharply.

'Because Mum went shopping for those stocking bits. She *chose* them for you. Would it kill you to just take them? It might be our last Christmas here for God's sake.'

Aileen was dismayed; she hadn't known that Natasha realized that. She was about to intervene, when Doon roared, 'Oh my God, Natasha, will you ever grow up? It's not our last Christmas on Earth, it's just our last Christmas at Ballyclare.' She stomped out of the room, somehow managing to put her empty bowl in the sink first.

Aileen sighed. Yes, it really was Christmas now.

'Mum, I'm sorry but she was being a misery! She could just say yes. Don't you think?'

Aileen knew Natasha was expecting her mother to take her side but she didn't have it in her. 'She doesn't have to if she doesn't want to,' she said briefly, standing up and putting her teacup in the sink. She would wash it later; now was the time for a walk in the blessed

228

sunshine, and some fresh air and time away from her beloved girls.

As ever, Aileen felt immeasurably better after her walk. The girls seemed to have reached some kind of truce; she came back in to find Doon hanging up Natasha's stocking, and her own, which she was donating to Gabe. Aileen wasn't sure what he would do with the lipstick and miniature hand creams, but she supposed he could regift them. Natasha was in the kitchen peeling parsnips and carrots with Christmas carols playing on Lyric FM.

'Oh, thanks for doing that, pet,' said Aileen, pouring water into a plastic bowl so they could soak in it.

'Leave that, Mum. I'll do it,' said Natasha.

'Well, all right.'

'Actually, I've been thinking,' Natasha said. 'You know the way you always do the Christmas dinner . . . and serve up the drinks . . . and you basically don't sit down from morning till night?'

'It's not quite like that,' said Aileen, though it was true that she had still been wearing her apron last year when they sat down to eat.

'It is. So this year I want to do it all,' said Natasha. 'The whole thing. I'm doing the prep and it's mainly all done now. I'll do all the cooking and serve it all up. You just have to show up for it.'

Aileen looked at her doubtfully. This was a sweet offer, but Natasha had never served Christmas dinner alone and there was more to it than she probably realized. 'Why don't we do it together?' she suggested.

'No.' Natasha held up a hand like a policeman. 'Too many cooks. I can either do the whole thing or I'm out.'

'Well, if you're sure,' said Aileen, thinking she would still sneak in at one point with the meat thermometer and just make sure that the turkey was cooked through.

Before they knew it, dusk was falling and it was time for a favourite tradition; the lighting of the Christmas candle in the window. Natasha, as the youngest member of the household, did the honours and the flame cast its halo against the dark window. Aileen loved this ritual. She could almost imagine for a minute that the girls were chubby and little again, solemnly watching for Santa out of the window or sitting on Dan's lap as he read them *The Night Before Christmas*.

After they had lit the candle it was time for their traditional Christmas Eve supper of smoked salmon on soda bread, and then they played a few rounds of cards until it was time to get gussied up, in their various ways, for 'midnight' Mass at nine p.m. Natasha put on Aileen's old red mohair dress from John Rocha. Doon wore black trousers and a black wool polo neck and looked, Aileen thought, like Audrey Hepburn or some other sixties film star – Jean Seberg maybe. Aileen was proud of her two beautiful girls and took extra trouble with her make-up and wore her best cream cashmere jumper. They walked to the church to join the hundred-strong congregation. There was no point in driving, for every legal parking space and a fair few illegal ones would be full, with every man, woman and child in Rathowen and a few guide dogs too.

'All right, Doonie?' Aileen asked her daughter, squeezing her arm as they went in through the church porch. Doon nodded and smiled, but she looked pale still. Aileen sighed and then took a deep breath as they walked in, smelling the comforting scent of incense and candles.

They took their usual seats towards the front left, nodding to acquaintances. There was Natasha's gorgeous friend Billie, and Maria from the gallery, and Aileen's friends Susan Reilly and Jenny Fenton, and the rest of the Cuffe family minus David, who was in Australia. Charlie Cuffe was there looking very handsome in a black wool coat with a navy scarf. You could see your face in his shoes. Aileen thought briefly how nice it would be if Natasha could get together with someone like Charlie, rather than pining over unreliable London boys. But Charlie was his own brand of unreliable probably, judging from a few things his mother had mentioned about his many girlfriends.

As Father Doyle led them in prayer, Aileen found herself remembering the years when she had stopped coming to Mass here. She couldn't stand the feeling of being watched and whispered about, as the woman whose husband had disappeared. Most people were nothing but kind, but it was the others who stuck in her mind. To try to find some black humour in it all she divided them into categories. There were the ghouls, who said things like *Have they dredged the river?* Then there were the detectives. *My brother's neighbour's cousin works in Busáras and he said he saw someone who was the spit of your husband*... Then there were the gossips, who didn't speak directly to her but whose words seemed to seep everywhere like fog: *I heard he went to England*... *Debts*... *Another woman*... *Drink.* She knew that at least one of them, whether ghoul, detective, gossip or all three, had voiced the theory that she herself had something to do with Dan's disappearance. *She looks standoffish*... *Keeps herself to herself*... *You wouldn't know.*

She gritted her teeth and did nothing about these remarks until one night, over a glass of wine in her kitchen, she confided in Susan, expecting some sympathy. But Susan shook her head. 'Aileen,' she said, 'have you never lived in a village? Have you never lived in Ireland? This is just what people do. We talk about each other. And there's a lot to talk about. Look around you. You're not the only family with problems.'

Aileen had taken mild umbrage at first, but then she realized Susan was right. She began to see sadness and scandal hiding everywhere. There was the family whose elderly grandfather killed someone while driving without his glasses. There was the couple whose only son died in a motorbike accident, a week after his twenty-first birthday. There was the young woman who was heavily pregnant when Aileen saw her one day in the post office, then two weeks later was walking alone, no baby and a frozen face. You could miss all this amid the peaceful nature of life here, with blue skies and friendly faces and beautiful countryside.

Around this time, poor Susan's mother, who lived in the village, was diagnosed with Alzheimer's. She would greet Aileen with great cordiality every time they met, out walking with her carer. 'And how is Dan?' she would always ask. 'Is he away working up in Dublin?' Aileen would murmur something non-committal, and ponder that Susan was right; she wasn't the only person with problems.

In December 1999, over two years after Dan went missing, they had a breakthrough. A Scottish woman, a photographer, had seen Dan's poster while on holiday in Wexford. She recognized him from a ferry journey from Belfast to Cairnryan on Tuesday 12 August 1997. She had taken photographs of the view, and Dan appeared in the background of one of them. He had a cousin in Glasgow; Aileen remembered him talking about wanting to go and visit him and make a trip to the Outer Hebrides. He must have travelled up there after going to Dublin on the bus that Sunday. The private detective hired by Dan's parents went to make the trip and speak to the ferry staff and locals at Cairnryan. They found two witnesses, teenagers at the time, one of whom reported seeing a splash overboard and thinking that someone might have gone in, but he later thought he must have been mistaken. It was impossible to say if this was true, but either way there was no record of Dan after the passengers had disembarked. The guards surmised that Dan had most likely had some misadventure and fallen overboard; or, given his illness, that he had had a fatal impulse of some kind.

In a sense it was a horrifying discovery. Aileen found herself imagining so many terrible scenarios. A tragic accident; a fight with another passenger even. She would come awake, bathed in sweat, from nightmares in which she saw his last hours. She was haunted by imagining what had happened to his body, picturing it corrupting and dissolving under the water. But at least she had an answer, or as close to one as she would ever get. Which was what she needed; not to move on, exactly, but to end the agony one way or another and have something to tell the girls. But Dan's parents disagreed. They wanted to keep searching for more information, even when the police investigation was officially closed. That was the start of the rift between them and Aileen.

Back in the here and now, Aileen registered that they were already on to the Prayers of the Faithful. *We pray for our extended families* ... Dan's father had died five years ago and his poor mother, by then very frail and forgetful, had moved into a nursing home in Donnybrook. Some cousins in Kildare had taken charge of her care, and the house in Waterloo Road had been sold for an eye-watering sum, over two million euro. 'She's leaving it all to some charity,' one of the Kildare cousins had told Aileen bitterly, when Aileen had phoned to get the details of the nursing home. Aileen had been vaguely insulted that they thought she might be hanging out for a legacy, but she was mainly relieved that she didn't have to be responsible for her mother-in-law's care.

When Miriam went into the nursing home, Aileen felt sorry for her and started calling or visiting at least twice a year, once in spring and once in autumn. This was only possible because the animosity of the years gone by had faded with her memory. Aileen wasn't ever sure that she knew exactly who she was, but she greeted her like an old acquaintance or neighbour; their relationship was the best it ever had been. And then, of course, she had died in the spring. Aileen hadn't even known she had died until she'd read about it on RIP.ie. Poor woman, it had been a sad ending to what had undoubtedly been a sad life.

She tried to still her mind and focus on the music, listening to Natasha and Doon singing beside her. They both had beautiful voices, true and sweet, inherited from Dan. Strangely enough, she had never heard them singing like that until after he left. Not immediately after he left, of course; there had been no singing for months. But at one of their little friends' birthday parties, a year after he left, she had heard them piping 'Happy Birthday' beside her and had been startled at the change in sound.

It might have been just that their voices had

matured, of course. But Aileen remembered her mother saying, years ago, that when a person died their gifts left them and took up residence in someone close to them. It had stayed with her, partly because it was such an uncharacteristically poetic thing for her mother to say. Maybe Dan's voice lived on in the girls; certainly his other characteristics did – his fire and enthusiasm in Natasha, his sombre depths in Doon. Aileen herself couldn't sing a note, though she did find consolation in music, spending the long evenings after she got the kids to bed listening to songs by Nina Simone and Mary Coughlan, women who understood pain and anguish.

In November 2000, a year after the discovery of Dan's ferry journey, Susan Reilly had held an intervention.

'Aileen,' she said, 'it's been three years since you lost him now. When are you going to allow yourself to enjoy life again?'

Aileen had felt briefly offended again. What did Susan know about her situation – Susan whose ex-husband was alive and well and living in Mullingar?

'I don't know what you mean by "enjoy life",' she said.

'Well, how about some plan for your evening that doesn't involve sitting around for hours listening to your Mary Black CDs?' said Susan.

'Mary Coughlan,' Aileen corrected her, but she took Susan's point. The trouble was, she didn't see where she fitted in to the social life of Rathowen. The married women, she felt, looked at her with, not suspicion exactly but pity and a kind of relief. *There but for the grace of God*, she could feel them thinking. And the single ones, like Susan, were few and far between and were by definition less able to go out of an evening, or if they were able to, they wanted to go on dates, something Aileen felt she never would do again. But Susan was right. She wasn't even forty yet; it was too soon to hide herself away.

'I know,' said Susan. 'Why don't we do something for Nollaig na nBán?'

'What's that?' asked Aileen, and Susan laughed at her Dublin ignorance, though to be fair she herself had only learned about it at school but never celebrated it.

'Women's Christmas, or Little Christmas, it's called. The sixth of January. It's the traditional day for women to have their own celebration after doing all the cooking and cleaning for two weeks for everyone else.'

Aileen liked the idea of doing something with all women. 'That's a great idea. Would we have it in Keogh's?'

'Keogh's, sure, or the Rathowen Arms if we wanted to get fancy.'

'Actually,' said Aileen, 'why don't we do it at Bally-clare? It's plenty big enough. I could make a big chilli or something, and we could have wine . . .'

'Are you sure? That would be brilliant!' Susan's fingers started to dance over her BlackBerry, a new acquisition. 'I'll help you. Who will we have?'

237

'Everyone! All the women anyway.'

And that was the start of Aileen's famous Women's Christmas parties. Women came from miles around, brought their kids or left them at home according to their ages, and ate and chatted and drank and, around midnight or just after, pushed back the furniture and danced. The last car left at three in the morning, and Susan Reilly and Laura Fenton were still there for breakfast. Aileen couldn't remember the last time she had had so much fun – had had fun at all really. Even her hangover the next day was enjoyable and felt vaguely illicit. She drove Susan home at lunchtime, both of them still giggling over nothing like a pair of schoolgirls.

Aileen thought about the final conversation she had had with Susan's mother, who was at her house with her carer when she dropped her home. 'And how is Dan?' she had asked for the tenth time. 'Is he away up in Dublin?' Aileen had been about to explain gently that, in fact, Dan was missing presumed dead, but then she had caught Susan's eye and remembered her explanation that her mother lived in a perpetual present moment. 'He is, Mrs Reilly. I'll tell him you said hi,' she said, and was rewarded with a smile before they all parted ways.

Back in the here and now, Aileen realized the Mass was ending, and everyone was standing for the final hymn – 'O Come, All Ye Faithful'.

Afterwards they all filed outside. Someone ahead of her exclaimed and she soon saw why. More snow had fallen while they were inside and the little village street was coated in white.

22

Natasha's first impulse, when she woke up on Christ-mas morning, was to check her phone. She had sent Ben a further message yesterday, to follow up on her Taylor Swift text. After about twenty drafts, she had put, Sorry, that was a crazy text. Maybe we could chat when I get back, though? She didn't want to completely row back on the substance of what she had said, just in case there was still some chance for them, but she obviously couldn't let it stand as it was, as she looked insane. Late on Christmas Eve, he had replied with – a thumbs-up emoji. She couldn't quite believe that that was it. Prob-ably his real reply would arrive overnight, like Santa Claus.

But she stopped herself from checking. She didn't want that to be the first thing she did on Christmas Day. Instead she pulled on her jumper, fleece dressing gown and extra socks, all piled in readiness beside her bed, and opened up the curtain to see if the snow had stuck. She gasped aloud. Even more had fallen in the night, blanketing the fields and woods all around and lying thick on the mountains. It was magical. She sighed, her breath misting on the windowpane.

She put her phone away, then she turned to the doll's

house, to distract herself. She would never have wanted anyone to know that she still sometimes played with it. Not played with it exactly, but maintained it, you could say. She moved the two little girl dolls from the bedroom downstairs to the drawing room and lined them up beside the tiny Christmas tree. The tree itself was modern, made by Aileen from an old wire brush years ago, but the house and the furniture were very old, and Natasha touched them carefully, stroking the satiny top of the little piano and the soft green velvet of the drawing-room curtains. Then, and only then, did she allow herself to check her phone.

Nothing. He had sent nothing since the thumbs-up emoji yesterday. The humiliation was terrible. She turned her phone off. If this was the way he was able to treat her, after they had been such good friends, she was done with him. That wasn't how you treated a friend. It didn't matter how busy he was with Lucy or whatever else. She deserved better than that. She was busy too. She had a Christmas dinner to make.

She ran downstairs, still in her dressing gown, and without glancing into the drawing room at her stocking, she went to check the fridge. The vegetables and the turkey were all ready to go in the range; she just had to finish off the stuffing, which she did quickly and efficiently. She put the turkey in the range and set the timer, ticking it off on her list. Then she was free to lay the table for a special Christmas breakfast. She put out all the good china and found a posy of dried flowers.

Then, feeling the need for more action, she looked up a recipe on her phone and started cracking eggs.

The door creaked open and Doon came inside, wearing her usual fleece and leggings. 'My God,' she said, taking in the scene: the tidy kitchen, the table laid for three.

'Happy Christmas, Dúnóg!' she said. 'I'm making a surprise breakfast. Are you hungry?'

She tensed slightly, expecting a typical Doon reply, such as that microwave porridge was fine or she couldn't possibly eat a breakfast as well as a lunch. But Doon had obviously woken on a better side of the bed this morning and she smiled.

'Yeah, sure. Sounds amazing.'

'Oh, watch out,' said Natasha, as Doon gave her an unexpected hug. Her tracksuit bottoms and Smashing Pumpkins T-shirt, both older than she was, were covered in flour. She would shower later, before Gabe arrived.

'You're up early. Can you believe the snow?'

'I know! It's gorgeous.' Natasha looked around, feeling energized and hopeful. With every egg beaten, every serving dish dusted and every herb added to the stuffing, Ben had receded even further. Ballyclare had worked its magic and she was behind its protective shield, in a world where he just didn't matter as much as he had even a day ago. She added, 'Have you seen Mum? Is she not up yet?'

'Presumably on her walk. Aren't you glad we're not

one of those families that does a Christmas Day swim at Bray Head?' said Doon, and Natasha shuddered.

She replied, 'Yes, or, even worse, a run. Though won't you be out for a run next Christmas with Ciarán? I'm pretty sure you told me they do one.'

'Oh yeah. They do.' Doon poured herself coffee, looking strangely downbeat. Or maybe she was just sad, like Natasha, that this would be her last Christmas spent on her own with her mother and sister. Ciarán had told them all that the first married Christmas was traditionally spent by the couple with the bride's family. He was full of these rules. Where he got them from Natasha had no idea, but somehow he knew all these things that Aileen had never taught her and Doon, like how much to spend on a friend's child's first Communion present or that you had a year after a wedding to give a wedding gift. If he ever got tired of teaching he could definitely write an etiquette column – a sort of Irish Emily Post.

Aileen came inside at that point and they all exchanged Christmas greetings and Aileen poured herself and Natasha a weak Buck's Fizz before they all sat down for breakfast. Then Natasha carefully set down the black cast-iron saucepan containing her Dutch baby: a giant fluffy pancake dusted with icing sugar. She had made a luscious creamy lemon sauce that Doon said she would have licked off the plate if it wasn't that she knew it would upset the others.

'Tasha, this is seriously delicious,' Doon said, and Natasha beamed.

'You wouldn't get better at the Gresham,' Aileen said.

With breakfast over, they processed into the drawing room for the ceremonial exchange of presents. Natasha opened her stocking, feeling a bit foolish at being the only one to get one, but also appreciating the gorgeous miniature toiletries which she could use for trips all year. Then she gave her presents out first, as the youngest.

Aileen opened up cashmere bed socks in a beautiful oatmeal colour.

'Just the thing for my shivery toes, thank you honey,' said Aileen, feeling the wool appreciatively.

Doon opened hers next: a beautiful leather-bound notebook with creamy white pages, stamped on the front with her initials in gold. 'Do you like it? I thought it could be handy for wedding planning!' Natasha added excitedly.

'Oh yes, thank you,' said Doon, smiling, but Natasha felt disappointed; it obviously wasn't quite right. Perhaps Doon did all her planning on apps. Oh well, maybe Ciarán would like it.

Natasha opened up her presents last, and shrieked when she saw her gift from Doon. It was the candle she had wanted to buy Aileen: fragrant with cinnamon, orange and cloves.

'Doon,' she said, her eyes bright, 'you're so good. And sneaky! How did you manage to buy it on the sly? God, she'd make a great spy, wouldn't she, Mum?'

Aileen laughed in agreement and suggested that if that was the end of the presents they should all go and get dressed for the day.

'Good plan,' said Natasha. 'Ooh, and, Mum, could I wear that big blue dress with the boat neck?'

'Sure,' said Aileen, and Natasha ran off to get ready. Just because she'd been in the kitchen was no reason not to dress up for the day that was in it. She found a strapless bra, a little tight but still doing the job, and hoiked herself into the dress. Then she did her hair and make-up, thinking that her skin and hair always looked better when they got a break from the London water. She had just finished doing her eyes when the doorbell rang. That must be Gabe – he wasn't invited until one, but he must have decided to come early. She felt a slight rush of anticipation, and as she ran downstairs she found herself giving her hair a last pat. *Showtime*, thought Natasha, flinging open the door.

'Oh, hi!' she said, astonished. For the man on the doorstep wasn't Gabe at all; it was Ciarán. 'Come in! This is a surprise.'

'Yes. I just woke up this morning and I said to myself . . . Why am I not with the woman I love? So I thought I'd surprise her! I've been a bit worried about her, to be honest,' he said, coming inside.

'Oh yeah? Why so?' Natasha said, hanging up his coat for him. She was a little depressed to see that he was wearing his GAA county jersey for Christmas dinner, but Ciarán's gonna Ciarán, she supposed.

'She's been sounding a bit funny when we've been texting – distracted, I suppose.'

'Well, there's been a lot going on here. Did she tell you about the house?'

'No! What about it?' Ciarán looked concerned.

'Um, I'll let her fill you in. Doon!' she yelled over her shoulder up the stairs. 'Look who's here!' She waited till Doon's voice could be heard overhead, then gave Ciarán a quick wave and darted off in the direction of the kitchen. She didn't want to spoil their romantic reunion; plus, she had a turkey to baste and another place to set at the table.

23

Doon had rarely felt so shocked and dismayed in all her life. Every time she tried to speak normally to Ciarán, all she could think about was Charlie Cuffe. She was just so unprepared; why had he not told her he was coming? The arrival of Gabe, smartly dressed in a jacket and shirt, was a welcome distraction and so was the fact that it was Christmas morning and acceptable for everyone else to have a drink. Natasha served up Buck's Fizz all round and banished them all into the drawing room while she did last-minute prep. Doon would have loved to join her, but Natasha was absolutely determined to cook the whole thing single-handed.

Ciarán seemed a little surprised to meet Gabe but he immediately understood once the family connection with the house was explained to him. 'Welcome home to Ireland,' he said solemnly, which made Doon cringe a little but she knew was kindly meant.

'Thank you,' said Gabe. 'These are for you,' he added to Aileen, placing two bottles of wine and a small gift-wrapped package on the coffee table.

'Oh, lovely! Can I open it now?' Aileen asked. She opened the package and exclaimed in pleasure. It was a small framed pen-and-ink drawing of Ballyclare in the snow. Even Doon, in her befuddled state, could appreciate that it was really good as well as being a very thoughtful present.

'I had no idea you could draw, let alone draw like this. It's excellent. Thank you, Gabe. I will treasure it,' Aileen told him, putting it on the mantelpiece. 'Gabe was a great help the other day when the surveyor came around,' she added to Ciarán.

'What surveyor?' asked Ciarán.

Doon's stomach plummeted a further few inches.

'Oh God,' she said. 'Sorry! I haven't actually had a chance to tell you yet. It's all happened so fast.' She managed to be almost grateful of the drama, as it provided such a welcome distraction and also hopefully went some way to explain her flustered state. Well, it was good to know that she was capable of new lows.

'Ah, here, that's terrible,' said Ciarán when all was concluded, shaking his head. 'Sorry to hear it. Stressful enough now.' Doon looked at him gratefully, thinking how good he was in a crisis. What a pity he couldn't help her with the particular one she was facing right now.

'Does your house insurance not . . . ?' said Ciarán, and poor Aileen's face fell.

Doon shook her head at him, and he tried to nod understandingly, though he looked horrified. Ciarán didn't have a single possession or activity that wasn't insured to the hilt. The idea of falling behind on your paperwork and letting your insurance lapse was as foreign to him as bank robbery or drug addiction.

'Anyway,' Aileen said, wanting to change the topic, 'are all your family well, Ciarán?'

Going through all the family news took a considerable amount of time, considering the size of Ciarán's clan, and Aileen looked more cheerful by the time he had finished. She said, 'Doon, have you heard anything else about this raid on the Christmas tree farm? Poor Laura was telling me all about it.'

'No. Or, nothing else, just that there was one,' said Doon, wishing that this purgatory would end. But Aileen, for some reason, seemed keen to make a saga of the whole thing, with Charlie chasing off baddies like Bruce Willis in *Die Hard*. What a mess. Doon had never been more grateful to see Natasha at the door.

'Lunch is served!' she said a tad breathlessly. 'Come on through.'

She threw open the double doors that connected the drawing room to the dining room, like a magician whipping a cloth off a hat.

'Oh, Natasha,' said Aileen.

'Wow,' said Gabe.

They all gazed at the room, which had been transformed. The white-linen tablecloth was barely visible beneath the sprigs of holly and ivy and the candles that glowed and guttered in antique candelabra. Where had they come from and when had Natasha had time to whip this all up? Doon, despite her bleak mood, felt her spirits lift as they all walked over to the table where Natasha had laid each gilt-rimmed plate with a folded napkin of the whitest linen and a single sprig of mistletoe. Remembering that it was poisonous, Doon moved the sprig carefully to one side.

'I was going to do a table plan,' said Natasha. 'But I thought *some* people might laugh at me.' She glanced at Doon.

'Nobody would dream of it, pet – this is absolutely gorgeous,' said Aileen. 'Let's take photos, before we mess it all up.' She looked around. 'Gabe, would you? The three of us.'

They stood in front of the table, Aileen with her daughters on either side, and smiled.

'And now – let's get all the family or soon to be family!' Aileen added, quickly. 'Gabe, do you mind, again? And then we'll do one of us with you. Ciarán, in you get! Good man.'

'Good man' was right, Doon thought, as she beamed obediently and felt the familiar strong arm around her. Better than she deserved. Maybe she should actually tell him after all. He might understand – maybe?

'You OK, Doon?' Ciarán asked her quietly, and Doon realized the immediate need to snap right out of it.

'Totally fine,' she said.

'Dig in,' said Natasha. 'This is just a little starter.'

Doon gave herself up to the feast. A starter no less; this was fancy. There was soda bread fresh from the oven, where it had been roasting with the turkey, with ramekins of butter and smoked salmon. There was champagne for the others, and elderflower for Doon to drink. And, thankfully, there was a new topic that everyone could agree on: the snow.

'Were you OK driving here?' Doon asked Ciarán, who shrugged and said, 'Snow chains. No big deal.'

'You know what I thought?' Natasha said. 'The waterfall at Powerscourt. It might be frozen. I was looking online but I couldn't see. I might go and check it out tomorrow.'

'Really?' said Gabe. 'Waterfalls don't freeze. Not in these temperatures.'

'I think you'll find they do,' said Natasha, but her tone was arch rather than cross. 'Will you give me a hand in the kitchen, D? You can keep your side plates and all your shooting irons, folks.'

'Can I –' Gabe, and Ciarán, both did the same half-rise.

'No, you're good, just sit and enjoy,' said Natasha over her shoulder as she swept out with swishing skirts, Doon following in her wake.

Doon was fearful at first that Natasha wanted to ask her why she was so distracted, but she needn't have worried. Natasha was all business, whirling around the kitchen like an acrobat. She loaded her own and Doon's arms up with dishes, and they marched back in with the feast. Natasha set down the turkey, a giant bronze glistening beast, and the Limerick ham studded with cloves. Doon set down three deep china dishes: one full of roasted carrots and parsnips and two filled with the fluffiest, crunchiest potatoes. The gravy was rich and fragrant, as smooth as brown silk. And the stuffing was made to Aileen's recipe, which was simplicity itself: just breadcrumbs, sage and onion, but Doon could eat it by the spoonful.

'This looks divine, pet,' said Aileen.

'This is seriously delicious – thank you,' said Gabe.

'Good stuff. Oh! Wine,' said Natasha, suddenly looking as if she was flagging. 'Forgot to get that. It's on the sideboard.'

'Let me,' said Gabe, and he got up to uncork it and poured it in four expert pours.

'You've done that before,' said Natasha, raising her eyebrows.

'I have. Three summers at Maison Robert in Boston.'

'Is that where you went to university?' asked Doon, and he nodded.

'This is like Guess Who. Did you go to Harvard?' asked Natasha, and Gabe said, 'No, to a place called Tufts. I studied architecture initially. But I didn't feel like I had the talent for it. So I switched to art history.'

'I think you're talented – look at that lovely drawing you did for us. Oh, Natasha hasn't seen it.' Aileen got up and fetched the pen-and-ink drawing from next door. Natasha gazed at it for a long moment in silence, before looking up at Gabe. 'It's beautiful,' she said with that sudden smile that transformed her face.

'How did you get it framed so quickly?' said Aileen.

'I just bought another picture from the gift shop, and

used the frame and mount,' he said, looking a little embarrassed. 'So you've got two pictures in one.'

'Whatever it is, it can't be better than this one,' said Aileen.

Ciarán said, 'I'm not one for art, but I'd hang that up for sure. I might have to get you to do one of our GAA clubhouse, if you're taking orders.'

Gabe looked as though he welcomed the change of subject. 'That reminds me of something I've been meaning to ask. When people say they're playing GAA – does that mean Gaelic football, or hurling, or both?'

Doon would have given the short answer of 'Gaelic football', but Ciarán, delighted at the question, gave him a longer explanation, before asking, 'What's your sport?'

Gabe said, 'I ran track in high school but that was it really for team sports. I like hiking, swimming, biking – that kind of thing.'

Solitary pursuits in nature; Doon knew exactly the type, and no harm either. Natasha and Gabe started talking about riding in Wicklow. Doon liked riding, and would have joined in, but beside her Ciarán had embarked on a long story about his GAA fixtures and how they might affect their summer plans.

'So if Man O'War beat Good Counsel by more than three points, we go through to the next round and we'll play the winners of St Jude's versus Fingallians. On the other hand, if Good Counsel win that match, then we're out of the championship, but there might be a friendly match the same weekend, though I don't know yet if it will be the Saturday or Sunday . . .'

'Right! Time for the pudding,' said Natasha eventually, and whisked out of the room.

Now Aileen was talking to Gabe about UCD, which was her alma mater. Again, Doon would have liked to join in, but she didn't feel she could interrupt Ciarán, who was still – still! – going on about his team; something about Killian being no good under a dropping ball.

'Ta-da!' said Natasha.

She came in with the pudding held aloft, flaming proudly; everyone oohed and aahed, and Natasha served them all up, looking pleased. After the briefest of pauses, Ciarán was off again about Jamesie Byrne who was sick of being a sub. Had he always been such a bore on this subject? Doon wondered. But that wasn't fair; it was his passion. She listened idly, wondering if there was a burning smell somewhere.

'. . . so then he threw a hissy fit and says he won't come to training any more . . .'

'Oh no! The table!' exclaimed Aileen.

A bright flame had started, either from the pudding or a candle, and was snaking its way up the length of the table, crisping all the holly leaves. There was a stunned silence, then everyone started yelling at once.

'Grab the water!' said Doon, and Natasha said, 'There's no more water! Will wine do?'

'Grab a blanket!' said Aileen. 'But not the Avoca one!'

'Which one is that?' Doon said, half out of her chair.

'Don't you have a fire extinguisher?' Ciarán asked them all, while the flames licked higher.

Gabe, meanwhile, had pulled off his jacket, rolled it up and placed it down on top of the flames, which went out immediately.

'Oh no, your good jacket!' said Aileen.

'It was just from Old Navy.'

'I don't know what that is! But thank you!' Aileen said.

'How did that happen, Natasha?' Ciarán was saying, in a slightly judgy way. Doon looked at him and remembered the almost identical fire when she had first cooked for him, and how different his reaction was now. What happened to things going wrong making the best memories?

Finally they all calmed down; the bits of burned cloth were taken out to the bin and everyone finished the rest of the pudding, assuring Natasha that it was even more delicious after the bit of excitement. Then Doon insisted that Natasha sit with the others in the drawing room while she made tea and coffee.

The kitchen was blessedly quiet after the drama of the fire. Doon cooled her hot forehead against the window while looking out at the darkening gardens, the snow glowing whitely against the dusk. Part of her wished she could just open the door and step outside into the fresh air and start walking, with no noise except the crunch of snow underfoot and the whoosh of the occasional car from the road below.

'Are you OK?' It was Ciarán, coming into the kitchen with some extra plates. 'I'm surprised your mother doesn't have a fire extinguisher; she really should in a house this old.'

'It's not the fire,' said Doon.

'What is it then?' he asked in a kinder tone. 'Is it about the house? That's a terrible worry. I don't know why you didn't tell me.'

Doon felt another twinge of conscience. She decided it had to be now or never. 'Can we have a chat actually? After we've had the tea?'

Looking surprised, he said, 'Sure.'

They had their tea – or, rather, tea for Aileen, Natasha and Ciarán, and coffee for Doon and Gabe – and then Natasha suggested a game of cards, while Doon caught Ciarán's eye.

'What is it?' he said, when he had followed her upstairs to her bedroom. 'You're not upset about Amy and Setanta, are you?' he added, joking. 'That's good news, I would have thought.'

'Oh, gosh, of course not. It's great news.'

She didn't know where to start, so she decided to open with what she hoped was the least controversial thing.

'I met Cara in the pub the other night,' she said. 'She said you'd invited her to the wedding?'

'Oh yeah, of course. I was going to say it to you. She's a lovely girl, isn't she, and her fella is sound as well. I thought we could put them on the same table as –'

'She might be now,' said Doon, knowing how absurd she sounded, 'but she was really cruel to me in primary school.'

'Oh,' said Ciarán, looking baffled. 'Like what? Bullying you?'

'There was an incident, yeah.' Hating to say it, Doon forced herself. 'She made fun of me for not having a dad.'

'Oh,' he said again. 'Are you sure? She wasn't just confused herself? You know what kids are like.'

'No,' she said.

'OK. I'm sorry to hear it. But it was what – one time?'

'That's enough, isn't it? You don't forget these things.'

Various expressions were fighting themselves on Ciarán's face, but Doon could tell he was trying not to smile.

'So it was one comment, what, more than twenty years ago? More? I'm sorry, Doon, but – well, OK. I'm sorry I didn't know. But you won't have to speak to her. There's going to be a hundred and fifty people there.'

'That's the other thing,' Doon said. 'I'm sorry. I know I should have said this earlier, and I did try, but I really don't want such a big wedding. I never have. Every time I think of it I feel sick.'

Any trace of smile was gone now. 'But, Doon, we've discussed this. It's too late to change it.'

'But we haven't sent the real invitations yet,' she said, almost pleading. 'Just save the dates.'

'It's the same thing. Anyone we did that to would never speak to us again.'

'Surely not,' she said. 'Surely they'd understand. And if they didn't, well, so what?' It was the kind of thing other people said all the time, so she thought it was worth a try.

'So what?' he repeated. 'You're talking about insulting half my family here. That kind of thing would literally never be forgotten. It would be held up over us for the rest of our lives. Honestly, families have fallen out over far less.'

It was more or less exactly what Amy had said. Obviously she and Ciarán knew what they were talking about, and Doon, the eternal outsider with the lopsided family, had no clue.

'OK,' she said tonelessly.

The silence buzzed between them and then Ciarán said, 'OK? That's it? I don't understand, Doon. I thought we both wanted this. But now you're talking about it like it's a trip to Lough Derg.'

Doon didn't know what to say. She had somehow agreed to the big wedding, though now that she came to think about it had she really? They had discussed it, and discussed it, and then it was a hundred and fifty.

She didn't even know any more. All she could think was that a trip to Lough Derg, where traditionally you went for a silent penitential retreat, sounded like heaven compared to the prospect of this wedding.

'Actually, I'd prefer Lough Derg,' she murmured.

'I beg your pardon?'

Ciarán was in full teacher mode now. He was raising his eyebrows, arms folded.

Doon closed her eyes; she hadn't meant to say that out loud. She felt as if she might be sick. *Tell him*, she thought to herself. *Tell him about Charlie and then it will all go away. The wedding – and everything.* But she couldn't do that to him.

'Tell me something,' Ciarán said. 'Is it really the wedding that you don't want – or is it the idea of marrying me?'

She looked up, startled. That was a great question. How had she not asked herself this already?

'If we did do something small,' Ciarán said, 'some hole-and-corner thing, in the church here or something, would you be happy then?'

Doon opened her mouth and closed it again.

'I'm not sure,' was all she could say.

Ciarán looked stunned. 'Well,' he said eventually, 'this is some Christmas.'

Doon felt a moment of panic. What was she doing? It was as if she was the one who had set the tablecloth on fire, after dousing all the china, glasses, food and candles with petrol. But she couldn't stop now – she didn't want to. She wanted to be honest, even if it set the whole house on fire.

'I kissed someone else,' she said.

'You what?' Ciarán looked completely shell-shocked. 'When?'

'The other night. I'm sorry,' she said again. 'I didn't mean for it to happen . . .'

Oh no, this was making it worse.

'Stop talking.' He turned away and she looked down, listening to the silence humming in the air.

'Who was it?'

'Nobody. A local. I barely know him –'

'OK, that's enough. You don't want the wedding and you've kissed someone else. I don't want to know any more.' He looked faintly nauseous. He added, 'Your timing is impeccable. What am I supposed to do now?'

'Well –' Doon had the mad impulse to suggest they go downstairs and play cards with the others, but thankfully she managed to stop herself. What was wrong with her? She was trying to mitigate damage, but everything she did seemed to be making it worse. 'Let's just get through Christmas,' she suggested weakly. 'And we can talk after that.'

'I don't think so,' he said. 'Do you know what, I've more dignity than this.' He picked up his Elverys sports bag and started putting things into it.

'Where are you going?' she asked stupidly.

'Home! Or a hotel if the roads are too bad. Maybe

that's better. Don't want to ruin Christmas for them all too.'

'Oh, Ciarán. You don't have to leave! And haven't you had a drink?'

'One glass, Doon. You know red wine gives me a headache. I was almost going to bring some beers, but, again, I'd more dignity than that.'

Doon watched him get all his stuff together, feeling weak with guilt and self-reproach. Then he zipped his bag up and held out his hand. She put out hers with caution, thinking that maybe he wanted to shake hands, but he swatted it away impatiently.

'The ring, Doon!'

'Oh God. OK.' She took it off, feeling terrible. Poor Ciarán. How could she have done this to him? But it was undeniable that something within her seemed to unspool and relax, as the ring came off and he zipped it away in his bag's smallest compartment. She could barely dare to look at him, dreading to see the pain in his eyes or even a tear. But to her relief there was just pure fury. He looked incandescent with rage. She wanted to ask if he was safe to drive in his state of mind, but some belated instinct told her, finally, to shut up.

When he had everything, she stood up too. 'I'll see you out,' she said.

'You're too good,' he said sarcastically. And then he was stepping smartly downstairs, down the two wind-ing flights of steps to the hall, where he picked up his jacket. He hesitated outside the door of the drawing room, and she knew he was weighing up the social sin of leaving without saying goodbye, with the mortification that would ensue if he did.

'Give them my regards,' he said shortly in the end. 'And whatsisname.'

He opened the door and stepped outside without saying goodbye. She watched as he got into his car, wondering what the etiquette was. Should she wave? Or just give a sad salute? But he didn't even look at her; he just did a neat three-point turn and set off down the drive.

She exhaled, watching him go, and looked up at the sky. It was a clear night and the stars were all out. Somewhere out there were all the families, households and phones that would soon be hopping and buzzing with the news of her disgrace. But for now it was just the night sky, the snow and the line of forest that hid the road. She listened to the noise of his car until it was gone, and then she took a few minutes to listen to the silence and breathe the fresh air before stepping back inside.

24

Aileen had long been a believer in the Christmas stranger – someone to help dilute the atmosphere of the nuclear family and to keep everyone on their best behaviour. It didn't even have to be a complete stranger; someone close but not immediately related could fit the bill, like Ciarán. And yet here they were with both Ciarán and a real stranger, Gabe, and it had backfired. Gabe had been a delight certainly; his drawing was something she would treasure. But Doon had been barely able to look at Ciarán earlier, even when the table went on fire. What was going on?

It was nearly night now. Gabe and Natasha had finished playing cards and were talking about watching an old film on television. He would be staying in the blue room originally intended for Ben; it was too dark and cold to walk home, particularly after all that wine. Doon and Ciarán were off somewhere together in the house, talking things out, she hoped. It was romantic of him to turn up, but nothing could be less romantic than the atmosphere between them.

Aileen was drawing the curtains in her bedroom upstairs when she saw Doon was outside, wearing her coat but not her hat or gloves, and watching as a car headed down the drive, the fan of its headlights illuminating the snow-capped gates and wall. It was Ciarán's car. Aileen stared in astonishment that anyone was braving a drive in this weather, at this time of night; what could he possibly need, unless it was a medical emergency? But then she saw how Doon was standing, staring after the car, heedless of the cold. Something must have happened. No ordinary disagreement or change of plans could possibly make the sensible Ciarán set off on a drive at this hour, in this weather, on Christmas night. Something must have happened.

Aileen was perplexed. Had they just had a row – or was it more serious than that? But she fought the urge to hurry downstairs and see what was the matter. Doon needed such a light touch. And anyway, she was probably jumping to conclusions. It was probably a family emergency of some kind; though that was worrying too.

Downstairs, she heard the front door close and Doon's footsteps in the hall, heading back towards the kitchen. She wished for a minute that they had the kind of relationship that would lead Doon to knock softly on her door, saying, 'Mum?' Or even to turn to her if Aileen found her in the kitchen. But if there was a family emergency, Doon would tell her, wouldn't she?

Aileen made a decision. She wouldn't pry, but she would go downstairs on the pretext of making some camomile tea and see how Doon was. If she was still in the kitchen, perhaps they could chat.

She went softly downstairs and past the drawing room, and the study where the TV was, hoping that Natasha wouldn't hear her and ask her to come in and watch the film with her. Doon was in the kitchen, sitting by the fire and waiting for the kettle to boil. She looked sober, as ever, but not actually shell-shocked. Though that in itself didn't mean anything; Aileen could imagine an earthquake leaving Doon looking no more than thoughtful.

'Are you making tea, love? I could do with a cup; is there enough water for two?' Aileen tried to pitch her tone correctly between soft and cheerful.

Doon said, 'Might not be quite, but that's OK. I can wait.'

'I'll top it up.' Aileen interrupted the kettle and added water before putting it back on to boil. *What would we do as a nation without tea?* she thought. *How would these conversations ever start, without a cup of tea?*

'Was that Ciarán's car I heard leaving?' she asked, as casually as she could, over her shoulder.

'Um, yeah.' Doon cleared her throat. 'He had – a family thing actually. Not an emergency, but he needed to get back.'

'I see. Not to worry. I hope he has a safe drive,' Aileen said as calmly as she could. This was something she knew how to do anyway: go along with a lie. God, this was reminding her of conversations with Dan when he was telling her he'd found gold in the river or the Renoir in a charity shop. *That's great, honey. We'll get it valued.* She would say nothing, not until Doon herself was ready to talk. She made mild chit-chat, observing how nice it had been to have them all, and then, as she handed Doon her tea, she saw the engagement ring was missing from her finger.

'Thanks, Mum. I think I'll take this upstairs to bed.'

'Of course.' Aileen went over to her daughter and hugged her. She hoped the hug would say what she needed it to, that she knew what had happened, that she supported Doon, and that she wouldn't pry.

Doon left the room, her head drooping sadly, and Aileen suddenly remembered her walking into that very room all those years ago, looking so grown-up that Aileen had almost offered her tea. *How will Daddy know where to find us?*

Her heart leaped slightly as Doon turned round.

'It was a lovely Christmas, Mum,' she said. 'Thanks for doing it. And having us all.'

She put on a smile. 'Any time,' she said.

Then Doon was gone. Aileen felt so helpless, knowing something terrible had happened but not being able to help her. Suddenly she remembered CJ, whose daughter must only be a few years older than Doon. She was glad they would be having lunch tomorrow. Maybe he could advise her on how to help an adult daughter in distress; Aileen felt she hadn't a clue.

25

Natasha had set her alarm for eight a.m. to take Gabe to Powerscourt, a plan they had made last night when they were up late together watching TV. But she managed to sleep right through it and saw to her horror when she awoke that it was a quarter to twelve. How had that happened? She dressed quickly and ran downstairs; the house was quiet and she thought Gabe might easily have left already. But when she went into the kitchen she found him waiting there, reading *Brooklyn* – he was over halfway through it – and drinking coffee.

'I'm so sorry. I totally overslept,' she said. 'Thank you for waiting for me.'

'That's OK. Do you want some coffee?'

'Yes please.' She put some soda bread on to toast, noting that it was running low; Doon the gannet must have eaten half the loaf. Where was Doon anyway?

'Where is everyone?' she asked.

'Doon went out for a run, I think, and your mom said something about meeting someone for lunch.'

'Oh, gosh, it is late.' She was glad Ciarán was out too, presumably with Doon, so she didn't have to face more interrogations about how the fire had started.

'I'm sorry again about your jacket,' she said.

'Hey, don't mention it. It was a bit of excitement. And the least I could do after you guys welcomed me in.'

'Have you had breakfast?'

'Just some toast . . . I can't eat much after the feast yesterday.'

'Oh yeah,' she muttered, watching for her toast to pop. She buttered it extra thickly, and contemplated adding some brandy butter before opting for the healthier option of raspberry jam. She would start cutting out sugar at New Year's; no sense in shocking her body yet.

'So, are you ready to go?' Gabe asked.

'Sure,' she said. 'Just give me five minutes to brush my teeth and go to the loo.'

By the time she had found a warm coat and a dry pair of boots, brushed her hair and teeth and applied extra lip balm, it was closer to fifteen minutes, but Gabe made no complaint. He was sitting in the hall with his backpack beside him, as if he was used to waiting for women. They went outside. The sun was out, striking sparkles on the snow, which had not thawed even slightly. However, by some miracle, the driveway had been shovelled clean, the snow and slush piled neatly to the sides.

'Who did all this?' she asked. 'Was it you?'

'I had some time, and I found the spade in the porch,' Gabe said.

'Did you? That was so nice of you! Mum will be

thrilled. Thank you!' She looked around. 'Now ...
where's your car?'

'My car? It's back at my place. I got a ride here.'

'Oh gosh,' Natasha said. 'Who with? It doesn't
matter,' she added, as he started on an explanation of
John Gallagher's sister's friend who was driving up to
Dublin. 'We can walk.'

Natasha had pictured driving there for a leisurely
ten-minute stroll rather than an hour-plus hike, but
there was no alternative as everyone's car was gone, bar
Doon's fancy sports car, which she would be too scared
to drive even if she was insured for it. She and Gabe
looked as though they were dressed for different excur-
sions; he in his high-tech winter gear and she in Aileen's
old fake fur coat and a pink bobble hat. But at least she
had hiking boots.

Before they had gone five minutes, she was glad they
were walking. The landscape was as lovely as she had
ever seen it. The snow was piled on every drystone wall,
making the shapes blobby and cartoon-like. The scen-
ery all around was still white, or blue where the shadows
lay under the trees. They walked in silence, breathing in
deep draughts of the fresh crystal air.

Just after the Protestant church, she led him off the
path she knew, into the woods. Here there was a still
deeper silence except for the birds and the occasional
softest flop of piled-up snow falling from the branches
above on to the pine-needle-coated ground. Natasha
breathed in the scent of snow and conifers and

wondered again why on earth she was going back to London.

Gabe wasn't checking his phone or looking at a map, seemingly trusting that she knew the way. Which she did; it was left at this giant oak – or was it right? She hesitated a moment, but then she saw the peak of the Sugarloaf just above the trees and knew where she was.

As they emerged from the woods into the paths that wound around the foothills of the mountains, she saw his gaze rise towards the horizon, where the white crests of the peaks met the blue sky. He looked down at her and smiled.

'Pretty good, isn't it?' she asked.

'It's gorgeous.' After a few more minutes he added, 'In fact, it's so beautiful, I'm having a hard time understanding why you live in London.'

'London is different. It's . . .' She looked around, and words failed her for how different exactly it was. Bars, cinemas, restaurants, endless variety. But nothing like this. 'It's got other things,' was all she could come up with. 'And I don't know what I would do here.'

'Well, what would you do if you could do anything?'

Without thinking, she said, 'I'd run the house here as a B & B.'

'So why don't you? It would be perfect.'

She frowned. 'I have no experience. Running it, staffing it, all the cooking and cleaning . . . Not to mention I set the place on fire yesterday if you remember.'

'Some people might pay extra for that,' he suggested.

'Ha, ha.'

'That kind of thing doesn't matter really. It's all about the food and the welcome. And you have those for sure – you're an outstanding cook.'

'I'm not so sure,' she said. 'But thank you. Anyway . . . even if I don't live here, this will always be home.'

'I can see that. You're lucky,' he said.

He stopped to get out a camera, an expensive-looking Sony with a strap, and took a few photos of the surroundings.

'Do you want to be in one?' he asked her.

'Sure,' she said, blushing slightly and taking off her pink bobble hat. As the camera clicked, she thought of the sketch he had given to Aileen. 'Do you draw a lot? Or take more photos?'

'A bit of both. I also sketch from the photos, which some people would say is cheating.'

'No it isn't! That sketch you did for my mum is so lovely. I think you're really talented, you know.'

Gabe said, 'I'm not so sure. But thank you.' She smiled as she realized he was echoing her words. He added, 'I just practise a lot – that's my talent, if I have one.'

They walked on while she pondered this. Was it really true that the key to being good at something was less about being naturally brilliant and more about daily practice? Ben would say naturally brilliant, but she didn't want to think about Ben right now.

'Anyway . . . we were talking about home, weren't

we?' she said. 'How about you? Is Massachusetts home?'

'Well, it's complicated. I grew up there, and my oldest sister still lives there, but my parents have just turned snow birds.'

'What does that mean?'

'It means they're spending September to March in Florida. They sold the family home last year and bought a place in Fort Myers. They've got a small apartment in Hingham, but for the spring and summer. Hence, snow birds.'

'Snow birds,' Natasha repeated, charmed with the phrase. 'So where is everyone for Christmas?'

'My elder sister Colleen is in Hingham. Megan, my younger sister, lives in New York, and she's going to Florida to be with my folks. Which I could have done, but it's really expensive. I'll go next year probably. But I will miss Christmas in Hingham. It's really pretty.'

'So why did they leave?'

'My dad had a work opportunity – and he and my mom were sick of winter in Massachusetts. It really is so long and cold.'

Natasha tried to imagine how she would feel if Aileen had suddenly decided to move to the south of Spain, even if only for half the year. America was so vast; she was lucky really that Doon and Aileen's options were narrower, comparatively speaking.

'Are they all excited about you finding Ballyclare?' she asked.

'Oh yeah. My mom even wanted to arrange a Face-Time call with your folks, but I said no to that, you'll be glad to hear.'

Natasha laughed. 'Ah, we could have FaceTimed them! There was a lot going on, though, in fairness.'

Gabe said, 'You know, when I first heard that my great-grandfather was from Wicklow, I pictured a tumbledown cottage on a hillside.'

'That would be more on brand, all right,' Natasha said. She pondered Gabe's story again: Tom Foley, the servant's illegitimate son, and the kindly childless couple who helped raised him. 'Have you ever managed to find out who your great-grandad's father was?'

'No, no clue.'

'Hmm.' If this was a book or film, she thought, Dr Redmond would probably turn out to be the real father, which would somehow make Gabe the long-lost heir to Ballyclare. She didn't love that idea, but she didn't hate it as much as she might have only a week ago.

'I did consider that it might be Dr Redmond,' Gabe continued.

'Yes!' She clutched his arm. 'I was just thinking that!'

Gabe laughed, and she dropped his arm, blushing slightly. 'But I really hope it wasn't him. It would have been sketchy and gross; not to mention he was, like, sixty years old at the time.'

'True. And if he *had* been the father, the Redmonds probably would have done the right thing and left Tom the house. Which would make you the rightful owner.'

Natasha's mind was racing ahead, filling in the gaps of the rags-to-riches story.

'Sure, except that I wouldn't exist,' he said mildly. 'Had my great-grandparents not met in Boston, back in the day.'

'Oh, true. I hadn't thought of that. OK, scratch that.'

'Thank you,' said Gabe mock seriously.

'Unless!' She held up a finger. 'What if they met back in Boston, and then got a letter from Ireland saying that they were being left the house?'

'I mean, sure,' he said. 'That works. Though my grandparents would still need to meet somehow. Have you ever thought of writing a novel?'

'I haven't,' she said, quite taken with the idea. 'But maybe I could. While I run my B & B.'

They were still laughing when they came to the end of the final winding woodland path that opened out on to the valley. Ahead was the waterfall, a hundred feet high, sparkling in the sunlight. It was too far to tell if it was frozen; she could see the glitter of something but couldn't tell if it was ice or white water.

'You win the bet,' said Gabe. 'It's frozen.'

'Is it? How can you tell from here?' She looked up at him in surprise, wondering if he had bionic vision through his glasses. But he smiled and said, 'No noise.'

He was right. The normal roar and crash of the water was silent. There was no sound except distant birdsong and the crunch of their feet on the icy path.

They walked closer, both hypnotized by the sight of the mighty torrent frozen silver against the whitened cliff. Natasha was so mesmerized that she forgot to look where she was going and felt her foot slipping from under her. She would have fallen, had it not been for Gabe catching her.

'Careful,' he said. She looked up at him while he released her arm slowly. He added, 'The spray from the falls will have frozen on the path. So it's icy.'

They came to the pool of boulders that she had played in so often as a child, stepping from the wood side to the waterfall side. They both clambered across, placing their feet carefully. Then they reached the bank closest to the waterfall, and stood right beneath it, gazing up at the white ice, the silver cliff and blue sky. There was nobody else about to witness the miracle, just them. Natasha didn't even want to take a photo, because she knew it would never capture it.

'I feel like I'm in Middle Earth,' said Gabe after a minute, his voice hushed.

'I know what you mean,' she whispered back. There was something special about Powerscourt at the best of times. But this morning it was something unearthly.

She glanced at Gabe beside her and remembered her initial impression of him as being like Ben. Now she knew he wasn't. They shared an interest in history, true, and a love of old books, but Gabe was different. How she couldn't say exactly, except that he was more serious but also had less ego. More substance maybe, she thought. She couldn't imagine Ben getting up at dawn to shovel snow off her mother's path or flinging off his jacket to put out a fire. Or doing that sketch of Ballyclare – the most thoughtful present of all the ones Aileen had received without question.

She could have stayed there all day. But it was damp and cold, so after Gabe had taken a few photos they agreed to head on.

'Would you like to walk up to the hotel?' she said. 'It's crazy expensive but we could warm up while we look in the gift shop.' She paused, suddenly thinking that maybe he wasn't such a gift shop fan, or a fan of fancy hotels in general, any more than Ben would be. 'Do you like a gift shop?' she asked doubtfully.

'I love a gift shop,' he said, and they set off up the snowy path towards the Powerscourt Hotel.

26

Doon woke up on the morning of Stephen's Day feeling terrible. Everything was overlaid with a sticky residue of shame that reminded her of her long-ago hangover back when she had drunk herself ill over David Cuffe. She felt sick with remorse when she thought of Ciarán driving home through the night with the weight of disappointment and anger on him. She wondered if it would be OK to text him to check if he had arrived home safely, but thought on balance it probably was not.

But regarding the wedding, she simply couldn't feel regretful. There would be so much to do – cancelling the venue for starters, the photographer, the DJ, and the nightmare of informing all the guests; though, to be fair, once one was told they all would know. And the irony of it all was she and Ciarán would really have to do it all together. Or would they? Could she tell people herself that it was off, or did she have to wait until Ciarán had told his own family and friends – including their mutual ones? It was a minefield. But the consolation was the fact that she wouldn't have to walk down that aisle. That in itself gave her hope.

She went downstairs and made herself coffee. She saw the lemon shortbread Natasha had bought at the tree farm left open on the counter. Doon dipped one in her coffee, enjoying the decadence of biscuits for breakfast. Doon felt a sudden surge of love as she realized that no matter how dismayed or confused Natasha would be, she would fundamentally be on Doon's side. She was less certain about Amy. Doon dreaded the conversation that awaited her with Amy, but that could wait.

The weather outside looked absolutely gorgeous; there were bright blue skies above the snow-capped hills and the snow was turning to slush on the drystone walls. Gabe was outside, shovelling the path; that was nice. He and Natasha were meant to be going to Powerscourt but no doubt Natasha was still dead to the world.

Maybe she would go for a walk, or a run. It was freezing and snowy and a stupid day for a run. If he was here, Ciarán would tell her to give it a miss so she didn't break an ankle. Which made her want to do it even more.

She changed quickly into her gear, and after a quick chat with Gabe set off down the drive at a trot. It was a challenge to run in the area around Ballyclare even without the winter weather. The roads were narrow and sharply cornered and the few paths that existed were hidden to the casual eye. But Doon crossed the road at a brisk walk and climbed the field at the edge of the woods until she came to the path in the woods that led towards Powerscourt. The way underfoot was clearer here and she set off at a moderate pace, enjoying the sensation of her muscles working while her mind rested. It was strange how that happened. As was the fact that she seemed to be running in the direction of Charlie Cuffe's place.

Charlie. Charlie Cuffe. Doon dodged a tree stump as she processed the dizzying fact that now, if she wanted to, she was free to visit Charlie Cuffe, maybe even get involved with him. Except, of course, that he was total--ly unsuitable; he was younger than her and a terrible flirt, not to mention his entire family were forever associated with the most humiliating episode of her life. So she would be wise not to take the path she seemed to be currently taking, which led down towards his cabin in the woods. *The Cabin in the Woods*, wasn't that a horror film? Was this the point at which she should be screaming to herself to turn back? No. These were the woods she had known since she was a child, and she was running the familiar sunken path beneath the larches that dropped the occasional plop of snow beneath a blue sky.

Here was the fork that led down to his cottage. She could see it now, not the building itself but the drive – with his car there. They had parted on an awkward note last time. So perhaps it would be a good idea to go down and say hello. A little voice told her this was foolish, but she knew that already. Everything she was doing this Christmas was foolish and selfish; why pretend otherwise?

She went down the steep hill towards his house, wishing that he lived closer to the main road so there could be some pretext for dropping by. But no, she would have to own the fact that she was coming to see him. She cringed as the memory of their goodbye came back more clearly to her. He had wanted her to stay or to see her again; she had responded by asking for his help in selling the house.

It had seemed OK at the time but now it made her feel terrible. She thought she was getting them back on a sensible footing. But to him, together with how she'd reminded him of her engagement, it must have sounded as if she was using him. She hadn't thought Charlie was sensitive enough to mind about that, but, as she kept finding out, she wasn't great at predicting what people might mind. Now she was torn between apologizing and just running away.

She knocked tentatively at the door. From inside she could hear the dog barking. She would have been tempted to turn round and run, were it not for the fact that she could see he had a Ring doorbell installed, meaning that she was already on camera. Feeling worse by the minute, she hovered, hoping for some last-minute excuse to leave, until she saw him coming.

'Hi,' he said, opening the door.

She couldn't decode his expression – was he puzzled? Pleased? Wary?

'Come in, it's freezing,' he said. 'Down, Bella.' The dog was weaving around Doon, beating her tail and sniffing enthusiastically. Doon bent to pet her, registering that Charlie looked less thrilled to see her than the dog was.

'Thanks,' she said, coming inside and just about remembering to wipe her feet, which were coated in pine needles and slush.

'So what's going on? Happy Christmas by the way. Or happy Stephen's Day.' He paused. 'Coffee?'

'That would be great,' she said, feeling pleased that things seemed to be on a friendlier footing already. 'Thanks.'

'I was making it anyway,' he said. 'Latte, cappuccino, espresso?'

'Cappuccino, please.' Doon edged her way into the kitchen area of the open-plan downstairs. She took in details she'd overlooked the first time: the black stove with its tall slate hearth that reached to the top of the vaulted ceiling; the little breakfast nook with views over the mountains; the pine panelling everywhere. The place even smelled of pine wood, like a sauna, mingled with the aroma of woodsmoke and coffee. She thought of her place in Ringsend; the paint colour had been called 'Wood Pigeon' but actually was just a bland grey. She could never make a place look like this; it was just another skill she didn't have.

Charlie was still absorbed in the coffee machine, and the roar, gurgle and hiss precluded any conversation.

Doon should have been grateful for the chance to marshal her thoughts, but nothing seemed to have appeared; instead she sat at the table, absent-mindedly stroking the dog.

'So, what can I do for you?' Charlie asked, setting down her coffee.

Doon took a sip, grateful for the distraction. 'Wow – great coffee,' she said.

'Thanks. But I'm sure you didn't come here for the coffee,' he said mildly. He didn't sit down but stood with his back leaning against the stove.

'I'm just here to say, um.' There was a nightmarish pause and she suddenly felt like a swimmer in a rough sea, unable to picture how she would reach the rocks or buoy. *Pull yourself together*, she told herself sternly. 'I'm sorry about how we left it the other day. You did nothing wrong and I was pretty rude to you. I didn't mean to make it seem like I only cared about selling the house – that's not the case at all.' She paused, feeling relieved that something coherent had come out.

'It's OK,' Charlie said. 'I get it. You're in a tough spot. It's nice of you to say I did nothing wrong, but that's not quite true. You're engaged and I should have respected that, not . . . what happened.'

'Well, that's the thing,' she said. 'I'm not any more.' She held out her hand. 'I mean, not as of last night. I broke it off. The engagement's off.' She felt herself growing taller, lighter. 'You're the first person I've told.'

Charlie said nothing for a moment, but he looked

stunned. 'Wow. OK.' He came round the counter and sat opposite her, looking again at her bare left hand. After a moment he said, 'I hope you didn't just do this because of what happened with you and me.'

She wished again that she was better at reading people. Did he mean that he wasn't interested in her after all? She wasn't, of course. Nothing could ever happen. She had just wanted to see him and make things better between them.

'No, of course I didn't,' she said too quickly. 'I suppose I just wanted to let you know that I'm sorry about the way I acted. That's all.'

The dog looked up at her sympathetically.

'OK,' he said. Then added, 'Thank you, I think?'

He was smiling now, and her heart swelled with relief and something else that she couldn't name.

'So I'm guessing it was not a great Christmas for you,' he said.

'Well, the person you should really feel sorry for is my ex. But thank you.'

She was almost relieved when they were interrupted by a buzz from his phone. He said, 'That's just my family. We're getting together for a walk up Djouce.'

'Oh yes. Blow the cobwebs away. Well, it's a great day for it.'

Bella, hearing the word 'walk', started whining and pacing up and down, retrieving her lead and bringing it to Charlie.

'Yes, Bella, I said "walk" and we're doing it . . . OK.

Doon, I'd better go. But maybe we could talk again soon?' said Charlie.

Doon nodded, all her sensible thoughts out of the window, as she wondered at how mature and confident Charlie was; anyone would think he had women turning up on his doorstep every day to apologize for this and that. *Maybe he does?* But she quelled the thought.

'Would you be free tonight for a drink, for instance?' Charlie said, putting on his coat. 'Maybe in the Roundwood Inn?'

'Oh . . .' Doon hesitated.

'Or dinner. I'm sure you've had their goulash. Unless you're not a fan of goulash?'

But Doon wasn't thinking about goulash. She was thinking that the Roundwood Inn was a place beloved of lots of people they knew. And talk would be flying if anyone saw them out on a date. Could she even be sure he was suggesting a date, and not a chat about property or something? But the look in his eyes told her this wasn't all business. Her heart surged with longing but also with fear. Fear of getting involved with someone new so quickly, yes. But also fear of what people would say. Not just the Cuffes but everyone. She could imagine the comments: that she had been obsessed with the oldest brother and now that she was sniffing around the youngest one. His mother alone – she couldn't imagine how mortifying it would be if Carmel Cuffe heard that something had happened between her and Charlie. The humiliation would be total.

She said, 'I'd love to, but . . . that's a popular spot. With everything going on, it might be wiser to keep a low profile? Go somewhere we won't meet anyone we know . . .'

'OK,' Charlie said. 'Doon, much as I would love to sneak around with you in a way . . . it would be very hot . . . The fact that you're suggesting we meet on the sly is making me think that it might be a bit soon for you. Which I can understand.'

'It's not just that. It's . . .' She wanted to explain, but she just couldn't find the words. Anyway, why should she have to explain? Surely he knew that her connection with the family made things awkward for her – and for him for that matter?

Charlie said, 'It's OK. I'm sure you have a lot to sort out. And I've got to head off and meet my folks. Let's catch up some other time – OK?'

And before Doon knew what was happening, he was pulling on his coat and striding towards the door followed by an ecstatic Bella.

She followed him outside and watched him whistle to Bella, who jumped into the car boot. He didn't seem in the least bit upset, just clear that he didn't want to waste his time with someone as messed up as her. And he was right. Turning up on his doorstep for a big apology, then telling him she didn't want to see him in public – she had just made everything worse. But didn't he understand how difficult it was? Clearly not.

'See you,' Charlie said, and with a brisk neutral wave he threw his car into a three-point turn and steamed off down the drive.

27

Aileen had left plenty of time for the drive to Powers-court. She was feeling oddly nervous, and not just about the road conditions. She had dressed carefully in a red silk blouse and black wool trousers, and a black wool coat instead of her old fake fur. She had let her standards slip a bit in recent years possibly. Comfort was all very well but she didn't *need* to walk around always looking as if she was in the middle of the gardening – even if she often was. She had even broken out her one pair of high-heeled boots, located with some difficulty after a rummage in her top cupboard.

The car park at Powerscourt was busy, despite the snow. She felt a flutter of nerves when she walked inside and saw CJ standing in the lobby, gazing out of the window. He was wearing a dark jacket over a blue polo neck jumper, and fawn trousers. He looked well. He had kept his hair and his waistline, which were the main things for men. It was a low bar. She wondered for a minute how she looked to him – did she look older? What a question. Of course she looked older. She walked over and tapped him softly on the shoulder.

'Aileen!' He smiled with what looked like genuine

delight and bent to kiss her cheek. 'You look lovely. It's great to see you. I hope this place is OK?'

She laughed. 'Oh, we'll make do.' It was more than OK. The place was like a 1920s ocean liner transplanted to the middle of Wicklow – all marble pillars and satiny wood panelling, and the gleam of soft light on marble floors and plush carpets. Jazzy Christmas tunes played softly and a giant Christmas tree towered over a pile of gift-wrapped packages and a beribboned reindeer figure. Beyond the lobby she could see the dining room, which overlooked the grounds of the estate, the white snow shining against the darkness of the interior.

'I've booked a table in the Sika restaurant,' said CJ.

'Oh yes,' she said, although she was pretty hazy on what all the various rooms were called here. She hoped they could get a table by the window; she wanted to drink in that glorious view of the surrounding white hills. Suddenly she wished she had brought her sketchbook. But poor CJ wouldn't take too kindly to her sketching while they lunched.

The place was still half empty – the other visitors must still be walking around the grounds – but the very charming young waiter showed them to a table right at the edge, close to the lobby.

'Is this all right?' CJ asked her.

'Oh –' She couldn't help but glance back at the view.

'Could we sit by the window? Would you prefer that?' CJ asked and she nodded.

Within minutes they were at a table overlooking the

formal gardens below, the frozen fountains and beyond them the woods and mountains. It was perfect.

'You're very thoughtful. It's silly to hanker after a view, when I live in Wicklow – I can see this any time.'

'But not from here,' CJ suggested.

'No, not from here.' She smiled at him, thinking how solid and reassuring he looked. Another of his college nicknames had been The Big Fellow, she remembered now.

'It's lovely. Thanks again for suggesting it,' she said, as the waiter poured sparkling water for both of them.

'It's a little different from our old haunts, isn't it?' he said. 'Do you remember sitting upstairs at Bewley's?'

'Could I ever forget it? We'd be there for hours on end, wouldn't we? One plate of chips between us.' She shook her head, remembering the afternoons spent whiling away the time in a haze of chat and cigarette smoke. 'You'd sit down with one crowd and get up with another. And I'm not sure everyone even bought anything, once we figured out how to get a spare cup and share a pot of tea.'

'Sure, we couldn't afford it. Do you remember the time that chap got out his guitar?'

'Yes! God. They did draw the line at that.' She could remember the waitress in her starched white apron nervously telling them they had to stop; their friend stopped but later got her number.

'Are you ready to order?' the waiter asked, and they both shook their heads. 'We'd better look now and decide on something or we'll never do it,' she suggested, and CJ nodded.

There were various soups and salads that looked appealing, but what stood out to her was the burger. Would that be a very unappealing thing to order, though – could they really catch up on several decades of personal news through a mumbled mouthful of burger? She was almost going to choose soup until CJ said, 'I think I'll have the burger.'

'Me too,' she said with a laugh, and closed her menu. 'And I'll have a glass of red wine, if you'll join me.'

The waiter came by again, and they both gave the same order, which Aileen always felt was such a companionable thing to do.

'I want to hear about your Christmas,' she said. 'But I also want to know what you've been doing for the past – I want to say twenty years, but I know it's more.'

'It can't be. Feels like ten.' The wine had arrived; they paused while the deep red liquid was poured into both their glasses. 'Well, I think the last time I saw you was probably just after Aoife was born.'

'I think I remember,' she said. 'A party after exams. I remember you showing me a photo of her. You were such a proud dad. And so young, weren't you?'

'Twenty-one,' he said. 'Yes, I was a proud dad, but I was also quite shell-shocked.'

'So what did you both do after we graduated?'

'Well, Maeve got offered a very good job in a solicitor's firm. I had planned to do the Bar but that was too precarious – you earn nothing for the first few years – so we agreed that I would look after Aoife while Maeve focused on work. And that was us for a few years, in a tiny flat in Rathmines. Then Aoife started school, and I got a job in IT . . . and Maeve and I split up. But we did it amicably, alternate weeks with Aoife. Not perfect but it worked.'

'Gosh. So you gave up the Bar to be a dad – and you shared the childcare after that. That's amazing,' said Aileen.

CJ laughed. 'Is it? It's less than what you did. And you didn't get a medal for it.'

True, Aileen thought. 'But then what about the States?'

'Yes, that was my belated bit of selfishness I suppose. Aoife was twenty-one and had just graduated, so I decided it was now or never. I thought it would be six months, and it turned into ten years. Aoife used to come out often for holidays. But I regret it now somewhat. I think in a way they need you as much when they're adults.'

Aileen nodded, thinking of Doon. Their food arrived and she realized how incongruous it was to be pouring out these confidences over burgers and chips. But why not? The first meal they had shared probably was a bowl of chips.

'Anyway,' he said, 'that's enough about me. What about you, Aileen? How have the years treated you? Not to make it sound like we're a hundred.'

'No. Um, they've treated me pretty well.' She paused

'A few rough years, of course. But we're all doing well . . .' *Mostly*, she thought.

'I'm so sorry about Dan. Again. I hope you got my letter at the time.'

'Thanks, CJ. I did. I remember it; I kept it.'

He shook his head. 'Poor Dan. Did you ever really find out what happened to him in the end?'

She took a deep breath and told him about the ferry to Glasgow, the private detective and how there was no trace of him after the ferry docked.

'So that was your answer?'

'As close to an answer as we'll ever get, I suppose.'

'That must have been awful. Living in that limbo.' He hesitated. 'Do you ever wonder . . . No, forget it. Sorry.'

'It's OK,' she said. 'Do I ever wonder if he's alive somewhere, living a different life or something? It's possible, I suppose. It does happen. But not Dan, I don't think. He wouldn't have done that to us.'

'No,' agreed CJ. 'God, what a tragedy. He was no age at all either, was he?'

'Thirty-five.' Aileen nodded, thinking how young that seemed now. She continued, 'The sad thing is, if it was happening now, there would be better help for him. He just never found the medication that would help him, which I think he would now. I used to keep up with it all, but I don't any more.'

CJ said, 'Hard not to beat yourself up.'

'I ate myself alive with it for years. After he went.

But I had the girls. I had to focus on them, and there was no time to sit around worrying. You know what that's like.'

'How old are they now?'

'Natasha's twenty-eight and Doon is thirty-one. And Aoife? She must be . . .'

'Thirty-five. If you can believe it. She's got two kids now. Traolach is six and Mantan is four.'

'Mantan! That's a good Wicklow name.'

'Isn't it? Her husband's local. I've got to show you photos now.' He took out his phone.

'Oh, look at them.' She smiled. 'I do envy you grand-kids. That's lovely. And nice to be young enough to swing them around and turn them upside down.'

'I didn't know I'd be a grandfather before I turned sixty. But it's great.'

She thought of the twenty-two-year old CJ, full of plans to be a lawyer or judge, and change the world. 'Do you ever imagine what would have happened?'

'Had we not had Aoife? Of course. I probably would have gone to the Bar. Worked my way up the ladder to whatever was at the top. Gone to a lot more parties. Gone backpacking!' He laughed. 'But I wouldn't have it any other way. As you know.'

'I do.' She thought of Doon and Natasha; them not existing was unimaginable. They were here, and she would always feel lucky in consequence. 'I know what you mean about the travelling. I never did any. We were always too broke, even when Dan was around. And the girls never wanted to go anywhere; they loved being home.'

'And who can blame them?' said CJ. 'Why travel, in a way, when you live somewhere so beautiful?'

'Well, true. And I find that lots of my friends have commitments here – they run B & Bs or farms or they have elderly parents, you know how it is. I could travel on my own, of course.'

'Where would you go?'

'Greece,' she said without hesitation. 'Greece and Italy. I can't believe I've never been.'

'Me neither, and I'd love to as well. It's easy not to get around to it, isn't it?'

'Yes! Well, I'm glad it's not just me. I know I sound as if I've been in suspended animation.'

'Not at all. You've been teaching, and I'm sure you've been a brilliant mum to the girls. You should be very proud of yourself.'

'Well, I don't know about that,' she said honestly. 'The girls are . . . they're both drifting a bit. Natasha still hasn't found her niche in terms of work. And Doon . . .' She hesitated, not wanting to talk about the broken engagement. 'Doon has problems too, it turns out.'

'That wouldn't be your fault, though.'

'I don't know. Maybe I could have handled things differently – when Dan left. I felt more worried for Natasha because she barely knew Dan . . . and she was so emotional. But looking back now, I think Doon needed me more.' She shook her head. 'Anyway. What about relationships? After you and Maeve split?' She knew she was being nosy, but she was curious; surely someone as eligible as CJ hadn't stayed single all these years. There might even be someone on the scene now.

'Nothing significant.'

'Really?' This surprised her. 'Now that I find hard to believe.'

'There was someone. There have been people. But nobody who stuck around – or who I stuck to.' He made a wry face. 'I've probably been a bit selfish there as well. In the early years I had to explain that Aoife came first. And I was wary of the possibility of starting a second family, I suppose. Which ruled out a lot of relationships for a while. So I stuck to what I knew. And the longer you go on like that, the more it becomes a habit. Like travelling, or not travelling,' he added.

'I can understand that,' Aileen said. She was the same. She hadn't had the heart for romance at first, and then later she had no interest. 'Well, as long as you've no regrets – that's the main thing.'

'Well, I wouldn't say no regrets,' he said.

The waiter came by at that point to clear away their plates. The room had filled up now, and beside them was a couple with a small child of about three. The mother, in a hushed voice, was saying, 'But you need something with your chips.' To which the little boy replied urgently, 'Just chips! Chips and chips!'

They smiled at each other. 'They lose something, don't they – when they stop being able to say exactly what they want without worrying a damn about it?' said Aileen.

'That's true. Although, thank God, or the world would be a noisy place.' He looked up as the waiter approached again. 'You don't want dessert, do you?'

Slightly surprised, she said, 'Well, I'd take a look at the menu. But are you in a hurry?'

'I'm afraid I need to be back at Aoife's in about an hour. We're having some family over. And I'm supposed to pick up some hazelnuts. She wants to make hazelnut dukkah. It's far from hazelnut dukkah we were reared, isn't it?'

She laughed; there were no words to say how far. She felt a slight sense of disappointment as he signalled briskly for the bill. With the freezing snow-bound weather outside, and the festive atmosphere inside, it would have been a nice afternoon to while away beside the fire, talking of past, present and future. But maybe they would meet another time.

'Mrs McDonnell?' a voice said beside her.

She looked up, fairly sure this would be a former pupil. She didn't recognize this one, though: a tall, elegant woman with dark hair swept back in a bob and a very arty geometric-looking dress.

'I'm Eva Mulcahy . . . I was in your Leaving Cert art class in St Fintan's?'

'Eva! My goodness!' How could she forget the miserable-looking girl with the hunched shoulders? She was often surprised at changes in her now adult pupils, but this was a doozy. Eva had seemed like a lost soul, with a tricky home life and seemingly no ambitions or talents beyond sneaking naggins of vodka into the local discos on a Friday night. She had worked diligently on her portfolio, but she had been let down by her art history essays – despite Aileen's best efforts to remind her that this represented most of the marks.

'I'm sure you don't remember me,' Eva was saying.

'Of course I remember you! You're looking very well.' Aileen never commented on her pupils' changed appearance, but this seemed safe enough. 'This is my friend, CJ . . . So what are you up to now, Eva?'

'Well, I've been working for a gallery in London . . . but now I'm setting up a new commercial gallery in Dún Laoghaire. In the old Carnegie Library – it's been bought by a private investor.'

'That sounds brilliant!' said Aileen. 'Congratulations. I'll have to pay it a visit.'

'Please do,' said the new, poised Eva. 'And if you have any pieces you'd like to exhibit, I'd love to see them.'

'Me? Are you serious?'

'Absolutely. I loved your work.' Eva put her glossy head on one side and seemed to search for the word. 'I hope you're still exhibiting?'

'I mean, not recently.' Aileen was unsure which exhibits Eva could possibly be referring to, before she remembered the school's open evening when, against her better judgement, she had shown a few works,

299

though she had tried to argue that it would really be better to keep it to work by pupils. That must be what she meant. Her own painting, like the idea of dating, in fact, had mostly gone out of the window when the girls had arrived. She thought of the three paintings she had managed to complete in recent years; if they were too conservative for Maria, in the gift shop, she dreaded to think what Eva would make of them. But it was nice to be asked.

'Let me give you my card,' Eva said, and reached a black-manicured hand into her designer handbag. 'I'd love to see something – do get in touch.'

'Well, I will. Thank you!'

'Not at all . . .' Eva looked earnest, and suddenly Aileen could see the serious young girl again. 'You know, I often think of your classes. They were the only ones I liked.' She waved a hand suddenly. 'Anyway! I don't want to interrupt your lunch. It was lovely to see you. Happy Christmas.'

'Happy Christmas, Eva.' She watched as Eva glided across the room to join her companion, whose transparent glasses and futuristic trainers suggested that he too was something in the art world.

'I take it she's one of your success stories?' said CJ.

'I'd say she's her own success story,' Aileen said honestly. 'I did very little for her.'

'It sounds like that was enough.' The admiration on his face was very flattering, but Aileen felt it was unwarranted. She had truly done very little for the girl – just taught her art. But that wasn't nothing, she supposed. Well, it was nice to know that she had done something for one unhappy girl, even if her own girls weren't one hundred per cent living their best lives, as Natasha would say.

The bill had arrived. Aileen said, 'Let's go halves, CJ,' and he said, 'Put your money away. It's no good here.'

'Well,' she said, 'that's very kind. I'll get the next one?'

He said nothing for a minute until the waiter had left. Then he looked up and smiled. She had forgotten what a nice smile he had; it lit up his whole face. 'I'll look forward to it.'

They walked out of the lobby again and Aileen felt the luxurious sensation of having just had a nice meal out with an old friend – who also happened to be an interesting, attractive man. Of course there was no question of there being anything more to it than that. But it was still nice.

Now they were back in the beautiful lobby, which Aileen took a minute again to admire. Various low-lighted cabinets held gifts and other *objets* for sale, and she ran her eye idly over them. A couple were gazing into one of the little cabinet windows. They were casually dressed in walking gear, and Aileen instinctively knew that they weren't here to have lunch but had just come inside to warm up – as she herself had done many times. The woman's dark curly hair looked just like Natasha's. Then she blinked. That was Natasha. And Gabe!

Without quite knowing why she felt flustered. 'Let's get out of here,' she murmured to CJ, quickening her step and trying to slip off towards the exit.

But Natasha, obviously hearing her or guided by some other instinct, had turned round and seen her.

'*Mum?*'

28

Natasha and Gabe had spent a happy ten minutes browsing the gift shop at Powerscourt, considering various items he might get for his mother and sisters. She told him how she used to come here when she was little to play in the grounds and to visit an exhibition with a spectacular doll's house called Tara's Palace.

'It's moving to Dublin now supposedly, but I haven't seen hide nor hair of it. I hope nobody's nicked it.'

'Oh, that's too bad. I would have gone to see it. I . . .' He trailed off.

'What?' Natasha asked, intrigued.

'OK, there's no way not to make this sound weird, but I wrote my thesis on doll's houses. I know that probably sounds super creepy.'

'No, it doesn't. Because guess what? I have a doll's house,' she said. 'Not just a Sylvanian Families thing; it's an antique.'

'No way! How old? How did I not know that?'

'Well, I don't tend to shout about it either. But I'll show it to you, when we get home.'

'Oh,' he said. 'I was actually planning to head back to my place after this. I've got all my stuff and everything . . .' He hoisted his backpack on his shoulder.

'Of course,' she said, feeling a little foolish. He hadn't moved in with them; he was only ever supposed to stay one night.

'But I could come by tomorrow – say, in the morning?'

She smiled. 'Yes, brilliant.'

At that moment, out of the corner of her eye, she spotted a familiar face and turned to see her mother coming out of Sika, dressed to the nines with some guy in tow.

Natasha couldn't believe how shocked she felt. She knew, logically, that Aileen had every right to be out and about having lunch with some man, but it was the fact that she hadn't mentioned a single thing about it beyond something vague about 'a friend'. Which Natasha had assumed meant Susan Reilly or someone like that – not this silver fox who was a dead ringer for Liam Neeson.

Aileen was looking pretty startled too, but she recovered quickly and made introductions with her usual poise.

'Honey! What brings you here? This is CJ. An old college friend. CJ, this is my daughter Natasha – and our friend Gabe!'

Gabe shook hands with CJ and said, 'We've just been on a walk to see the waterfall. It's frozen solid – check it out.'

They all pored over the pictures of the waterfall on Gabe's camera. 'You'll have to go and see it, Mum,' Natasha said.

'I'd love to. Maybe tomorrow,' said Aileen. 'Well, what are you up to now? I'm driving home, Tasha. Do you both want a lift?'

Natasha glanced up at Gabe, and then back at her mother. She would have liked a lift certainly. She was freezing after the walk. But Gabe had just been saying that he had never had a real Irish coffee, and she had told him the bar here would do a fantastic one, and maybe some sandwiches too – she was starving again. And a small voice told her that if Aileen was on – gulp – a date, it would be a bit mean to bust it up.

'It's OK, Mum,' said Natasha. 'We're actually going to have a drink here.'

'If you think we're OK like this?' Gabe asked, looking down doubtfully at his hiking boots and high-tech trousers.

'You're dressed for walking, that's perfect for Wicklow,' said the silver fox, smiling warmly.

'How will you get home, though?' said Aileen, looking concerned.

Natasha suddenly felt how ridiculous this was; she was a grown-up and they did have taxis if she didn't feel like walking.

'Same way we came. Shanks's pony,' she said, patting her leg. 'Or an Uber. Don't worry, Mum! I'll see you at home!'

So Aileen went off, with her silver fox giving them a friendly wave.

Natasha said nothing as they went into the lounge

bar, got a table near the fire and ordered two Irish coffees, but she was still dwelling on what on earth that was all about. He was presumably a friend. But why the mystery?

'Are you OK?' Gabe asked. 'If you don't want to walk, you know, I could walk to the village and get my car and drive you home from there. I'd be happy to.'

'Oh no, it's not that. Thanks, though. I'm just surprised. I think that might have been a date. And I'm surprised that she would go on a date, that's all. It's silly, I know. She just never has, since my dad.'

'I get it. I would be pretty surprised if I saw either of my parents out on a date. I mean, they've been married for thirty years, but if they weren't, I'd still be surprised.'

Natasha was staring into the fire, unable to explain the unsettled feeling that had come over her on seeing Aileen with this man. 'It just feels like everything's changing,' she said. 'I mean, there's this problem with the house. And with Doon getting married . . . I don't know. It just feels like this time next year, we could all be in a really different place.' She didn't want to voice her deepest fear that Doon and Aileen would find new love and their own homes and that she would be left cast out and homeless somehow. It was too soon for that much crazy.

'So Doon's getting married?' he said. 'When is that supposed to be?'

'What do you mean, supposed to be? It's in July. I'm trying on bridesmaid dresses while I'm here.'

'Well, you might want to check with Doon first.'

'What are you talking about?'

'Um, the fact that Ciarán left really late last night? Did you not hear him leaving? In fact, I think I maybe heard voices arguing at one point. And then he drove off? You missed all that?'

'What? Did he? No, I didn't hear a thing!' She hadn't seen Ciarán or his car this morning, true, but she hadn't realized he was *gone* gone. 'Why didn't Doon tell me?' She had seen her late last night outside the bathroom, but Doon had said nothing at all except maybe a mumbled 'Goodnight'.

'Doon is such a secret squirrel. God. Are you sure they've argued, though? He probably just had to go off and buy a new pencil case for school or something.'

'I don't know, but they obviously weren't getting on so great yesterday. I'm sure you noticed.'

'Oh yes. Yes, of course I noticed,' she said, feeling embarrassed again. Because she hadn't. She had been far too busy with timing the turkey and keeping things hot, and obviously setting things on fire, to notice anything particular beyond the odd remark which was just Doon in her usual festive grump. But now she was worried. How was it that Doon and Ciarán had had a fight – a serious one – without her even noticing? If that was the case, with Aileen dating silver foxes and Ciarán and Doon falling out, what *else* hadn't she noticed?

29

Doon had returned to Ballyclare at a run, but it wasn't the ecstatic floating pace she had kept up earlier. This time she was stumbling over tree roots and branches, and slipping on patches of icy grass. The winter sun was low in her eyes, dazzling her and stopping her from thinking straight. She also found that she had left one of her running gloves at Charlie's place and groaned aloud.

At least it was quiet back home; nobody was about. Aileen must have gone out for a walk to enjoy the brilliant sunshine, and Natasha had presumably done the same, though probably not for as far or as long. Doon showered and dressed and went downstairs, drifting around disconsolately. What to do? She should probably get a move on with contacting people and explaining things. Or contacting Ciarán and seeing who he wanted her to contact. That was going to be truly awful.

The front door opened. She knew, from the step, that it was Natasha.

'Hellooo, anyone home – hey!' She came into the room and flung herself down on the sofa. 'I am sooo tired . . . I just walked to Powerscourt and back.' She sat upright. 'Guess who I saw there – on what I think was a date?'

'I dunno. Um, Bono. Timothée Chalamet.'

'No. Mum. If she's not back yet, it must still be going on.'

'Oh.' Doon hadn't expected that. 'Are you sure?'

'Um, yeah. He was a college friend, allegedly, but there was definitely something going on. Plus she was wearing her high heels – you know, the ones from M&S.'

'Those aren't high heels,' Doon said irrelevantly. She appreciated this was beside Natasha's point. 'Well, OK. She went on a date. She's allowed.'

'I suppose. Anyway . . .'

Doon was surprised at how quickly Natasha had dropped the subject, as normally she was like a dog with a bone with any topic like this. Instead she was looking at Doon with concern.

'Anyway . . . how are you? And where's Ciarán?'

Doon inhaled deeply and found herself curling her fingers into fists. *Here goes*, she thought. The first person she was telling. No, actually, the second. But she wouldn't think of Charlie now.

'He headed home to be with his folks. I'm afraid the wedding is off. We're calling it a day. I mean, we've split up.' How was she so bad at explaining this? Presumably it would get easier.

But Natasha didn't seem shocked. 'God,' she said. 'That's . . . I mean, that's big news. Are you OK?'

Doon was so grateful to be asked this, she almost felt herself tearing up. 'Yes. Yes, I'm OK,' she said. 'I feel terrible about it but I'm relieved honestly. It just wasn't right.'

'Well, good for you,' said Natasha. 'I mean, not that he wasn't nice and everything, but . . . maybe the feeling wasn't there.'

'No, it wasn't.' Doon curled up in her armchair, wrapping her arms round her folded knees. 'But I feel so guilty. And I'm dreading telling everyone. Not just the wedding venue people but friends and family . . .'

Natasha raised her eyebrows. 'Oh, God, yes. I hope you don't have many coming from abroad. Oh, wait, you do! Auntie Nuala and the Vancouver cousins.'

Doon sank her head in her hands. 'Oh God. They'll have booked flights probably. I don't know how to explain it to them.'

Natasha looked thoughtful. 'Why don't I do it?'

'What? What do you mean, you do it?'

'Well, all they really need to know is that the wedding's off, so not to come. And I can tell them that, and if they ask me other stuff I'll tell them to buzz off.' She grinned. 'I can be your spokesperson. Your PR.'

'Would you, Tasha? That would be . . . beyond amazing.' Doon gazed at her little sister in wonder. She hadn't expected her to take the news so well, let alone offer to help. 'I'm sorry you won't get to be a bridesmaid,' she added, guilt resurfacing.

'Are you kidding? I genuinely don't care about that,

Doon. If anything you're doing me a favour. Now I won't have to wear a bridesmaid's dress and go stag to the wedding.' She grinned.

Doon smiled gratefully. 'How are you anyway?' she asked, feeling bad that she hadn't asked this earlier. 'Have you heard from Ben at all?'

'Not really. I sent him an embarrassing text. Saying I liked him. And then I apologized, because it was drunken digits, and he just sent me a thumbs-up emoji back.'

'A thumbs-up?' repeated Doon. Was she hearing this right? What a clown.

'It doesn't matter. He's wrapped up with Lucy now.' She shook her head. 'I just don't know how he can go back to her, when she broke his heart like that. Not to mention they have nothing in common.'

'What's she like? Have you met her?' Doon asked, almost relieved to be distracted from her own inner turmoil.

'No. But here she is . . .' With a smooth practised movement, Natasha took out her phone and swiped straight to an Instagram profile, which she showed to Doon. Doon glanced at the pictures – all long limbs, pillowy pout and heavily lashed gaze – and nodded.

'OK. I'm not going to insult your intelligence by saying that she's not hot. Because she is,' Doon said. 'I can see that. But I will say she looks a bit vapid. All those bathroom selfies. I thought you said he was some kind of book-loving intellectual?'

'He is. That's what I don't get either. Anyway, whatever. We're talking about you.'

'I'm sick of me. Look, do you want to know what I think?'

Natasha nodded eagerly, and Doon felt bad that she seemed so starved of sisterly advice. When had Doon last talked to her about something like this?

'OK. Do you remember when Lorraine Ryan in my year got the points to do medicine? She didn't really want to do it, she wanted to work with horses, but she got the points so she felt she *had* to do the course?'

'Yes . . .'

'I think this is a bit like that. He got this very hot woman to show an interest in him, so he feels he has to follow it up. That's my theory anyway. Don't know if that helps.'

'Actually, it does! It really helps.' Natasha looked pleased. 'Thank you, Doon.'

'No sweat.' She stood up, feeling the stiffness descend, and did a quick side stretch. 'I tell you what. We're both freezing and I'm miserable, so why don't I make you my special hot chocolate?'

'Yes, yes! I'd love that.'

They went into the kitchen, where Doon got some squares of dark chocolate, melted them in a little pan, and poured over some full-fat milk, whisking it to perfection. She poured it into two mugs, and they sat there for a minute sipping the creamy, comforting hot drink, the one thing Doon knew how to make that tasted good.

'Who did you go to Powerscourt with?' Doon asked.

'Um, Gabe. We had a drink afterwards in the hotel, which is where we met Mum.'

'So you've forgiven him for his terrible crime of offering to buy the house.'

'I suppose.' She looked around the kitchen, staring at the dresser with its china glinting in the firelight, the rocking chair, the gingham curtains at the window. 'It's not his fault. I still just can't believe that we might have to sell. Can you?'

Doon was about to say yes, because it was all too likely, but she didn't have the heart to.

'I've been thinking. In case the bank won't lend Mum the money . . .' Natasha sipped her drink. 'I know you don't think this is real, but I really do remember Dad saying that he had found a gold nugget.' She added casually, 'It might be worth a look in the attic . . . ?'

'Yeah, that didn't happen. I mean, I do remember him saying it, but it was all in his head, Tash. There's nothing up there. Piles of junk, is all.' Doon shuddered as she considered the task that lay ahead if they were forced to sell, of sorting through the piles of stuff up in that attic: ancient toys, broken furniture, old cans of paint and sundry other clutter. Well, it would make a welcome change from wedding planning.

Natasha stood up. 'I know. But I might have a poke around up there anyway. There might be some good junk.' She put her mug in the dishwasher and straightened up, looking more cheerful than she had in days.

'Thanks for the chat, Doon. And as soon as you're ready – I mean, you and Ciarán – I'll start working through the guests. I know you've got a spreadsheet.'

Doon smiled. 'I do.' Natasha was standing up from the table when Doon said, 'By the way, Tasha . . .'

'Yes?'

'You know that business with the tree farm the other night? The raid?'

Natasha's eyes grew wide and she sat back down. 'Yes?'

Doon drew a breath. 'OK. Don't tell anyone, but . . .' But she couldn't say it. Not the full truth. 'I actually gave Charlie a lift to the Christmas tree farm. But I don't want anyone knowing about it – you know what people are like.' She stopped short of telling the whole truth, knowing it was cowardly, but also unable to come clean. She was all out of confidences and felt emotionally exhausted.

'Wow.' Natasha looked impressed. 'That's cool. You could have just said! Did you see the crims?'

'Just a grey van. Nothing else.'

Natasha shook her head. 'You're a hero. I bet Charlie was really grateful.'

'Yeah,' said Doon. She felt terrible; now she was compounding things, lie upon lie. But it was too late now.

'Exciting times,' said Natasha. 'Now, wish me luck, I'm going up to the attic.'

'Want me to hold the ladder?' Doon said, feeling awful.

'Oh, yes please. The last thing we want is for me to break my neck, that would really make it a Christmas to remember, wouldn't it?'

Doon smiled weakly and put her mug away, following Natasha out of the room. Natasha suddenly turned and threw her arms round her, almost knocking Doon over.

'It will be nice to be just the three of us again this evening, won't it?' she said. 'I love you, D-Dawg.' She hugged Doon tighter.

'Love you too,' Doon said, awkwardly giving in to the hug, and wondering how it was that everything was conspiring to make her feel worse than she already did.

30

Aileen was pleased to find, when she got back to the house, that the girls seemed to be on good terms again. Natasha was rummaging in the attic, while Doon was patiently sitting at the top of the stairs below waiting for her. Aileen noticed that she still wasn't wearing her engagement ring.

'What are you looking for, honey?' she called upstairs to Natasha. 'I might be able to help.'

'Just having a goo. Seeing if there's any good stuff. Like my school books for instance.'

'I wouldn't have put those in the attic.'

'It's OK. I'm just having a root around.'

'Suit yourself.' Aileen wondered whether to sit down beside Doon and try to talk to her, but she decided against it and made her way to her bedroom. That was the thing about having adult children. She remembered hearing, and then finding out for herself, that your kids completely disappeared in the teenage years, body and soul, and were swapped for some strangers. After which, hopefully, you got them back. Aileen felt that she had got them back mostly, but Doon remained elusive.

She changed out of her fancy outfit and into her

usual cold-weather uniform, full thermals top and bottom, followed by thin layers: a long-sleeved top, a jumper and a cardigan. As she packed away her 'good' clothes, she remembered her conversation with CJ and how they had said goodbye.

'Where are you parked?' she had asked, as they walked outside.

'Nowhere . . . I got a taxi here. I'll call another.'

'No you won't, I'll drop you. It's no bother. Where do you want to go, Rathowen? The Spar should be open, though I can't promise they'll do you hazelnuts.'

'Who was that with Natasha?' he had asked, as they drove out of the car park.

'Oh. He's a young American chap, the one who came to us for Christmas. We met him because he has a connection with the house.' She explained about Gabe's great-grandfather.

'What a story. She was lucky, wasn't she – the mother?'

'That's what I said. Anyway, he was delighted to look around; he's a really nice kid – he did a beautiful drawing of the house for me.' Her face fell as she felt the shadow hanging over her, briefly forgotten over their lunch. 'You know, I had some bad news recently about the house. We have subsidence. It's quite serious apparently, and needs a lot of funds for repairs. Which I don't have.'

'Gosh, I'm sorry. Does your house insurance –' He stopped short, as she shook her head. 'I see. No house insurance. They often don't cover things like that anyway.'

'No . . . anyway, that's the situation. I'm hoping that I can get a loan, with the house as security . . . It's not guaranteed, of course. I should have started enquiries, but I couldn't face it till after Christmas just in case they say no. Natasha would be devastated.'

'And Doon?'

'Doon is very practical. And . . . I don't think she has quite the rosy memories that Natasha does. In a way she's all about leaving the past behind. Now, here we are, the bright lights of Rathowen. It's busy enough, isn't it – for the day that's in it.'

She found a spot not far from the Spar and parked and turned to face him. Expecting him to say his good-byes and leave, she was surprised when he said, 'And what about you?'

'What about me what?'

'How would you feel about selling?'

'Well, I would feel guilty. All these years I clung on to the idea that we had to keep the house. The girls had lost their dad, so I was determined to keep Ballyclare, as a roof over their heads. And a place to come home to whenever they needed it. Now I feel like such a fail-ure that I haven't managed that.'

'But you have,' he said. 'They're grown-ups now, and they can make their own homes surely.'

'Doon, sure.' She felt a moment of relief that, what-ever the ropey state of Doon's own relationship, she had her little cottage in Ringsend. 'But not Natasha. She's working for buttons over in London. Even if she earned more, you know what property prices are like now. She's priced out.' Aileen realized, as she said this, how completely true this was. The few years between Doon and Natasha had made all the difference.

'Yes,' said CJ. 'We were lucky, I suppose. In that respect anyway.'

'We also had mass unemployment and had to get the train to Belfast for our contraception,' Aileen replied. 'But yes, in a sense we were. When I think of our mortgage back then, it seemed so huge at the time but now it seems like nothing. Ninety-five thousand euro for a six-bedroom house in Wicklow! That was just before the boom, of course.'

'Six bedrooms?' He raised his eyes. 'Gosh, that's a big old barracks to heat and light by yourself. What's the energy rating?'

She laughed at the question, so practical, and then said ruefully, 'It's rated F. Now, don't forget your hazelnuts.'

'I have a minute, thanks to your kind lift. One reason I'm asking is we went through a similar thing before I went to the States, when I had to decide whether to do up my place in Rathmines, which was a three-bed, and rent it out, or sell up.'

'What did you do?'

'I sold it. So Aoife got a chunk, which meant she and Graham were able to get a bigger place. And they're the ones who host Christmas now, which is as it should be.'

Aileen nodded. The same thought had crossed her mind. If she sold now, in theory, even with the subsidence bringing down the price, she could buy herself somewhere small and give Doon and Natasha a chunk – it could be a deposit for Natasha even. That was the logical, sensible option. But Ballyclare was their home. How could she sell it?

'I know what you're saying, but . . . I still feel – regardless of the practicalities – I told them they'd always have a home to come back to. And if I did sell, I'd be breaking that promise.'

'But they're grown-ups. So maybe it's not about making a home for them any more. Maybe it's about helping them to make a home for themselves.'

'Oh, gosh.' She stared at him. Somehow his simple words had cut through all the haze of her confusion and she saw the situation in an entirely new light. 'You're right, of course.' She couldn't help but add, 'But where does that leave me?'

She felt quite pathetic, saying it, and she wasn't sure if CJ would even grasp her meaning: that she was supposed to be the one welcoming the girls home and not the other way round. But he seemed to understand.

'I know what you mean,' said CJ. 'It does feel strange not to be the keeper of the keys any more. But that's life; our role is meant to change, isn't it? I think so anyway.'

'I suppose so.'

'Anyway, Aileen . . . I could stay here all day talking

to you. But I'd better tear myself away.' He smiled at her, and she felt a strange sensation deep inside, like a knot being undone or a page being turned. 'Could we do this again – sometime soon?'

The sounds of Doon and Natasha talking on the landing brought Aileen back to the present. She closed her eyes for a minute and allowed herself to think of that goodbye with CJ. How he had kissed her cheek. It was brief and friendly, but it sent a sensation down her spine that had kept reverberating as she watched him walk away. He had suggested dinner the following week, and, feeling a sudden doubt, she had said she would let him know. She wasn't sure whether she would go for it, or if perhaps life was complicated enough right now. There were other things she needed to think about first, and there was a call she needed to make. Aileen sat up, closed her bedroom door fully, and got out her phone.

31

'Tash,' Doon called up, 'if you're going to be there much longer, I'm going to go and watch TV, OK?'

Natasha made her way back to the trapdoor and looked down at Doon in a panic. 'Don't leave me up here! How will you know when I want to come down?'

'You can text me. You've got your phone, haven't you?'

'Oh yeah. Well, OK.' Natasha gave Doon a wave and went back to her search.

She had certainly found some treasure. Her Beanie Babies, well loved and mangled. A pile of notes from her Junior Certificate. Old sketchbooks of Aileen's, along with several boxes full of broken jewellery due for repairs. And a box full of Waterford-linen table napkins, slightly yellowed but miraculously untouched by mice. Her whole life was in this house, recorded in its objects and its walls. If it ever was sold, who would she even be any more?

She found some of her father's things – lever-arch files of notes from his law studies, textbooks and several books on house restoration. It was poignant to see his handwriting, so familiar though she had only a few examples of it. She found a box full of mementoes:

postcards and theatre tickets, and a strip of photos from a booth, showing him and an incredibly young baby-faced Aileen. Natasha gasped out loud when she saw it and clutched it in her hands. This her mum would want to see; she couldn't understand why it had ever been stuck up in the attic. These boxes hadn't been disturbed for decades by the looks of them.

And then she saw something. The edge of something, a shoebox from Carl Scarpa it looked like, just visible behind one of the joists. She pulled it out. It felt weighty and something loose knocked against the edge when she picked it up.

Then she noticed the writing on it. *Gold Mines River, July 1997*, it said in her father's handwriting.

She took in a deep shuddering breath. Then she opened the box. A padded envelope lay inside with something hard and heavy in it, about the size and heft of a big paperweight. She opened the envelope.

Inside were two rocks. They weren't gold but a dull grey granite. If she turned them, she could just about see a glint of something that looked like silver flecks, but she knew it wasn't even silver; mica or pyrite it was called. She had seen it lots of times. She remembered a geography teacher finding some on a trip to Glendalough and showing it to her and her class. 'It's called fool's gold,' he had said. 'I'm sure you can see why.' It was briefly interesting for kids to see the shiny flecks, but it certainly wasn't gold.

Natasha looked at the rocks for a long moment. Her

father hadn't been a fool; he had had an illness. She had always known that. Aileen had talked about it openly and they had understood that it was part of him but sometimes made life difficult for him and others. And that it was the reason that they lost him tragically – not because he didn't love them but because his brain was giving him information that wasn't helpful.

But Natasha didn't have his illness, so what was her excuse? How had she let herself believe that her father was finding gold in Wicklow streams and hiding away valuable nuggets that would somehow save their family fortunes? She made a quick search for 'gold nuggets' on her phone, just to be absolutely sure she wasn't missing anything. Within seconds she found one for sale on eBay for £1,000. So even if it had been genuine, it was hardly the solution to the problem of the house.

When she finally put the rocks away and climbed down the ladder with the strip of passport photos tucked into her pocket, she felt as if she had aged ten years.

'Tash?' It was Doon, coming upstairs from the drawing room. 'Hey, did you climb down all by yourself?'

'Yeah, of course I did. It was easy.' She considered telling Doon she wasn't a child, but there was no point. She had been acting like a child her whole life really. But not any more.

32

Doon, sitting at her post under the ladder, had had a birds-eye view as Aileen came inside. She had clocked her pretty appearance – a touch of make-up, the high-heeled boots – but what she noticed most was the smile on Aileen's face, the mixture of contentment and stimulation that you felt after a really great first date. She could just about remember that feeling herself, back when things were good with Ciarán. She didn't know if it was the upset over their break-up, the turmoil of dealing with Charlie or the stress over the house, but she suddenly felt in need of her mother's consolation for the first time in a very long time. After warning Natasha that she was leaving her post, Doon went to tap on Aileen's door. She could hear her winding up a phone conversation, with many 'bye bye byes', so she went away to the bathroom and came back five minutes later when it was quiet and knocked.

'Come in.'

Aileen was lying on her bed, still made up but back in her 'home' clothes and reading a book by the glow of her little fringed yellow bedside lamp. The room was so cosy; Aileen was the only person Doon knew who had an actual dressing table, with an embroidered stool in front of it, and a heavy old-fashioned dresser with a blue and white pitcher and bowl on it, the pitcher filled with dried flowers. There were framed paintings on the wall, all bought by Aileen over the years to support local artists. And the wallpaper was the striped yellow and white that Doon remembered her picking out when Doon was twelve, when they redecorated. It had seemed dated for a few years, but now it was back in fashion again.

'How are you, Doonie? What's up?'

Doon sat on the bed and ran her finger along the furrow of the yellow bird-patterned quilt, which she also remembered being bought around that time.

'I have some bad news, I suppose. You know how Ciarán left suddenly . . . well, there was no family emergency. I mean, there was, but only between the two of us. We've decided to call off the wedding.'

Aileen nodded. 'I'm sorry, darling,' she said. 'That must have been hard to do.'

Doon said, 'Yeah. It was awful.' She drew back and looked at her mother. 'You don't seem very surprised . . .'

'Well, he left late at night and you're not wearing your ring, so . . .'

Doon hung her head, realizing what an idiot she had been to think that their break-up had escaped everyone's notice.

'I'm really sorry, Doon. I don't think it's bad news, though.'

'Do you not?' Doon looked up, feeling a glimmer of

hope that her mother would have seen some silver lining that escaped her now.

'No, of course not. Bad news would be you getting married to the wrong person. Or feeling that you had to go through with the wedding at gunpoint, so as not to let anybody down . . .'

'Both of those have felt like they were on the cards if I'm being super honest.'

'Well, there you go. I'm very glad that you found the courage to do this. I know it's not easy. I'm proud of you, sweetie.'

Doon felt her eyes brimming with tears. Aileen held out her arms, and she went into them, breathing in her mother's familiar scent. She sat on the bed beside her, leaning her head on her shoulder. Why hadn't she told her how she was feeling weeks ago? She should have known that Aileen would understand what it was like to feel different or wrong.

'You don't think I'm a terrible person for how I treated him?' she said, muffled.

'No,' said Aileen. 'These things happen. Much better to decide now than after the wedding.'

'It's going to cause so much talk, Mum. I'm so humiliated.'

'It must feel like that. But I promise it will be a nine-day wonder. People will find something else to talk about. And he will be OK as well. He'll meet somebody else and they'll be happy.'

Doon nodded. She looked around the room again

and felt the consolation of being with her mother and being at home.

'I can give you that money back anyway,' she said, remembering the 3,000 euros Aileen had given her for the wedding. The deposits weren't coming back, but she could refund her mother at least.

'Water under the bridge,' said Aileen, which made Doon want to cry. She would give it back to her secretly somehow.

'I'm sorry I didn't tell you earlier, Mum. I was also thinking –' Doon gulped – 'if I had got married, and moved in with Ciarán the way I was supposed to, I could have sold my place. And then that would have been your funds for the repairs. Maybe I should have done that.'

'No, Doon! Don't be crazy. I wouldn't have let you.'

Doon said miserably, 'I could still sell my car, though. Why don't I do that? It would be something – not the whole cost but it would go towards it.'

'Don't be ridiculous now. Stop that – let's have no more chat about selling things, please.' Aileen added gently, 'Though I do appreciate the thought.'

Doon wanted to tell her mother about Charlie too, but that would be too much information even for someone as understanding as Aileen. The whole Charlie thing was forgotten now, and the best she could hope for was that he would be discreet about it.

'Come on,' said Aileen. 'We'll all feel better after some dinner. Turkey sandwiches all round, that will help you feel better.'

She slid off the bed and Doon followed her obediently, enjoying being told what to do for once.

'When are you thinking of leaving us, sweetie?' Aileen asked as they went downstairs. 'Not that I'm hurrying you away.'

'I'm not sure,' said Doon. 'Maybe tomorrow? Depending on the roads. I think I'll decide in the morning.' She looked worried again. 'Are you sure you don't want me to try to sell my car?'

Aileen laughed. 'Of course not. We don't want you walking back to Dublin,' she said, which got a watery laugh from Doon.

As they went downstairs, Doon looked at each picture on the landing and each turn of the steps as if it might be the last time. Which one day it would be, maybe sooner than she had thought. She hadn't allowed herself to feel what it would be like not to have this place, this base. It was where she had grown up; she had had good times here, as well as sad ones. Here was where they had gathered with Amy and her other friends for drinks before leaving for their debs' ball. Here was where she and Amy's family had spent Christmas together, kids in one room playing Twister while the two mums made dinner and drank wine. And the sofa where she and Natasha had spent hours over Christmas, arguing over what film to watch – those memories, which she had thought of as mundane or even annoying, now seemed golden in retrospect. And she could even remember the happier times with her dad, when she and Tasha were little. He used to run around the lawn with them riding on his shoulders. He pushed them on their swing, and helped them dam the stream. The place was filled with memories of him.

For the first time she could truly understand how Natasha felt about the house. They had been so happy here. Maybe it wasn't crazy to try to keep it, she thought. Maybe the bank would come good or they could figure something else out; for the first time she wanted to try.

33

Aileen rummaged in the fridge for the Tupperware box containing the leftover turkey, thinking that although she could never tell Natasha this, after the trouble she had gone to to make the full dinner, turkey sandwiches were her favourite Christmas meal. She put the cold meat on a willow-patterned platter and placed it on the table, along with mustard, mayonnaise and some cranberry jelly, as well as the leftover stuffing. This sandwich would be the food of the gods. But, importantly, it couldn't be made with soda bread, but with sliced pan from Brennans – the pillowy white slices, lightly toasted, lifted the humble sandwich to a new level. With a glass of white wine this would be her choice for her last meal on earth.

Turning round as the girls trailed into the room, she thought they looked a bit like they were going to their last meal. It was understandable that Doon looked tired, but Natasha also looked sombre. She must have been disappointed in her search for something or other. Or maybe they were both absorbing the news of Doon's broken engagement; it was a big shock all round. She decided to let them both eat a proper dinner before she said anything else. They ate mostly in silence, passing mayo or mustard as required.

'This is delicious, Mum,' Doon said eventually after finishing her plate.

'You can thank Tasha, not me,' she said. 'But I agree. A finer turkey we never had.'

'Thanks,' said Natasha, still looking downcast.

What was wrong with her? But Aileen couldn't pussyfoot any longer. She put her glass down and drew in a breath. 'Listen, girls, I want to talk to you both. About the house.'

They both looked at her, looking heartbreakingly identical as they rarely did.

'I know we talked about me trying to get a loan, to raise the money for the repairs. But . . . I've been thinking it over and I think that even if we did magically put our hands on the money, the sensible thing is probably to sell.'

Silence. She continued, 'If I manage to sell it, you could both get some of the payout, and it should be enough to help you both out. Hopefully a deposit for you, Tasha. Maybe not enough for a place in London, but you could buy something around here maybe . . . You could rent it out even if you didn't want to live here. Anyway. What do you both think?'

Natasha was looking down at her plate, looking blank but not especially shocked. Doon, to Aileen's surprise, was the one to object.

'But, Mum, are you sure? This is your home. And it's been our home for so long. Can't we find a way to hold on to it?'

'We could try. But think of the practicalities, Doon,'
she said. 'It's a huge house just for me. It costs so much
to run and heat. I won't always want to be going up and
down three flights of stairs. I could get a little flat or a
cottage – maybe in Greystones or Skerries . . .'

'You want to move to *Skerries*?' Doon asked.

'You say that like it's a death sentence – I'd be lucky
to get a place there! Or maybe I could find something
nearby, though there's less on the market,' Aileen said,
wondering why Doon was the one with so many objections. 'Tashie, what do you think?'

Natasha said, 'I don't know, Mum. Maybe you should.
Maybe it's the right thing to do.'

'Do you really think so?' Aileen was shocked. 'I
thought you'd be dead against it. What's wrong with
you, Tashie? Did something happen?'

Natasha shook her head. She seemed to make an
effort to stay calm. 'Nothing really. Just . . . facing facts,
I suppose. It was a nice idea to think that we could keep
the house. But I see what you're saying. The sensible
option probably is to try to sell.'

Both Doon and Aileen stared at her, as astonished as
if she had started speaking in tongues.

'I guess the only question is, what kind of price you
would get for it,' said Natasha. 'With the subsidence, I
mean.'

Aileen blinked. Was this truly Natasha talking or had
she been body-snatched?

'Hold on,' said Doon. 'Before going down this route,

Mum, why don't you at least speak to the bank? See what they can offer you. It could be more affordable than you think to get a loan, with the house as security . . .'

'I already have,' said Aileen.

'What?' they said in unison.

'Not the official bank itself – they're closed, of course – and I don't know who I would even speak to there, probably a call centre. But I phoned Susan just now to get her take on it.'

'Susan?' said Doon.

'Reilly. She's a bank manager, remember?' said Natasha.

'Yes. She reckons it's a very slim chance. Best-case scenario, I'd be looking at a twenty-year mortgage at a horrible rate. For someone like me, on the brink of retirement, it's just not feasible.'

The girls exchanged glances. 'Well . . .' Doon said. 'Can we just see? We don't want to rush into anything . . .'

But Aileen could see, looking at them both, that the fight had gone out of them. The idea of selling was out in the open now, and they just had to come to terms with it. But they would be OK. She hoped so anyway.

Then the knocker rang. Not the doorbell, but the heavy knocker Dan had bought on Kildare Street over twenty years ago.

'Who's that, at this time of night?' Aileen said.

'I don't know,' said Doon, glancing at Natasha.

'I'm not expecting anyone,' Natasha said. 'Who

would call around so late on Stephen's Day anyway – Stephen's Night?'

They looked at each other for a second longer. Aileen was about to say something sensible, about how it must be a passing friend or maybe Gabe had forgotten something, but she didn't want to break the momentary spell that she felt had descended on them all. She didn't want to dispel the hope that it might be the last person they expected and the one they wanted most.

'I'll get it,' said Natasha, standing up, and she walked quickly down the corridor.

34

Natasha opened the front door and immediately she felt foolish, disappointed and also, even, a little relieved. For there on the doorstep was Charlie.

'Oh, hi there,' she said. 'How's it going? What brings you here?'

'Nothing major. I have something of Doon's.'

'Oh, I see,' Natasha said, remembering the lift Doon mentioned. She was about to ask him in, but Charlie didn't seem to want to hang around.

'Just give her this, would you?' Charlie held out a soft crumpled item. Natasha, looking more closely, saw that it was Doon's running glove. 'She left this the other night. I found it, I mean, in the pub.'

'No you didn't! Come on, Charlie. I know what happened.'

'She told you?' He took a step backward, his handsome face pale. 'What did she say? How did she sound? Forget it. It doesn't matter.'

'She told me she gave you a lift to the tree farm,' she said. 'But I'm beginning to feel like that wasn't the full story?' Natasha added slowly.

'There's no story,' Charlie said almost sternly. 'She gave me a lift and – and somehow I ended up with her glove. That's all. Look, I've got to go, OK? I'll catch you before you leave. See you, Tasha.'

And before she could stop him, he had thrust the glove at her and set off down the driveway, turning up his collar against the cold. Natasha stared after him. *Curiouser and curiouser*, she thought. That was not just a lost-property scenario. Combined with Doon's dodgy story about staying over at Amy's and the sudden departure of Ciarán, it was all suddenly clear. Doon had been shagging Charlie Cuffe!

Had it been anyone else, it would have been a fantastic piece of gossip, but, as it was, Natasha couldn't help feeling foolish. After their heart-to-heart in the kitchen – all the hot chocolate and sisterly confidences – nothing had changed. Doon was still keeping things from her. It was like the engagement all over again; Natasha was the last to know. She closed the door, feeling fed up and undermined, and also a little bit peeved that Charlie, the acknowledged stud of their year, had shagged Doon and clearly still had the hots for her. Why did Doon have two men on the scene, and she couldn't even get a reply from Ben?

A text pinged in her pocket. She checked her phone and did a true double-take, for there on the screen *was* Ben. A missed call, plus a photo message. It was a picture of a shop window, probably a department store like Selfridges, with a tiny tree-ornament doll dressed in an outfit almost exactly like one Natasha owned: a red dress with a full circle skirt. There was no message, just a hashtag: STATOY. Their shared hashtag.

She stared at it and then saw that he was typing. The message came through a moment later, followed by two others.

> How are you? Xx
> Things not 100% great here.
> I'm feeling confused. Wondering could we talk?
> Please call me?

Natasha drew her breath in sharply. This was literally the message, or messages, she had dreamed of ever since saying goodbye to him in the airport. So why didn't she feel more thrilled?

'Tasha, who was that?' called her mother from the kitchen.

'Nobody,' she said, Charlie almost forgotten. 'Just – just Billie. She's gone now.' She wouldn't let Doon be busted now; she would give her the glove later and not even ask about her shenanigans with Charlie.

Her thoughts in a whirl, she walked upstairs to her room, still holding Doon's glove, and composed herself. Even if she was less sure now about Ben, they were friends, or they had been. She would give him one final chance to explain himself. Should she text? But she was tired of playing games; if he wanted to talk, she would talk. She picked up her phone to return his call.

It rang out. After a minute, Ben messaged again.

> Sorry. I'm tied up right now – will call you shortly when L goes out.

Natasha frowned. Why couldn't he call her openly? The only reason she could think of was that he didn't want Lucy knowing he was in touch with her. Or that he wanted to talk about Lucy behind her back. Neither of which was very appealing.

It was a full five minutes before his next message came through.

> Thought L was going out solo but actually she wants me to come with.
>
> I'll call you tomorrow instead?
>
> Might not be early but will get to it when I can?

Then, as a final afterthought: xx

What the hell? How had they gone, within minutes, from him practically begging her to call him, to him telling her he would *get to her when he could*, like she was a pile of laundry? Well, maybe he was feeling mixed up. She was about to type out, Sure, no problem, another time, but then she stopped. Why even offer? She had already spent hours listening to him about Lucy when Lucy was his ex; why spend more time listening to his problems now that he was back with Lucy? Who did he think she was, the Samaritans?

She put down her phone on her bedside table, knocking something over. It was the so-called 'gold nugget' that her dad had carefully saved from the river. Just a rock, of course. Poor Dad; he had been panning for gold in all the wrong places. *Just like you and your love life*, said a voice in her head.

She put it down, feeling a new sense of clarity. Barely an hour ago she had been telling herself off for all her illusions about the house. What was Ben but yet another illusion? She had thought they were soulmates, but he was more like an emotional gold-digger, getting close to her when he wanted to and then dropping her when it suited him – all without intending to let it become anything real. Whether he truly was confused, or flaky or selfish, it didn't matter. She needed someone who knew what he wanted. She tapped out a quick reply. Hi Ben. Things pretty busy here too. Hope you sort things out. Take care. And she pressed send and then she archived their chat. Now *that* was closure.

She got up to go downstairs to the others, remembering to grab Doon's glove, which she dropped into her pocket on her way down. She would tell her later, in private, that Charlie had called by. What had seemed such a big deal just half an hour earlier now, after the talk about the house, seemed less important. Life was complicated and Doon no doubt had her reasons. Though if she did come clean, Natasha would tell her for free that he was a much better bet than that dry ould Ciarán – or indeed, Ben.

35

Left alone in the kitchen, Aileen and Doon had stayed quiet until they heard the sound of voices at the door; it was obviously some friend of Natasha's. Doon let out a breath, so quietly nobody else but Aileen would have heard it. Without looking at each other they went back to the topic they had just been discussing, the house.

'Well,' Aileen said, 'I have to say I'm surprised, Doon. I thought you would be all for me selling. But you seem more upset than Tasha was.'

'It's a big thing, Mum. It's our house. Our memories. And it's been a busy day or two. A lot of upheaval.'

'It certainly has,' Aileen said with a sigh, pouring herself another glass of wine.

'By the way, how was your lunch today?' Doon asked casually.

'Oh, it was very nice,' said Aileen. 'An old college friend, a man called Conor Jameson – CJ. I bumped into him in the village and we arranged to have lunch today. Very pleasant.'

It all sounded very normal and nothing-y, but a lunch at Powerscourt seemed a little more significant than a random meet-up. Doon was about to ask Aileen more when her attention was distracted by the unmistakable sound, unmistakable to her anyway, of Natasha saying goodbye to her friend at the front door. That was Charlie's voice; she could hear it now. She remained frozen, unable to register what Aileen was saying until she heard the front door close and Natasha stumping upstairs with her usual heavy tread.

'Are you OK, Doon?' Aileen asked. 'Do you want some tea?'

'Oh, no. Not just now. Just going to ask Tasha something.' She hopped up and went cautiously up the stairs. She was about to go and knock on Natasha's door to find out what Charlie had wanted, when she saw the text from Amy.

Doon? What's going on – call me? xx

Doon drew in a deep breath. Here it was: the showdown she had been dreading the most. Amy would try to understand, no doubt, but she would also be disappointed that their idyllic set-up – two best friends dating two best friends – would be wrecked. And she would be upset at Doon for not telling her earlier; this seemed to be the mistake Doon kept making. She would probably feel extremely sorry for Ciarán, and rightly so. And that was without even mentioning Charlie!

But it had to be faced eventually. Doon went into her room and sat down on her neatly made bed and prepared to call Amy, just as she had done hundreds, maybe even a thousand times before. She had never dreaded it like this before. She took heart from the double 'x' at the end, though; Amy probably wouldn't have put those if she hated Doon.

Amy answered seconds later. 'Doon! What's going on? Will we switch to video call?'

'No, no, it drains my battery,' said Doon, though that wasn't actually true, unless she meant her mental battery. How was every single thing she said lately a lie?

'Hang on, I'll just come out of the front room. No, Mam, it's Doon. One sec.' There was some rustling while, Doon surmised, Amy went to her own room.

'What happened?' Amy said, seconds later. 'I've just heard from Setanta. He said Ciarán just texted him and said the wedding's off? That's not true, Doon, is it?'

'It is, Amy. I'm really sorry. I should have told you. I've been having doubts for a while. We had a row and it just all blew up. I've been dreading the wedding, and I also just don't think we're right for each other.'

Doon was proud of herself for being truthful, if not coming totally clean. The whole Charlie thing could follow later, maybe. But then there was a pause so long that Doon said, quailing, 'Amy? You there?'

'Yes, I'm here. Doon, I can't believe it. Why didn't you tell me?'

Doon felt her voice choke. 'I tried. But it was hard. I was worried you'd be disappointed.' She gasped and realized something was closing up her throat. Tears! She never cried. 'I did try.'

'Doon, don't cry! You poor thing. You must have

been going mental.' Amy paused. 'I'm so sorry. Is that what you were trying to say the other night in the pub? I thought it was just cold feet.'

Doon sniffed. 'Yes. It was. But that's not all, Amy, there's worse. I kissed someone else.'

'Oh my God! Doon. Who? When?'

'I don't want to say who. But it was just the other night.'

A pause. 'Was it Charlie Cuffe? It was, wasn't it? You know what, Doon, I would. He is a ride, no two ways about it. Is it serious?'

Doon groaned, but she was so relieved that Amy didn't sound upset with her that she forgot to deny it. 'No, no. Please don't tell anyone.'

She waited to see if Amy would bring up the whole Cuffe thing, but she didn't. Instead she said, 'Of course I won't. Doon, I'm your oldest friend. You know I'll always have your back. And I would never want anyone to get married if they didn't want to. You know what my mam always said?'

'What?'

'I've told you. She tried to tell her mother, before the wedding, that she was having doubts, but her mam didn't want to hear it. So there's no way I would do that to you.'

Doon lay back on her bed and looked at the ceiling, weak with relief. 'So you're not angry with me?'

'Of course not . . . Look, it's going to be difficult I suppose, with Setanta and Ciarán; we'll still be seeing him a lot. But that's just how it is. You come first, no question.'

'Thank you.' Doon cleared her throat. 'I feel so stressed about the wedding. We'll have to cancel everything, and we won't get deposits back either.'

'True,' said Amy. 'Unless . . . how about we buy the whole wedding from you? That would be quite handy actually. A bird in the hand. I'd even take the dress off you if I could get into it.'

'Oh, Amy, you're not serious, are you?'

'Well, I'm not sure Setanta would go for it, and it might be a bit of a slap in the face to Ciarán. But still, waste not want not, am I right?' They both laughed, and in the sound of the shared laugher Doon knew that somehow things would be OK.

She hung up the phone ten minutes later, feeling limp and drained but deeply relieved. The fact that Amy didn't think she was a terrible person was all she needed to know. And maybe it was a sign that honesty was the best policy – and not just with Amy.

Hoping for a second miracle, she slipped out of her room and went upstairs to knock on Natasha's door. She would see what Charlie had wanted, and she would come clean about him as well; otherwise it would only make things worse.

'Come in,' her sister said. Doon went inside and found Natasha sitting cross-legged on the floor by her doll's house.

'I'm not playing with it,' she said quickly, turning as

Doon came in. 'Just checking the mice haven't been at the curtains or anything.'

'Oh, Tasha,' Doon said. 'It's fine if you are. I'm not one to judge.' She sat down beside her sister, looking properly at the doll's house again; it really was a little beauty. She wondered if any of hers or Natasha's children would ever play with it. Less chance of that happening any time soon now that she and Ciarán were no more, of course, but that was too depressing a thought to pursue.

'Charlie called by. He gave me this for you,' Natasha said, handing over Doon's running glove.

'Oh!' said Doon. 'Was that it? Um, look. I meant to tell you – the other night –'

'It's OK, Doon. I don't need to know. It's your business – whatever.' Natasha soberly put one little doll back upstairs in its bedroom. 'I don't need to know everything about your life, honestly. I just think it would be nicer if we talked more sometimes.'

'But we do talk.'

'Not really.' She was staring into the doll's house. 'I feel like I'm always the one calling you. And when you do text me, I feel like it's out of duty almost. Not to mention I never see you.'

'It's not! Natasha, I don't – we see each other loads, don't we? Last summer, every Christmas.'

'Yes, but have you noticed where? It's always here at home. The planes go both ways, you know?'

'The planes?'

'To London. I've been there six years, and you've never once been to visit me.'

Doon was about to say that she had seen Natasha once for a coffee when she was over on a work trip, but then she realized that wasn't the point, any more than the night with Charlie was. It was bigger than that.

'But you come here so often – and Mum's been loads of times . . .' She stopped short, realizing that this also wasn't the point.

'Yeah, but you're my sister!' Natasha sat up and piled her curls on top of her head. 'Look, I don't want to make a big deal of it. Just – don't be a stranger, OK?'

'OK,' said Doon. 'I get it. I will. I'll come over and visit. Actually, I'd love to.'

'Great,' said Natasha. 'And by the way. Charlie?'

'Yes,' Doon said, quailing.

'He's cute, and a nice guy! You could do worse.'

'Oh no. Nothing can ever happen between us.'

'Why not? Because it's too soon?'

'Yes, but also – you really don't know?' Doon said.

Natasha shook her head. Doon sighed, and told her all about what had happened when David Cuffe had dumped her: the phone calls to his mother, the bottle of gin, Sheryl Crow, the awful episode when Aileen had to drive her to hospital to have her stomach pumped. Natasha listened, wide-eyed.

'Are you serious?' she said finally. 'How did I not know this? Where was I when this all happened?'

'I think you were at a sleepover. Thank God.'

'Oh, maybe.' Natasha shook her head. 'That's gas. Sorry, Doon, I don't mean it's funny. But it's so unlike you.'

'Did you really not know about it?' Doon asked. 'I thought everyone must have heard about it.'

'What? No. It's not such a big deal anyway. Wind any woman up and stick half a bottle of gin in her and you'll get a similar effect, I'd say.'

'I just always feel like his whole family must be judging me whenever they see me,' Doon admitted.

'But they only know about the psycho phone calls in fairness. If that. Not the gin and the stomach pumping. I didn't even know about that.'

'I can't believe you didn't.'

'Who would be bothered saying it? I'd say even his mother has long forgotten it.'

'Really?'

'Listen,' said Natasha, 'the other night I sent Ben a Taylor Swift song and a message asking him why we're not together, and I'm not a teenager.'

'God, sorry, Tasha. Do you want to talk about it?'

'I don't actually.' She smiled mysteriously. 'I'm kind of over him now. But my point is: if I can get over that, you can get over this.'

'OK. Thanks for telling me,' said Doon, feeling as light and unburdened as she used to in the olden days when she went to confession. But there was one little sin remaining on her conscience.

'Tasha,' she said. 'I'm sorry I didn't call you to tell you I was engaged. That was crappy of me. I get it now.'

'It doesn't matter, Doon. Just . . . next time you get engaged, tell me sooner, will you?'

'I will,' said Doon, thinking it was a very remote possibility.

She stood up, thinking they should go back down to Aileen, but Natasha stayed sitting, gazing into the doll's house. 'Do you remember giving me this?'

Doon sat back down. 'Of course.'

Natasha said, 'You know earlier – when Charlie knocked on the door . . .'

After a minute, Doon said, 'I know. I thought the same thing, just for a minute. Just for a second maybe.'

'Did you, Doon? I thought it was just me.'

'No, it's not just you. I think Mum thought it too, only for a minute.'

'It's not ever going to happen, though, is it?'

Doon shook her head. 'No. It's not.' After a minute she added, her eyes bright, 'But I think we'll always wonder.'

'Even you?'

'Even me,' said Doon.

Natasha squeezed her hand, and they sat in silence for a minute longer. Then Natasha closed the front panels of the doll's house so that the rooms were all hidden, revealing the graceful Georgian facade with its bow windows and the fanlight over the door. She got to her feet and held a hand down to Doon, to pull her up. 'Now, you're heading off tomorrow, right?' she said.

'That's the plan,' said Doon, though she wasn't sure if that was really going to happen. At the rate she was going, she was going to disappear into some kind of multiverse before she managed anything as sensible as packing up her stuff and driving up to Dublin with her leftover turkey. But she felt a shred of hope now, that no matter how crazy things were, they would somehow all work out.

'OK. So let's go downstairs and do something, all three of us. Any last requests?'

'Well, I was about to offer to help Mum go through her old post,' said Doon. 'But we can do something fun instead.'

'It's OK, Doon. I know that's fun for you,' said Natasha, and poked her sister in the ribs. Poking her back, Doon followed her downstairs, feeling better than she had in weeks, months or even years. She felt closer to Natasha now than she had since they were tiny. And not only that; another burden had been lifted. She had been convinced that the whole town knew about her antics with David and his family – and yet Natasha, who heard everything, had no clue about it. If only she had realized this before, she might have handled things differently with Charlie. But maybe – just maybe – it wasn't too late?

36

Aileen had just finished the washing-up when the girls came into the kitchen, both looking, somehow, more like buddies than they had since they had arrived. She smiled at them. 'Well, girls. Who's for tea or another glass of wine?'

'Wine for me,' said Natasha, heading for the fridge. 'Thanks for doing the washing-up, Mum. I promise I didn't just disappear to dodge it.'

'I'll make tea,' said Doon. She put on the kettle, adding to Aileen, 'Mum, as a Christmas treat, would you let me go through that pile of paperwork with you?'

Aileen groaned. 'Fine. Let's do it. Pass it over to me there and we'll tackle it now.'

She hated this chore but she had to smile at Doon's air of quiet satisfaction, as they started opening the envelopes, sorting Parish Dues, notes from the county council about works and bank statements, into piles of 'file', 'action' and 'recycling'. Natasha, of course, was into everything, scanning each little bit of paper for local news and gossip. Everything was so much more lively when they were here. She would miss them so much when they left. She hoped she wouldn't cry.

'Mum,' said Doon suddenly, 'this is from the solicitor's.' She handed the envelope to Aileen. 'I haven't looked at it.'

'Oh Lord,' said Aileen. She opened it and saw the familiar heading. It was Dan's old firm, his father's firm, which continued to handle their family affairs even now. *The late Miriam McDonnell, née Fitzpatrick* . . . The probate process for Dan's mother's estate must have concluded.

'It's about your grandmother's will,' she told the girls.

'Her will?' said Natasha. 'I thought you already saw that?'

'No. I only heard about what was likely to be in it.' Aileen scanned the letter. When she read and reread the relevant part, she almost didn't know whether to laugh or cry.

'Well?' Doon said, her face alive with hope.

'Well, she's left me ten thousand euro,' said Aileen.

'Mum, are you serious?' said Natasha.

Aileen nodded. 'He says – the solicitor, I mean. He didn't have to put this, but I suppose he did since we're family. Or maybe she wanted me to know. He says she left the rest of it, half to the RNLI. The Irish Lifeboats.' She felt her eyes fill up with tears. 'And the rest was a donation to the National Missing Persons Helpline.'

'Oh, God . . . I'm sorry, Mum. I see why she did that, but . . .' Natasha said. 'Like, the house sold for what, two million, and she leaves you ten grand?'

'It's really OK, Tashie. They will help lots of people. I'm happy she did that.'

'So why are you crying?' asked Natasha, distressed.

'Oh, it's not the money. Though I'm sorry she didn't leave anything to you girls. It's just – the poor woman. And your poor father.' Aileen stretched out her hands to both girls, squeezing them tight. She couldn't put into words her sadness at the quest that had lasted all the rest of Miriam's life, and even beyond. 'I'm sorry, chicks. I don't mean to upset you.'

'What are you talking about?' said Doon. 'It's OK, Mum. It's not your fault. I'm just sorry she didn't leave you something more; you could have kept the house.'

'It's really fine, Doon. Like I said, I'm ready to sell. And those are two good causes.'

'That's true. At least it's not, like, a home for retired Persian cats,' said Natasha.

Aileen laughed and wiped her eyes. 'It's very nice to have ten thousand – that's a lot of money. It was kind of her. Now, I have an idea. Why don't we make a round of gin and tonics – or tonics, Doon – and have a game of whist for old times' sake. How does that sound?'

'Are you sure?' said Natasha. 'You seem tired, Mum. You sure you wouldn't rather, I don't know . . . talk about it all more? Or just go to bed?'

But Doon seemed to understand how Aileen felt; she wanted fun and action and a little bit of normality before they all went to bed.

'I'll play,' she said, and Aileen gave her a grateful smile. Doon was better at reading people than she thought.

37

The next morning, Natasha was up and in the shower before either Doon or Aileen had stirred, and was dressed and making coffee when the doorbell rang. That would be Gabe, who had texted last night to confirm a time to come and see the doll's house. She ran down the corridor, feeling oddly shy yet excited. She checked her reflection in the mirror and decided that it wasn't terrible; inspired by Doon, she was working the fresh-faced fleece-clad look and it wasn't bad.

Gabe was standing on the doorstep, looking back at his car in the driveway he had cleared. When Natasha opened the door, he smiled. She wanted to fling her arms round him, but she restrained herself.

'Hey,' he said. 'It's good to see you.'

'And you,' she said. 'Come in. Would you like some coffee?'

'That would be great.' He followed her down the passage to the kitchen. She felt as if she had so much to tell him – so much had happened since she had seen him last; was it only yesterday? She just didn't know where to begin. But he was so easy to talk to; he sat down at what she now thought of as his usual place, and they started where they had left off.

'I hope you had a good evening. Did you thaw out in the end?' she asked.

'Of course. How about you?'

'We had a bit of a family conference.' She poured him a coffee and herself a second cup. 'My mum has made her decision. She's going to sell.'

Gabe raised his eyebrows. He looked around the kitchen and then back at Natasha. 'That's big news. Are you OK?'

She was touched that this was his first question.

'I don't know. Maybe? It might hit me later. But I can see why she feels like she doesn't want to get into a massive debt at this point in her life. Not to mention the cost of running it, heating it, all for one person. It makes sense. That's what my head says anyway.'

'And your heart?' he asked.

Hearing him say this gave her a strange fluttery feeling; though, she reminded herself, it was a perfectly logical question.

'It's a bit broken,' she said.

'I can imagine.'

'In a fantasy world I'd find a pot of gold and run the place as a B & B, like I told you. But it is what it is. Anyway,' she said quickly, 'how about you? I just realized I don't even know when you're leaving.'

'Tomorrow. This is my last day.'

They looked at each other in dismay. Then he added, 'But maybe I'll be back.'

She looked down, blushing. 'Oh yes. Nobody visits

Rathowen just the once. They all come back in the end . . .'

'Or I could stop by London some time?'

'Of course, any time,' said Natasha. Why was she suddenly feeling so awkward and hot-cheeked? She found herself looking everywhere but at him, twiddling her coffee spoon and both hoping and dreading that Doon or Aileen would appear.

'Anyway,' he said, 'I still want to see that doll's house. Wow, there's no way to not make that sound weird. But it sounds cool.'

'Yeah, sure,' Natasha said. 'I'll take you up to have a look now.' As they walked upstairs she started to wonder what would happen to the doll's house when her mother sold up. Of course Aileen would offer to mind it for her, but the thought of it plonked in the corner of a tiny flat was depressing. She supposed she could put it into storage. Oh God, how sad it all was.

'Excuse the mess,' she said half-heartedly, as they went inside, but really it seemed OK; there were clothes scattered around but they were clean, no underwear, and her bedcovers were pulled up if not exactly made. Doon made her bed every single morning, but Natasha didn't see the point.

'This is it?' Gabe said.

Natasha watched him kneel down carefully beside it, examining each beloved room, from the tiled roof to the wooden floor, each tiny bed and miniature cabinet. It was a perfect work of art; she was glad he could appreciate it.

'Where did your dad get this?' he said without looking up. His voice sounded strange. Natasha said, 'In a charity shop, I believe. One Christmas. He gave it to Doon, but she went off it, or grew out of it, I suppose, and she gave it to me.' A minute later she said, 'Are you OK?'

Gabe was sitting on the floor, looking – flabbergasted was the word, she thought.

'Natasha, do you know what this is? Or what I think it is?'

'I don't know. I mean, a doll's house?' she said, not getting his meaning.

'I can't believe I'm saying this, but I think it's one of the Three Sisters,' he said. 'A wealthy industrialist had them built in the 1850s for his three daughters. One sold at auction recently. The other is in a museum in Philadelphia. I'd like to send my professor some pictures, but I'm ninety-nine per cent sure that this is the third. Let me look it up.'

'Gosh,' she said. 'That's amazing, isn't it? I mean, I've always loved it, but I didn't think . . .' Her voice trailed off as she started to grasp his meaning. 'So it's valuable?'

'You could say that.' He laughed. 'Here, look.' He showed her a news headline on his phone: *Victorian doll's house sets record price at auction*. Skimming the text, she gasped when she saw the selling price: 100,000 pounds.

'*What?* Who would pay that for a doll's house?'

'Lots of people . . . You see, for each one, he commissioned miniature pieces from all the most well-regarded artisans of the day on both sides of the Atlantic. The wallpaper is by William Morris. The lamps were made by Tiffany. They're completely unlike any other doll's houses – unique in the world.'

'So how did this one end up in a charity shop in Dublin?' said Natasha.

'I don't know. But you've kept it as it is, right? You've never changed the furniture or the wallpaper or anything?'

'No, I never did. I did let my Lego people walk around it a good bit. But they're not heavy on their feet.'

He laughed. 'In that case . . . I think you could be looking at double what the last one sold for. If not more.'

Natasha couldn't speak. Gabe looked at her, as if to check why she wasn't rejoicing with him, and then he seemed to get it.

'Oh,' he said. 'You don't want to sell.'

She was shaking her head, her eyes brimming. 'My dad bought it,' she explained.

'I see.' He took this on board and sat back on his heels. 'Well, you don't have to sell it, of course.'

'I'm just in shock,' she said. 'Are you positive?'

'You'd have to get it authenticated, but I am as positive as I can be. Look, here's a photo! I knew I'd seen it somewhere.' He showed her the screen again, and they cross-checked it with a grainy black-and-white photo. Each room was identical down to the lamps and chairs.

'God,' she said after a minute. 'I can't believe it.'

Gabe said suddenly, 'I won't tell anyone about it, though. If that's what worries you. You can just pretend I never saw it.'

She looked up at him, appreciating the genuine sacrifice this would involve.

'Thanks. But if we could sell it and fix the house, our real house . . .' Her voice trailed off. 'Oh God, you know what? It's Doon's anyway.'

'But you said she gave it to you.'

'Yes, but we were really young. She didn't know how much it was worth.' Natasha looked at it soberly. 'I have to tell her. Come on, let's get her.'

She got to her feet and pulled up his hand. Suddenly he was right beside her, their faces almost touching. 'It's going to be OK,' he said. 'I promise. Look, you have the story now behind your doll's house. That's really cool. And no matter what you decide to do, it will all be great.'

'I know,' she said. 'Thank you.' Without thinking, she put her arms round him and hugged him tight, just like she would with a friend. But then somehow their profiles were touching. He put his hands on her face, and bent to kiss her, and at the touch of his lips she almost swooned. It was the kind of kiss that made you feel like Ilsa in *Casablanca*, the kind that made your knees wobble and your head swim. Who cared about houses when a kiss could make you feel like this?

'Tasha? Tasha, are you here? Doon's car is missing – have you any idea where she's gone? She hasn't left yet, has she?'

It was Aileen.

Natasha looked up at Gabe, who said, 'Come on. We can do this again later.' She gave him one last kiss, then went to answer the door to her mother.

38

Doon had been awake for hours the night before. She never had trouble sleeping and had never understood how other people didn't just listen to a podcast and drift off. But that night she got it: the tossing and turning, the racing mind, the feeling of being tired but wired. Despite her foggy head, one thought kept preying on her mind: that she had to see Charlie before she drove back to Dublin, and talk to him properly. She had a few confused hours of dozing, when she wasn't sure if she was asleep or awake, before waking fully by seven. By eight o'clock the sun was beginning to spread a pink line above the horizon and she was in her car, going down the driveway.

She was at the bottom of the drive when she realized how crazy it was to turn up unannounced at his place – for the second time – for no reason. So she decided to drive first to the Spar in the village and pick up some croissants as a peace offering. He would probably still think she was crazy, but at least she would have a prop of some kind to make the interaction less mad. She knew that she could wait till she was back in Dublin and phone him or text him – that would be more sensible – but she felt an odd but very real sense of urgency;

she had to see him before the Christmas spell had vanished.

Rathowen was as quiet as a toy town; all its inhabitants were still at home, wiped out no doubt by the past few days' festivities. Doon parked in a prime spot right opposite the Spar and walked inside, hoping that whoever was on duty today would have switched the oven on and put the pastries on to bake while they were opening up. The aromas wafting through the store told her she was right. She bought half a dozen of everything, and was just leaving the store when she saw a figure up the road, dressed in running gear, his dark hair ruffled.

Without thinking she called, 'Charlie!'

The handful of passers-by on the street turned to look at her. She gulped. This was literally her long-term nightmare being enacted for real. She was in the main street of Rathowen and everyone was staring at her. But what did it matter?

'Charlie!' she called again, not caring who heard her.

He turned round, his face beaded with sweat. He looked divine, like an ad for something masculine and outdoorsy. He started walking slowly down the road towards her.

'Hi!' she said, grinning, and his wary look dissolved as he clocked her obvious delight at seeing him.

'What are you doing here?' they both said at once, and Doon laughed at how they would sound to an observer, stunned at their chance encounter in a tiny town.

'I just went for a run – obviously,' he said. 'And I didn't have breakfast, so I was running to Bear Claw Coffee to get something. Which sort of defeats the whole purpose. What are you doing?'

She thought of various fibs she could tell, but instead she held out the bag. 'I was going to bring you these. As a peace offering. Thank you for bringing by my glove last night by the way. I appreciate it.'

'Hey, no worries. Can I get you a coffee in return?' He looked down at her doubtfully. 'Look, I do understand why you want to keep a low profile. We could always grab a couple to go and have them in your car.'

'No, no,' she said. 'Bear Claw is a great idea. Why don't we go up there? I'm sure they won't mind that we've brought some pastries. We can pay corkage or whatever it is for pastries – crumbage. Or I can bring them home for the family.'

'Are you sure, Doon?' he asked. 'I mean, it's a pretty public spot. Anyone could be stopping by there – we'd be the talk of the town.' He was half smiling, but she could tell that he also really wanted to know what her reply would be.

'Charlie,' she said, 'you know how I went out with your brother when we were younger? Does it bother you?'

'Does it bother me?' he repeated. 'No. Not at all. But I was worried that maybe it was bothering you. Does it bother you?'

She looked up and down the main street of the

village that she'd known almost her whole life. This was the very street where David Cuffe had crossed the road to avoid her, the same street where she remembered feeling so deeply traumatized at the posters advertising her father as a missing person. But that was a long time ago. She was a different person now; it was a different place. And Charlie wasn't part of her past; he was a whole new chapter, and she didn't know how it ended but she wanted to find out.

'Not at all,' she said. 'So let's go and get coffee.'

'You sure?' said Charlie.

'Yes, positive. Come on, I'm famished,' said Doon, and she took his hand to pull him up the road.

39

Aileen would normally have been surprised to see Gabe up in Natasha's room so early in the morning, but really nothing surprised her any more; it was officially the oddest Christmas since records began, and she had seen a few doozies.

'Oh, hi, Gabe,' she said politely. 'Tasha, have you any idea where Doon went? I was going to go out for my walk but I don't want to miss her, unless she's headed back to Dublin already?'

'She wouldn't have done that,' said Natasha. 'But let's go downstairs – there's something I want to tell you.'

They all trooped downstairs, Aileen wondering what this was all about. Were they about to get married and run off to Dublin together? Or had Gabe decided to purchase their house after all, and let them live there as his tenants? All bets were off. But whatever happened, she was quietly hopeful that it would be OK. The sun was shining on the remains of the snow; the sky was a perfect winter blue. It was a miserable thought that this was their last Christmas there, but at least it had been a good one all in all.

'Oh, look,' she said with pleasure, as the front door opened while they came back down the stairs. 'She's back. How are you, Doon?'

'I'm great.' Doon came inside, glowing – literally and figuratively. 'Hi, Gabe,' she added. 'I just went to the village for pastries. I bumped into Charlie and I had coffee with him.' She glanced at Natasha when she said this.

'Did you now?' said Natasha. 'Very nice. I hope he was very well.'

Aileen looked back and forth at the two of them, noticing the code messages flying.

'Anyway,' said Natasha, 'can we all go and sit down? I want to tell you guys something.'

Aileen felt alarmed at first, but it was clear from Natasha's demeanour that it was good news. They all trooped down towards the kitchen and sat down at the long pine table, except Gabe who said, 'Should I give you guys some space, Tasha?'

Aileen noticed the 'Tasha' and smiled to herself; lots of her friends called her that, but he was seeming like more than a friend today. Natasha said, 'It's fine, Gabe. You were here at the start after all. And you can tell them.' She looked at him expectantly and he began.

'Well, this is a little random, but Natasha told me she had a doll's house . . .'

Aileen could barely believe her ears as he explained. The doll's house was quite a good antique, but the idea that somebody would pay six figures for it was beyond her imagining. But Gabe seemed to know what he was talking about and had found a picture online that appeared to show the doll's house or the spitting image of it. The irony was striking. She remembered sitting in that very kitchen over twenty Christmases ago, when Dan had come in buzzing from his purchase of what he thought was a priceless painting. But all the time the real treasure had been sitting there under all their eyes, a child's toy. What were the odds?

'That's amazing,' Doon said when Gabe had finished. 'But you wouldn't sell it, Tasha, would you?'

'Well, it's up to you really,' said Natasha. 'Because it's yours. Remember? Dad gave it to you originally.'

'Yeah, sure. But then I gave it to you.'

'But you didn't know what it was worth. So I'm letting you know now so you can have it back if you want.'

Doon shook her head vehemently.

Aileen felt stunned at this new turn of events.

Then Gabe started to laugh, and they all turned and stared at him. 'I'm sorry,' he said. 'It's just that most families fall out over who gets to keep stuff like this – but you're fighting over who gets to give it away.' He smiled. 'You're all awesome. You did a great job, ma'am. I mean, Aileen. If you don't mind me saying so.'

'I don't mind actually, Gabe.' Others might have felt patronized at this gold star from such a young man, but Aileen thought it was sweet. 'I can decide, girls. I think it belongs to both of you. Your dad always pictured you both playing with it.'

She had thought this would solve it, but neither looked satisfied.

'I know,' said Natasha. 'Maybe we should agree

something this valuable belongs to *all* of us. And if Gabe is right, then selling it is going to mean we have the money for the repairs. So I vote we get it valued as soon as possible and sell it. And if we do make a few quid from it, and we get the repairs done –' Natasha paused for dramatic effect – 'I would like to have a go at running Ballyclare as a B & B.'

There was a stunned silence and Gabe smiled.

Natasha continued, 'Wait, Mum. I know I'm liable to set the place on fire, but I also know the perfect person to help . . .'

'Billie?' guessed Aileen.

'Yeah, Billie. She's said she'd love to manage a place like this. And I'd love to give it a go too and keep it in the family that way. I thought it was just a pipe dream. But if we can raise the capital . . . why not at least try it?'

They all looked at her.

Doon said, 'But what about your life in London?'

Natasha shrugged. 'What life? It's a few boxes of junk and two weeks' notice at work. I haven't missed London for a second that I've been here. I think I could have stayed drifting there forever. I just needed a push. And here it is. I know it sounds a bit wild,' she added, looking at them all. 'And I know it might not work out. But I want to give it a try. I can get work in Billie's hotel while we suss things out; I hope so anyway. Honestly, even if the doll's house is worth nothing and we have to sell up, I'm not going back to London. I want to stay here and try to make a life here.'

Aileen would normally have tempered her joy at this idea with some sensible objections, but she couldn't think of any. It wasn't so much Natasha's suggestions themselves, though they seemed reasonable enough, but her attitude. This didn't seem like one of her old crazy notions, like finding gold in the river or treasure in the attic; it seemed like she knew this would be a challenge but she was up for it. She must be determined, to sell her most cherished possession.

Even with her thrill at the idea of Natasha moving home, Aileen felt a pang at the idea of her giving it up. 'But your doll's house, darling,' she said. 'You've always treasured it so much.'

Natasha sighed. 'I know, but . . .' She glanced at Gabe and said, 'Compared to the real thing, I know which is more important.'

Nobody had an answer for that. Aileen was looking at her youngest daughter and wondering how it was that somebody could grow up seemingly overnight. And Gabe was also looking at her in a way that made it clear that however valuable the doll's house was, to him Natasha's happiness was the most priceless thing imaginable.

'Well,' said Doon. 'Let's vote on it, will we? All in favour of selling the doll's house and keeping Ballyclare – as Natasha's B & B.' She raised her hand. So did Natasha. And finally Aileen's hand went up. 'Gabe, you can't abstain,' said Doon, and he raised his hand too.

'I'm so glad, Mum,' said Natasha. 'I don't know how you'll feel about living in a B & B, but . . .'

'Well, actually, I do know,' said Aileen.

They all looked at her. She continued, 'You're welcome to give it a shot, Tasha. But I'm not going to get involved in it. What I'd like to do is to buy myself a little flat, which was my plan all along. And as soon as I'm retired, I'm going travelling.'

'But, Mum, you wouldn't leave Ballyclare!' said Natasha.

'How are you going to buy yourself something if Natasha's living here?' said Doon practically. 'She can't exactly buy you out.'

'We'll have to work that out. She could pay me rent,' said Aileen. 'We'll have to wait till we get the doll's house evaluated first, and sold, touch wood. But, either way, I'm ready for something new.' She smiled at how alarmed they looked. 'Girls, I've never been anywhere. I want to go backpacking in Italy and Greece – and Albania, Croatia – bring my sketchpad with me and see what adventures I find.'

She would have expected Doon to be the first to voice objections, but instead she was nodding away. 'That sounds really cool, Mum. For how long?'

'I don't know,' said Aileen, savouring the freedom of it. 'Maybe for as long as the building works take,' she added on a more practical note.

'But you won't stay away forever?' said Natasha, sounding much younger than she had a minute ago.

'Of course not,' said Aileen. 'I'll have three more years till I retire – and I can move in with Susan during the works; she's always suggesting it. And I'll be here for the grand opening of Ballyclare B & B. You can be our first guest, Gabe,' she added.

'That would be awesome,' he said.

'Can we agree something, though?' said Doon suddenly.

'What?' said Natasha.

'If you do manage to get a B. & B. going, could we keep it free over Christmas? So that we can all have Christmas here every year. If it's financially viable and everything,' she added quickly.

'I think we can make that work,' said Natasha with a grin.

The chat moved on, and Natasha made more tea as Gabe explained how to go about valuing the doll's house. Aileen kept marvelling at how much had changed since Gabe had first sat at that same table with them – was it less than a week before? Yes, it was.

'So soon?' she said, when Gabe stood up and said he really had to go. But he said he wanted to go to Glendalough, and she was secretly pleased when Natasha said she was going with him. She and Doon waved them off, after the sisters had exchanged many hugs and promises to meet up soon.

'If I'm living here,' said Natasha, 'I can go up to Dublin and meet you, can't I?'

Doon smiled. 'Of course. And I can always come

down.' She added, 'You'll have to learn to drive again anyway.'

Aileen was about to intervene, to tell Doon to be nicer to her sister, but she stopped herself just in time. Natasha was laughing and agreeing that, yes, she would.

'Have a lovely time, both of you,' said Aileen.

'We will,' said Gabe.

Aileen beamed, not doubting this for a minute. And, with that, Natasha hopped into the car with Gabe, waved goodbye to them all, and off they went down the drive.

Aileen turned back to Doon. She was glad that she seemed happier now; she had been so worried about her, but a weight seemed to have lifted from her.

'Would you like some turkey to take home?' she asked Doon, and Doon said, 'Definitely.'

'You and Natasha seem to be getting on better,' Aileen said once they had finished loading Doon's two bags into the car.

'Of course we are,' said Doon simply. 'We're sisters.'

Aileen was relieved. 'I'm glad to hear it. Keep in touch, my chick. And don't worry about the wedding or any of that stuff. It will all be OK.'

'Thanks,' Doon said. She gave Aileen a big hug, and with promises to talk soon they said goodbye.

Doon drove off, but Aileen noticed that instead of turning right for the road to Dublin, she indicated left, up into the hills. Odd. But maybe she was saying good-bye to someone.

Aileen closed the door and sighed with the happiness of finding herself alone again in the house. She walked slowly down the passage, trailing her hand along the dado rail. The memories of this last Christmas seemed to settle like dust motes, joining all the other memories of the house. She remembered carrying Natasha in as a baby; she remembered Dan bringing in the tree for their first Christmas. She remembered coming home, after taking Dan to St Patrick's hospital and trying to hold it together over dinner with the girls after he left. She remembered all the nights sitting up late with Susan and Laura, talking and laughing, and all the Women's Christmas parties she had had. She would have to make sure her new place would be big enough to hold them for maybe just a few select friends.

It was so hard to imagine not living here, but at the same time she felt a stirring of excitement about what might lie ahead. She pictured sunshine, deep azure seas, worn stone steps, trailing branches of scarlet flowers over whitewashed walls. Why wait till she retired? She could go next summer, as soon as school finished. And always she would be able to come home to Wicklow. It would be good to see Ballyclare filled up with people again, busy and humming with activity the way it was meant to be. And it would be a relief really to have a smaller place. One bedroom even, or maybe two. Of course I might not always be living alone, she found herself thinking, and then blinked. Where had *that* come from?

She dismissed it with a smile, but it reminded her of something she'd been meaning to do for a while. She located her phone on the kitchen table and typed out a reply to CJ's message. Dinner would be great, she wrote and pressed send. Then, on a wild impulse, she typed out, And also, how would you feel about going travelling? Then she laughed at herself and deleted it. There was no point in rushing anything; they could start with dinner. She put her phone in her pocket, and went outside to start her walk, closing the door carefully behind her.

Acknowledgements

Rathowen is not a real village, and the characters and all their circumstances are imaginary. However, the charm of Wicklow itself is completely real, as are the Powerscourt Hotel, Glendalough and all the other places mentioned. Thank you very much to Angela F. for telling me Wicklow tales and showing me the spectacular view from her home. Thanks also to my brother Gavan for putting us in touch. Barry Doherty and Anne O'Mahony kindly read the manuscript and set me right on many points of fact – thanks, guys! All my love and thanks go to Alex who has supported my writing for so many years – and to Stella for cheering me on too.

A big thank you and lots of love to Rowan Lawton, Eleanor Lawlor and all at the Soho Agency. I'm so grateful as ever to Rebecca Hilsdon and Clare Bowron, who helped me turn a shaky first draft into a proper story. Thanks also to Sriya Varadharajan, Nick Lowndes and the rest of the team at Michael Joseph, as well as the team at Penguin Ireland. Thanks to Jennie Roman for her insightful copy-edits, and to everyone else who worked on the manuscript. And huge, huge thanks to all the booksellers, bloggers and readers who've enjoyed my novels and spread the word about them.

Lastly, this book is dedicated to my parents, Brendan

and Noreen, who first introduced me to the beauties of Wicklow. The county was the constant backdrop to their long, happy life together, which they shared so generously with me and my brothers. Thank you to them, and to the staff of Glengara Nursing Home who continue to care for my mother with such kindness. I hope that somewhere in another world, Mum and Dad, you are enjoying a walk up Djouce on a bright winter day without a cloud in the sky.